9-20

COME HOMICIDE
OR HIGH WATER

Come Homicide or High Water

Denise Swanson

THORNDIKE PRESS
A part of Gale, a Cengage Company

LIBRARY OF CONGRESS CIP DATA ON FILE.
CATALOGUING IN PUBLICATION FOR THIS BOOK
IS AVAILABLE FROM THE LIBRARY OF CONGRESS

ISBN-13: 978-1-4328-7879-5 (hardcover alk. paper)

Published in 2020 by arrangement with Sourcebooks, Inc.

Printed in Mexico
Print Number: 01   Print Year: 2020

COME HOMICIDE
OR HIGH WATER

CHAPTER 1
I'LL BE HOME FOR CHRISTMAS

Monday morning, school psychologist Skye Denison-Boyd stood on the small metal porch in front of the RV she had been living in with her husband, Wally, and their twins, CJ and Eva, since a tornado destroyed their house last June. No matter how hard she stared across their property at the construction site near the river, there was no sign of the silver pickup that belonged to their general contractor, Beilin Quinn.

Sighing, Skye stepped back inside the motor home and took a quick peek at the babies, who were napping in their bassinets. They were getting so big that they would need to move to a crib soon, but there wasn't room for two in the RV's small master bedroom.

Their new house was supposed to be finished the Friday before Christmas, but the holiday was only a bit more than five weeks away, and their general contractor kept making excuses. First, it was the building inspector who didn't show up, then it was the well guy, and finally Beilin claimed that he and his wife were fighting over their daughter's education and he couldn't concentrate.

While Skye was sympathetic, by the time Beilin called with his latest excuse — the painter had mixed the wrong color — her inner psychologist turned off, and she wasn't listening anymore. In truth, by then, all she wanted was to get the GC off the phone, find the nearest cookie jar, and drown her sorrows.

She was ready to kidnap any stray inspectors, use whatever shade of paint was available, and, if necessary, start couples counseling with Beilin and his spouse. To say spending the holidays in an RV with three-month-old twins would be a challenge was like declaring that the Scumble River was a little wet.

The thought of trying to celebrate the babies' first Christmas in such crowded conditions was enough to make her cry. But what she really dreaded was the holiday's aftermath. Between May, Skye's grandchild-obsessed mother, and Carson, Wally's über-rich father, there were sure to be more packages under the tree for the twins than snowflakes on the ground. And the meteorologists were all predicting a very white December 25.

Frowning, Skye looked outside one more time and groaned. Still no sign of Beilin. You would think that if he and his wife were fighting, he'd want to get out of his own house and work on Skye and Wally's. She just hoped he wasn't in a bar somewhere drowning his sorrows.

Skye was reaching for her phone to text the missing contractor when she felt it buzz in the pocket of her jeans. She dug it out and slid her finger across the picture of her handsome husband's face.

Instead of a greeting, she blurted out, "He's not at the house."

Her voice held a hint of hysteria, and Bingo, their enormous black cat, hopped off the windowsill and streaked under the couch.

"Beilin didn't show?" Wally's baritone went up a notch. "Again?"

"Nope." Skye sucked in a deep breath to stop herself from whining. "And it's past ten. He promised he'd be here first thing in the morning to get the kitchen ready for the cabinet guy."

"Son of a bi . . . bishop!" Wally corrected and Skye snickered. They were both trying to stop swearing before the twins started talking, but it was a lot harder for Wally. "I'll get ahold of Beilin. Or since he was my father's suggestion, maybe I'll let Dad deal with him."

"Sounds like a plan." Skye grinned. "Remind your dad that he can only buy CJ and Eva one Christmas gift each if we're still living in the RV." That would make Carson light a fire under Beilin's butt for sure.

"Okay. Back to the reason I called." Wally's tone was brisk. "Are you still planning to take the twins over to your mother's today for her to watch?"

"Yes," Skye answered, puzzled that Wally would telephone her about that. "I promised Piper that I'd come by the school to give her a hand with a parent meeting scheduled for one o'clock, so I told Mom that I'd drop the babies off at her house around noon."

Officially, Skye still had six weeks left of maternity leave. She wasn't due back at school until January 2, when classes resumed after winter break. However, because her psych intern, Piper Townsend, wasn't getting as much help or supervision from the special education cooperative's psychologist as he'd promised them, Skye felt bad for the poor woman.

While Skye was gone, the co-op had

agreed to provide eighty hours a month of psych services to the Scumble River school district. It was supposed to include intern supervision as well as other duties, but after the first month, the man assigned to them rarely made an appearance, which left Piper attempting to handle the whole load by herself.

And sadly, a rural community in central Illinois had about as much chance of finding a substitute school psych as it did of being fully funded by the state or federal government. Which meant that Skye's conscience had her going in a few half days a week to rescue her intern from drowning in referrals and meetings.

"Do you think May would be available to babysit any earlier?" Wally asked. "Like, say, in a couple of hours? Or even less if at all possible."

"Probably." Skye took another peek at the babies and saw they were waking up. They'd be ready to eat soon. "What do you need?"

"I'd like you to come with me to talk to the husband of a missing woman."

Wally was the chief of police in Scumble River, and as well as working full-time as a school psychologist, Skye also served as a psychological consultant to his department. That might make Wally her boss at the PD, but he was too smart ever to try to order her around at home.

"Anyone I know?" Dread settled like a concrete blanket over Skye's heart.

Scumble River was a small town, just a shade over three thousand, and she was at least acquainted with most of them. Heck, she was related to half of its citizens. Then there were the people she knew from her work at the elementary, middle, and high schools and from attending church.

"I don't think so." Wally rustled some papers, then said, "Her name is Edie Baker. She and her husband live in Bord du Lac. They moved down here from Chicago about six years ago when Mr. Baker retired."

"Oh," Skye said. "You're probably right. Unless they have kids in my schools or go to St. Francis, I probably haven't run into them."

Scumble River was a bit cliquish. It took more than half a dozen years to be accepted as anything but "the new people" and be invited to any weddings or parties thrown by the original town citizens. Then there was the matter of the Bakers' address.

Bord du Lac had been built as a resort village that offered weekend and vacation cottages on the river. That was until some smart attorney discovered a loophole, and people, especially retirees, had begun to live in the holiday community full-time.

They added close to a thousand people who, while not in the city limits proper, were in the police, fire, ambulance, and school districts. Skye didn't understand exactly how it happened, but they paid less in taxes than those living in town, and there was some unrest about their water usage as well. There had been a feud and lawsuits between the Scumble Riverites and the newcomers ever since.

"So when do you think you can get to the police station?" Wally broke into Skye's musings. "I'd really like to get out there pronto."

"I'll call Mom, get CJ and Eva dressed and fed, then head out ASAP." Skye was already packing the babies' diaper bags. "How long has Mrs. Baker been missing?"

"The husband's not sure." Wally sighed. "They went to bed last night after the ten o'clock news — they have separate rooms — and she was gone when he called her to breakfast about eight thirty. He spent some time looking for her and called here a few minutes ago."

"I thought someone had to be missing twenty-four hours before the police got involved." Skye wedged her cell phone between her ear and shoulder as she swiftly changed Eva before moving on to CJ.

"It's at the discretion of the law enforcement agency. In Scumble River when the missing person is under age sixteen or has mental health issues, we start the search immediately," Wally explained. "And Mrs. Baker has the beginnings of dementia."

"Oh no," Skye gasped. "Okay. Let me call Mom, and if she isn't available, I'll let you know. Otherwise, I should be at the station in about an hour."

"Great." Wally paused, then asked, "When do we start interviewing nannies again?"

"The Wednesday after Thanksgiving. Remember we agreed to wait until after the holiday," Skye said patiently, having answered that question what seemed like a million times already.

The previous nanny had only been working for them a couple of weeks when she handed in her notice. She'd said that between May's constant advice and Carson's security cameras, she didn't feel trusted to do her job.

"Have you had a chance to go over their résumés?"

"Yes. I told you we're only talking to the ones that I liked." Skye kept her tone light even though she was getting tired of repeating herself. "We don't really need a nanny until I return to school."

"Right. I . . ." Wally trailed off.

Wally had confided in Skye that he was worried about her wearing herself out. His ears had reddened when he'd added that he missed their time as a couple too. She wanted that as well, but finding the right nanny wasn't easy.

Making sure she didn't sound impatient, Skye said, "I've got to get going. See you soon. Love you."

"Love you too. Bye." Wally disconnected.

Having finished with diaper duty, Skye put on black dress pants and a geometric print tunic, then called her mother, who was overjoyed to get her hands on CJ and Eva for longer than expected.

After Skye thanked her mom and hung up, she hurriedly fed the twins. Once they were burped and warmly dressed, she put on her coat, placed a diaper bag over each shoulder, and snuggled a baby in each arm. Opening and closing the door was tricky, but by now she was a pro.

Carefully walking down the metal steps, Skye smiled as she took in the shiny Mercedes SUV sitting before her. Skye's old Bel Air and Wally's Thunderbird had been totaled during the tornado when the garage collapsed under the impact of a blown-down tree. However, Wally had already ordered the new car for her as a surprise thank-you-for-having-my-babies gift, so they'd only been without transportation for a few days.

Once she reached the Mercedes, Skye began the task of getting the twins buckled into the SUV. She and Wally had selected a travel system that was both a double stroller and car seats. Thankfully, the seats were already in place and the frame was in the rear of the SUV so she didn't have to monkey with them.

With the babies settled into the back of the car, each playing with spinning rattles, Skye tossed their gear onto the passenger seat, slid behind the wheel, and headed toward her parents' place. Her parents lived a few miles outside of town. Their house was a sprawling redbrick ranch built on an acre of land carved from one of the fields that her father, Jed, farmed.

Her folks took great pride in their property. Jed kept the outside in pristine condition and May made sure that the inside was immaculate. As Skye pulled into the white pea gravel driveway, she noted that the autumn decorations were out in full force. They would be completely replaced with

Christmas paraphernalia by noon the Friday after Thanksgiving, but for now the colored leaf wreath, hay bales, cornstalks, and pumpkins shone in the fall sunlight.

The SUV had barely rolled to a stop when May appeared at the Mercedes's back door. By the time Skye grabbed the diaper bags, May had a twin in each arm and had returned to the house.

Skye strolled down the sidewalk, stopping to stare at her mother's concrete goose. Often, the cement fowl's costume was a good indication of whatever May was plotting. However, today, the bird was decked out as a pilgrim and Skye blew out a relieved breath.

May had been laying low since the extravagant baby shower she'd thrown for the twins. Skye crossed her fingers that the upcoming holidays would keep her mother occupied and out of her kids' business through January.

Entering the familiar utility room, Skye stepped out of her black pumps before proceeding. May had already removed the twins' jackets and had CJ in the swing. She was settling Eva in the bouncer as Skye entered the kitchen.

May had immediately purchased her own set of baby equipment when Skye's brother,

Vince, had presented her with April, her first grandchild. She had added another set to her collection when the twins arrived.

Once Eva was safely buckled in place, May turned to Skye and asked, "Did the parent meeting get moved up to an earlier time?"

"No." Skye leaned a hip against the counter. "Wally needs me at the police station."

At sixty-three, May had the energy of a twenty-five-year-old. In addition to keeping her house immaculate, she exercised at a nearby community's fitness center three times a week and worked the afternoon shift at the PD as a police, fire, and emergency dispatcher. Wally was technically her boss, too, but as she had told Skye more than once, mother-in-law always trumps superior officer.

May's biggest fault was her tendency to meddle, and with both Skye and her brother Vince married and having children, her interference had only gotten worse. Between Skye's twins and Vince's wife Loretta ready to have a second baby any minute, May was in heaven.

"What's up?" May wrinkled her brow. "I haven't heard anything on the scanner."

Many Scumble River citizens had their own personal police scanners and May's was a top-of-the-line model. She never turned it off and listened to it every waking hour, determined not to miss any juicy tidbit of gossip.

"A woman from Bord du Lac is missing and Wally wants me to interview the husband." Skye glanced at the kitchen clock. "So I need to scoot."

"Those people out there are always sucking up our public services." May *tsked,* and her short salt-and-pepper waves seemed to bristle with her displeasure.

Trying to change the subject, Skye said, "Your hair looks really nice. Did Vince just cut it?"

"I had the first appointment at his salon." May frowned. "And would you believe that when the next woman canceled, your brother suggested that I let him dye my hair?" Before Skye could comment, her mother added, "I told him that I don't have strands of gray. I have wisdom highlights." May crossed her arms. "That shut him up."

Skye smiled in approval. "Good one, Mom."

With the exception of her hair, Vince could do no wrong where their mother was concerned. It was good to hear that for once he was in the doghouse instead of Skye.

"She probably had a fight with her husband and went shopping."

"What?" Skye couldn't always follow her mother's leaps in conversation.

"The Bord du Lac woman."

"Oh. Maybe." Skye twitched her shoulders. "But she has some mild dementia, so the police have to look into her disappearance."

"Of course." May scowled, yanking at the neckline of her sweatshirt. "But Dante needs to get those Bord du Lac property taxes raised."

"I'm sure he will," Skye assured her. May's brother, Dante, was the mayor of Scumble River, and while there were a lot of things Skye didn't like about her uncle, he was good at his job, so the fact he hadn't found a way to increase the Bord du Lac property taxes was surprising.

"That dang lawyer of theirs keeps messing things up. Dante needs to let Loretta take a shot at it." May's eyes sparkled, their emerald green the same brilliant color she'd passed on to both Skye and Vince. "My daughter-in-law would make that guy go crying to his mama with his tail between his legs."

"True." Skye straightened and went to kiss Eva and CJ goodbye. "But is Loretta still taking on clients this far along in her pregnancy?"

"Yep." May shook her head. "You know your sister-in-law. She always has all her ducks in a row. She'll be writing briefs as they wheel her into the delivery room."

"Sadly, I don't have either ducks or a row." Skye shook her head. "All I have are squirrels, and they're too ADD to line up." As she started toward the utility room, she said, "Okay. I have to get going. I should be back by three at the latest. Call me if you need anything." She put on her shoes and paused with her hand on the back doorknob. "Oh, get the twin's bottles out of the diaper bags and put them in the fridge. Don't use any old ones you have in the freezer. I only want them to have the combo formula and breast milk that I prepared this morning."

"I was taking care of babies before you were born." May shot Skye a look. "Eva and CJ and I will be fine." She made a shooing motion with her hand. "You go find the missing woman and rescue your intern."

"Thanks, Mom!" Skye waved and hurried to the SUV.

She slid behind the wheel, buckled up, and reversed out onto the road. She hoped the interview with Mr. Baker wouldn't take too long. She really needed to get to the elementary school early enough to review a

21

student's file and go over Piper's findings.

At the insistence of the child's mother, Piper had evaluated a first grader as a candidate for the gifted and talented program. The woman had been unhappy with the results of the assessment, and she was now demanding additional testing. However, from what Piper had reported to Skye, there wasn't much chance the new scores would qualify the girl.

It was a shame Skye couldn't just tell the mother that Scumble River's gifted program wasn't any great shakes and her daughter would get just as much from being assigned to one of the better first-grade teachers.

Sadly, while gifted programs were mandated, they weren't funded by either the state or federal governments. And truth be told, the district just didn't have the money to run a stellar one.

Sort of like how the town didn't have the money to launch a massive search for the missing woman. A woman who more than likely had fallen into and drowned in one of the many lakes located in the Bord du Lac community. There were usually a couple of drownings a year in those lakes, and with Mrs. Baker's impaired mental status, an accident like that was high on the list of explanations for her disappearance.

CHAPTER 2
EDIE BAKER, WON'T YOU PLEASE COME HOME

After leaving her parents' place, Skye glanced in the rearview mirror at the empty car seats in the back of the SUV. It still felt weird to leave the twins, but she'd better get used to it before her maternity leave was over. Having had the nanny for so short a time, Skye hadn't had a chance to acclimate to being apart from her babies for any length of time.

Even though she regularly helped out Piper at school a couple of times a week, the two or three hours she was gone didn't seem as if she was really separated from CJ and Eva for long. But come January 2, she'd be gone at least nine hours for five days in a row.

Skye's throat closed and she blinked back a tear. What if they said their first word or got their first tooth when she wasn't there? They were already smiling, cooing, and reaching for objects.

Shaking her head, she rolled her eyes. She'd promised herself she wouldn't be *that* parent. Skye was fully aware of maternal separation anxiety and determined to focus on minimizing her guilt and fears. She knew the babies would reflect her feelings, and if she was uptight leaving the twins, they would be a screaming nightmare for the nanny.

It wasn't as if whomever she and Wally hired wouldn't be thoroughly screened — they'd probably known more about the previous nanny than she did herself. And because of Carson's enormous wealth and high-profile position as CEO of one of the biggest oil and gas companies in Texas, there was a full-time security team assigned to guard CJ and Eva from any outside threat.

At first, Skye had been reluctant to have a security detail watching the twins' every move, but her father-in-law had assured her that his men were among the best in the country. He'd promised her that most of the time Skye wouldn't even be aware of their presence.

When she'd raised a doubtful eyebrow at his assurance, Carson had pointed out that there had been a team on him since his arrival in Scumble River and that she'd never even known it. He'd added that while he'd love to have guards on both Skye and Wally, he accepted that they would refuse them, but babies would be a much easier kidnapping target than an adult.

With that warning, Skye had caved in. Having lived through her husband's abduction, she wasn't sure that she'd survive if her children were snatched. Evidently recognizing her weakened resistance to the idea of security, Carson had offered to install cameras in their home that she could operate to keep an eye on the nanny and Skye had accepted.

Although that had turned out to be a part of the reason their first nanny had quit, Skye was not about to remove the security devices. She'd just warn the women they were interviewing, and if they didn't like it, they shouldn't take the job. She rolled her eyes. Too bad nothing could prepare them for May.

Heck! With the surveillance cameras, if she missed a first with CJ or Eva, she could at least watch the recording.

As Skye turned into the police station's lot, she scanned for a parking place. The PD shared the building with the library and city hall, so it wasn't unusual for the lot to be full and today was no exception.

Skye waited patiently for a spot to open up, and once it did, she pulled the SUV between the faded white lines of a slot recently vacated by a teen driving a bright-blue Chevy Spark. Exiting the Mercedes, she began to make her way across the lot, keeping a watchful eye out for cracks in the murky gray asphalt. The increase in business at the city hall and police station after the tornado had taken its toll on the black-top.

They'd had a mild fall with temperatures remaining mostly in the sixties and seventies, but today there was a nip in the air and the meteorologist's promise of a snowy winter appeared much more likely than it had seemed in the balmy autumn. The odor of burning leaves had Skye's nose twitch-ing, and she quickened her pace before she started sneezing. While she loved the sea-sonal smell, her sinuses did not.

She made a beeline for the police garage and used her key to let herself in through the PD's back entrance. Stepping inside, she was surprised by the silence. Usually she could at least hear the daytime dis-patcher clicking away on her computer's keyboard or talking to someone on the telephone, but not today.

As she walked down the narrow corridor,

she glanced at the break room's sparkling window. Her mother always cleaned it just before her shift ended at midnight. And woe be it to anyone who got a fingerprint or smudge on it during the next sixteen hours.

Wally's office was on the second level, as was the mayor's. And while Dante was Skye's uncle, there was little love lost between her family and his. On the other hand, since Wally had come clean about his family's wealth, Dante had become *his* new best friend.

Skye climbed the stairs, but before she could make it down the short corridor to Wally's office, Dante burst out of his like one of those pop-out snakes from a fake can of peanuts, and Skye barely swallowed a scream.

His resemblance to the Penguin in the old *Batman* television shows was pronounced and it was always a bit of a surprise when his voice didn't match as he snarled, "Tell me you aren't here because of that old woman?"

"But if I lie, I'll have to go to confession." Skye smirked.

"Shit!" Dante pointed an unlit cigar at Skye. "She's probably gone shopping."

"You know, you sound a lot like your sister." Skye crossed her arms.

27

"And now we have to pay your salary." Dante ignored her comment about May, and his gaze grew crafty as he said, "With your husband's money, you should waive your fee. It isn't as if you need it."

As usual, Dante rubbed her the wrong way and she smirked, "You know what they say. Life is like a doughnut. You're either in the dough or in the hole." More often than not, Skye didn't complete the paperwork to get paid the hours she spent consulting for the police department, but she'd never admit that to him. Making a "get out of my way" gesture, she added, "You're costing the city each minute you delay me here in the hall."

"What?" Dante squawked. "You're not on the clock yet, missy."

"I am from the moment I enter the building." Skye smiled sweetly. "But since we're related and all, I don't charge you for my walk across the parking lot." She put her hands on her hips. "Can I go now?"

"By all means." Dante narrowed his dark, beady eyes. "Hop to it."

When Skye turned away from her uncle, she saw Wally leaning against his open doorway grinning, and she asked, "Been there long?"

"I think I caught the whole show." Wally

enveloped her in a hug and after kissing her breathless asked, "How come you didn't tell Hizzoner that you rarely take any money for your work here?"

"He ticked me off." Skye jerked her chin in the direction of Dante's closed door and scowled at it. "His and my mother's attitude about this poor missing woman just . . . just burns my grits."

Wally chuckled. "You've been hanging out with my dad too much, sugar."

"At least your father doesn't curse." Skye wrinkled her nose. "Which is more than I can say for his girlfriend. I thought that relationship would be over by now." She raised an eyebrow at Wally. "Didn't you?"

It had been quite a surprise to find out that Carson and Bunny Reid were an item. Even more of a shock had been the way they found out that the couple were cohabitating. Especially since Bunny was Simon Reid's mother and Simon was Skye's ex-boyfriend.

"Yep." Wally frowned and rubbed his chin. "Unfortunately, Dad and Reid's mother seem to be getting along like a house afire."

"Or a bowling alley blown up." Skye giggled, then when she remembered that someone had lost their life over that incident, she slapped her hand over her mouth and swallowed her laughter. "Well, we'd better get down to business before Uncle Dante docks both of our pay."

"Yep." Wally's voice dripped with sarcasm. " 'Cause Hizzoner never wastes the taxpayers' money taking time for his personal affairs."

"Is Mr. Baker here or are we going to his place?" Skye asked.

"His place." Wally gestured to the steps. "I'll fill you in on the drive out to Bord du Lac." Skye descended the stairs and Wally followed. Once they reached the first floor, he led her out of the garage door and toward his squad car. "I've got Martinez and Anthony out there combing the development, but I'm hoping Gerald Baker can tell us something that will help us narrow down the search."

"I'm curious why you needed me." Skye slid into the cruiser, and once Wally had settled behind the wheel, she added, "Not that I'm not happy to help."

"When Gerald Baker called to report his wife missing, he was agitated to the point of incoherence." Wally slid a quick glance at Skye. "My impression of Baker is that he is a bit of an odd duck."

"You got that from a single phone conversation?" Skye admired her husband's craggy

30

profile but noticed that the silver frosting his dark hair at his temples had increased. "I hope you'd be a little frantic if I was missing."

"He's one of those three or four guys that are always bellyaching about something in the *Star.*" Wally took another hasty peek at Skye. "You know, in that column where people call in, record their complaints, and the editor writes them up." Returning his attention to the two-lane blacktop, Wally commented, "Most of the people prefer to remain anonymous, but not Baker and those others. They sign their names to every single rant."

"Interesting." Skye hadn't had time to read the paper since the tornado. "But I don't think someone who is willing to take responsibility for his opinions is a crackpot. I think it's admirable."

"Maybe." Wally's expression darkened, indicating Skye hadn't won him over to her way of thinking. "But in last week's paper, someone wrote that Baker had better mind his own business or he'd regret it."

"And now his wife is missing." Skye frowned. "That's not a good coincidence."

"No. And believe me, Baker was quick to point out that fact." Wally tugged on his tie. "He's one of those conspiracy theory nuts."

31

Wally looked at her sharply. "And don't say that just because he's paranoid, doesn't mean someone isn't after him."

"I won't." Skye blew out a breath.

Wally couldn't understand her fascination with doomsday and apocalyptical books and movies. But there was something about people starting over with nothing but their wits that reminded her of her own return to Scumble River. And after the tornado, they were even more interesting.

"Look, this Baker guy comes off like a real fanatic." Wally braked for a stop sign. "I want you there to help keep him calm enough to answer my questions without going off on some tangent."

"I'll do my best." Skye checked her Bulova chronograph diamond watch, a gift from Wally to celebrate the twins' baptism. Although she usually stuck to her trusty Timex, when attending high-stakes meetings at school, she'd found the more successful she appeared, the more the parents respected her opinion. "But I need to be in my car driving to the elementary school no later than twelve thirty."

Wally glanced at the dashboard clock. "That gives us ninety minutes." He took his turn at the four-way, then said, "Plenty of time."

A frisson went down Skye's spine and she joked, "You better not have just jinxed us."

"Seriously?" Wally's expression was wary. "You don't mean that?"

Skye shrugged and hid her smile. Wally used to tease her about being superstitious and believing in ghosts. However, their encounter with a fairy godmother who was in possession of facts she couldn't possibly know had made him a lot less quick to spout off about Skye's gullibility.

Wally turned into a private drive, then braked. Bord du Lac was a restricted community and the entrance was blocked. The guard waved at them and quickly raised the gate arm. Wally drove along a narrow street and Skye glanced at the houses on either side of the road. All were adjacent to the small lakes that inspired the development's name and had their own docks.

Skye had never been inside the enclave before, and the houses weren't quite what she was expecting. The words "private gated community" had her imagining large structures on spacious lots, but these were mostly modest modular homes packed tightly together.

"Here we are." Wally pulled into the driveway and gestured at the large ranch-style house. It sat on a double lot and had a detached two-car garage and shed.

"Wow!" Skye gestured to the house and landscaping. "From what I've seen, this place is by far one of the nicest homes in Bord du Lac."

"I believe Baker pointed that out in several of his complaints against his neighbors that were published in the paper." Wally parked next to a Scumble River squad car and behind a shiny black sedan. "He also bragged it was twice the price."

"So he'd probably have money for ransom if his wife was kidnapped."

"Or . . ." Wally got out of the cruiser, walked around the hood to Skye's side, and opened her door. "People might think he does."

"True," Skye agreed as they walked toward the house. "Is Mr. Baker expecting us?"

"Yes." Wally rang the bell. "I told him we'd be here within the hour."

Almost before he finished speaking, the door opened and a tall, thin, sixty-something man wearing crisply pressed khakis and a starched button-down shirt said, "It's about time you got here."

"Mr. Baker," Wally said, "I told you when to expect us and as you can see" — he pointed to the other squad car — "officers are already searching."

34

"Sure." Stepping aside, Gerald said, "Come on in. And just to warn you, I am keeping a record of how this investigation is handled."

"So are we." Wally crossed the threshold and gestured at Skye. "This is Skye Denison-Boyd, our department's psych consultant."

"Nepotism at its finest," the man grumbled under his breath, then held out his hand. "Nice to meet you, Mrs. Boyd. I'm not sure why a missing person requires a police psychologist, but I'll reserve judgment."

"Where's the best place for us to sit?" Wally asked, his tone neutral.

"Let's go into the great room." Gerald led them across the foyer and down a short hallway. "I can keep an eye on the lake from there. I need to make sure that the residents and guests follow the rules."

He showed Wally and Skye into a spacious room decorated with military memorabilia and dominated by a large telescope. There were no throw pillows or curtains, and the coffee table's top was completely empty.

Gerald waved them to a large black leather sofa, then seated himself on the matching recliner and demanded, "What's being done to find my wife?"

"I have two officers going door-to-door and searching the yards," Wally said, his gaze never leaving the older man. "You mentioned that you called your friends. Does that include the neighbors?"

"We don't socialize with the riffraff around here. Well, my wife does talk to the gal next door, but she's in Florida for the winter." Gerald ran his fingers over his short gray hair. "Edie wouldn't be with any of the others."

"Maybe someone here who she knows from a card or book club?" Skye suggested.

"She doesn't do any of that." Gerald scowled. "With the lady next door down south, Edie spends most of her time with me."

"Because of her dementia?" Skye asked gently. "To keep her safe?"

"Yeah." Gerald's chest deflated. "She's drifting more and more."

"Would she have gone out on the lake?" Wally leaned forward. "And perhaps fallen in?"

"I . . . I don't see how." Gerald shook his head. "I keep my key ring hidden, but . . ."

Wally and Skye exchanged glances and she raised a questioning brow.

When he nodded, she asked, "But she finds them, right?"

"Not often." Gerald's perfect posture sagged. "But I couldn't locate them this morning."

Wally stiffened and Skye put her hand on his knee, then said, "Why didn't you tell Chief Boyd that when you first reported her missing?"

"The car and boat are still here, so I didn't think it was relevant," Gerald protested.

"What other keys are on your ring?" Wally asked.

"The front and back door of the house, our post office box, and the shed."

"Have you checked the shed?" Wally jumped to his feet, and when Gerald shook his head, he said, "Let's do it now."

Gerald retrieved a set of keys from his pocket that Skye assumed were spares, and the three of them trooped outside. She held her breath as the shed's door opened and let it out when it was clear that Mrs. Baker wasn't inside.

Returning to the house, Gerald said, "I'm sorry I didn't mention the key ring." He shrugged. "I guess I didn't want to admit how careless I'd been." Gerald's expression was shamefaced. "It was a moron move. I should have protected her better."

"You really can't do that by yourself," Skye murmured soothingly. "Do you have any help? Someone that gives you a break?"

"I hired a home health aide by the name of Krissy Ficher for the weekends and Edie loved her." Gerald exhaled loudly. "But Ms. Ficher didn't show up on Saturday or Sunday."

"Could Mrs. Baker have gone to find Krissy?" Skye asked.

"Maybe." Gerald twitched his shoulders. "But she wouldn't have any idea where the woman lives. I have that data on my phone, but Edie doesn't know the password." He took his cell from his pocket and said, "Do you want Ms. Ficher's address and number?"

After making a note of the health aide's contact information, Wally commented, "You said there was no family in the area, but are there folks farther away she might try to see?"

"Her son." Gerald shrugged. "But they aren't on good terms."

"Her son," Skye repeated thoughtfully, then asked, "He's not your child?"

"Edie was married briefly the day after she graduated from high school and Ford is from that union." Gerald held up his hand. "Before you ask, that husband is dead and Ford lives in California."

"I'm going to need his number," Wally

said, then asked, "Have you called him?"

"Right after I talked to you." Gerald stared out the windows. "He said that he hadn't heard from her and if I was smart, I'd count my blessings and just let her disappear forever."

CHAPTER 3
NOBODY'S HOME

It took only a few minutes to establish that Gerald Baker didn't have a clue as to where his wife might go and that it was highly likely that she'd just wandered off. Gerald claimed that she'd never done that before, and after taking a look at Mrs. Baker's room, Skye was inclined to believe him.

The couple slept separately, but the missing woman's room was equipped with a baby monitor as well as sleigh bells mounted above the door in such a way that they would jingle if the door was opened. There were no signs of struggle, and Gerald swore that nothing was missing except a pair of jeans, a blue sweater, a pair of white tennis shoes, and her Coach purse, which were what she'd worn the day before. She had no access to any kind of credit or debit card and had at most fifty dollars in her wallet.

After they'd examined the room, Wally radioed the two officers looking for Mrs.

40

Baker and brought them up to date. They were about twenty-five percent through searching the Bord du Lac development and had nothing to report.

Skye checked her watch and gave her husband a significant look.

He nodded and said, "Mr. Baker, please notify me immediately if you think of anything or if your wife returns home." He put his hand on Skye's back and guided her toward the front door. "My officers will continue to search the community, and if they don't find her, we'll ask for volunteers to expand the scope."

"Can't we do that now?" Gerald demanded. "You should drag the lake."

"That will be considered after all other options are exhausted, but try to stay positive." Skye patted his hand. "I know how hard it is to have a loved one missing. The initial search will take some time to complete, so there's still a good chance that she'll be found safe and sound."

Before he could form another protest, Skye and Wally said a hasty goodbye and headed to the car. Gerald was still standing on the front steps when they reached the cruiser and climbed inside.

Skye buckled up and said, "Hurry. It's already half past twelve."

As they headed toward town, Wally said, "Instead of picking up the SUV at the PD, I can drop you off at the school to save some time."

"That's a good idea." Skye thought for a moment, then patted her tote bag. "Yep. I have everything I need in here so go ahead."

Five minutes later, Wally pulled up to the elementary school and said, "Give me a call when you're done and I'll come get you."

"Thanks, sweetie. Love you." Skye got out of the car, waved goodbye, then ran for the entrance.

She used her key to open the door, then rushed inside and made a sharp right turn into the main office. When Skye attempted to walk past the school secretary on her way to the principal's office, Fern looked up from her computer screen and handed Skye a pink slip of paper.

Before she could read it, the woman grabbed her arm and said, "I'm so sorry I couldn't let you know sooner."

"About what?" Skye examined the bird-like woman as she eased out of her grip.

Fern was always nervous, but today Skye could actually see the pulse beating on the side of her neck. Something had really discombobulated her.

"Mrs. Greer." Fern took a ragged breath

42

and held her hand to her mouth. "They rushed her to the hospital an hour ago. They think it's her appendix."

"That's awful." Skye's heart sank. Caroline Greer was by far her favorite principal. Although Caroline was nurturing toward the students in her charge, Skye admired the woman's no-nonsense attitude toward the parents and her staff. "Did they give you a prognosis?"

Fern wiped her brow with a tissue. "As long as they get her into surgery before the appendix bursts, they think she'll be fine."

"Well, that's a relief." Skye blew out a breath she hadn't realized she was holding. "And I certainly understand why you couldn't let me know while all that was going on here. I guess Piper and I are on our own for the parent meeting."

"You don't understand." Fern twisted the tissue until it started to disintegrate, then gestured to the square of paper in Skye's hand. "What I was sorry about not letting you know is that Mrs. Greer called the superintendent to request that another administrator sit in on the meeting."

Skye glanced at the note and saw that was exactly what Caroline had written.

"Neva?" Skye asked hopefully. Neva Llewellyn was the junior high principal.

43

While not as skillful with parents as Caroline, she had been a high school counselor and was better than the alternative.

Fern shook her head, then looked around as if she thought someone was spying on them. Skye followed her gaze, wondering if security cameras had been installed since the last time she was there.

"Dr. Wraige?" Skye crossed her fingers. The superintendent wasn't her favorite, but at least he had some grasp of special education laws.

"No." Fern stared at a button on her blouse and whispered, "Mr. Knapik was the only one available. Neva is on jury duty and Dr. Wraige is at a county meeting."

"Shi . . . oot!" Skye grimaced at her near slip. "That's not good."

Homer Knapik had been the high school principal for as long as anyone under the age of forty could remember. He treated parents as if they were annoying gnats that he'd like to slap and his behavior toward his staff was even worse. The man needed to retire.

"Mr. Knapik's in Caroline's office with Piper and Mrs. Quinn right now," Fern sniffed and clutched Skye's arm again. "He was quite rude when I told him he should wait for you to arrive before seeing the parent."

"Son of a gun." Skye pried the secretary's hand from the death grip the woman had on her wrist. "I better get in there ASAP."

"He didn't even take the child's file." Fern blinked rapidly, then thrust the manila folder into Skye's hands. "He said he didn't care what it said. That man is beyond disgusting."

"It'll be fine." Skye smiled reassuringly at Fern, then walked toward the principal's office. Before entering, she turned and said, "Wish me luck."

"You'll need it," the secretary muttered as Skye gave a brief knock on the closed door, then without waiting scooted inside.

Homer sat at Caroline's desk eating pumpkin seeds. Skye couldn't understand his recent obsession with the snack, and his habit of spitting the shells directly from his mouth into the trash can made her stomach turn.

Against the pastel-colored walls and delicate furniture of Caroline's office, Homer stuck out like a Sasquatch who had wandered into the Ritz-Carlton from the wilderness. Seated in front of him were Piper and an attractive woman in her forties who Skye assumed was Mrs. Quinn. They

45

were both watching the man eating and spitting with appalled expressions on their faces.

As soon as Piper spotted Skye, she jumped up and said, "Oh good, you're here. Take this seat. I'll go get another chair." She thrust a folder into Skye's hand and nearly ran out the door.

Piper Townsend might be twenty-five years old, but due to her petite stature and baby face, she could easily pass as a middle schooler. Homer had been treating her like a twelve-year-old since she started her internship and Skye could understand the young woman's desire to get away. She just hoped Piper would come back since Skye was completely unprepared.

Turning to the woman she assumed was the parent, Skye held out her hand and said, "Hello. I'm Mrs. Denison-Boyd, but please call me Skye. I'm the school psychologist for the Scumble River district, but I've been out on maternity leave and won't officially be back until after winter break. Can you bring me up to speed on your concern?"

"Call me Jerita." The slender woman shook Skye's hand. "My husband is building your new house. He thinks a lot of you and your husband. He's really intent on having it done on schedule."

Skye wanted to say that if that were true,

then the man would show up at the job site on time. But she bit her tongue and murmured, "Oh. So you're Beilin's wife." Skye smiled. "Nice to finally meet you in person. We've spoken on the phone a few times."

"If you two are done with your lovefest, can we get this over with?" Homer belched. "I have to get back to my own school."

"By all means, let's start." Jerita pushed a strand of chin-length dark hair behind her ear and held up her cell phone. "My attorney has advised me to record our meeting. Does anyone object?"

"Attorney?" Homer's caterpillar-like eyebrows rose to meet his shaggy bangs.

"Yes." Jerita glanced at the clipboard on her lap. "My husband and I have sought legal counsel. She isn't attending today because she said that would hold things up as you would probably demand your own lawyer be present. But she did suggest an audio record."

Skye shot Homer a silencing look and said, "That's fine as long as you agree to the school making its own copy." When the woman nodded, Skye took her own phone from her tote bag, activated the recording app, and put the device on the edge of the desk.

A moment later, Piper returned with a

folding chair. She set it up as close to Skye as possible, looked nervously around, then sat down and began chewing on her thumbnail.

"Why don't you begin, Jerita?" Skye nodded at the woman. "I understand Piper has shared her results with you and you have a concern."

"In a nutshell," Jerita said to Skye, ignoring both Homer and Piper. "I believe my daughter is gifted. Although the scores on Ms. Townsend's assessment did not fall within the district's parameters, I feel that those lower scores are due to Ms. Townsend's inexperience. Thus, I am requesting an independent evaluation."

Skye flipped opened both the student and the psych files in her lap. She noted that the girl was in kindergarten and one of the youngest in her class. She was doing well and there were no teacher concerns.

Next, she read Piper's report. Although there were a few subtests on which the girl had done exceptionally well, the others were in the high average range. Nothing in the report suggested giftedness.

Skye thought quickly and suggested, "How about I do an additional evaluation as soon as I get back from my maternity leave and we go from there?"

She hoped that six more weeks would show Jerita that while her daughter was bright, she did not need an accelerated program. That way by the time the second assessment was completed, the woman would be ready to accept the results.

Before Jerita could answer, Homer pounded the desk so hard the pencils in the cup rattled and Skye's phone teetered on the edge. She caught it just as it was about to fall onto the light-green carpet.

"No!" Homer pounded again, his face the color of an eggplant. "Your precious little Suzie had her chance and we're not giving her another bite of the apple." He narrowed his beady little eyes, which considering the contrast to the size of his enormous head looked like specks of pepper in sausage gravy. He turned his angry gaze to Skye. "Since you've been out on your little vacation, things that she can't do alone" — he pointed to Piper — "have piled up." He crossed his arms. "You aren't wasting a day retesting a kid who's already struck out of the game."

"My daughter's name is not Suzie and her future is not a waste of anyone's time," Jerita fumed. "I was hoping for a battle of wits, but you, my good man, are clearly unarmed."

49

"Jerita, Mr. Knapik didn't mean —" Although Skye hurried to step in, the woman ignored her.

"And since you feel that way, we can go directly to a private evaluation." Jerita shot a smug smile at Homer. "Shall I send the bill to the school or do you run a tab somewhere?"

Skye glanced at Homer, who was now ignoring everyone as he laboriously tapped something into his cell phone. Turning to the disgruntled parent, she said, "Jerita, I'm sure you're aware that Mrs. Greer is the elementary school principal, not Mr. Knapik. Did Piper explain that she had a medical issue and that's why she isn't here?"

"Yes." Jerita lasered Homer with a look of loathing. "I was sorry to hear she was ill, and even sorrier to be stuck trying to deal with this cretin."

"Cretin" about described Homer, but Skye ignored that and suggested, "How about I confer with Mrs. Greer once she's on the mend, and in the meantime, I'll speak to our district superintendent."

Homer looked up from the screen of his cell phone and snorted. "At her age, Caroline will be out for a month or more."

Skye frowned. It was almost as if Homer was trying to push Jerita into an outside eval. He was usually bad with parents, but this seemed like he was deliberately provoking the woman. Why would he do that?

"I'm sure she'll be able to talk on the phone before that," Skye said quickly.

"And Shamus will back me up." Homer returned his attention to whatever he was doing on the phone, probably playing solitaire. "As superintendent, he's aware of how much your maternity leave has hurt our district."

"He had six months to find someone to substitute for me." Skye tapped her fingernails on the open folders in her lap. "You two came up with the scheme to hire an intern and have the co-op fill in the gaps."

"That's not how I remember it." Homer shrugged, slipped his phone in his pocket, and flicked a glance at Jerita. "This meeting is over. Little *Suzie*" — he emphasized the wrong name — "stays where she is."

Piper edged closer to Skye and whispered, "Mrs. Quinn will get a private eval and it'll cost the district a fortune." She slumped. "They'll blame me."

Skye caught a tiny smile hovering on Homer's lips and scowled. Was that it? Piper had called the man on several illegal maneuvers regarding children's rights. Was this his revenge on her for standing up for the kids?

After all, the mess wasn't in his school.

"No, they won't." Skye assured Piper. "I won't allow that, which means they'll blame me."

"They won't blame either of you." Jerita rose from her chair. "I have it all here. In addition to the school district, I'm going to instruct my attorney to name Mr. Knapik specifically in our lawsuit and go after his private assets."

"You can't do that!" Homer lumbered to his feet. "I have immunity."

Skye held back a chuckle. Did Homer think he had diplomatic status?

"I absolutely can." Jerita waved her cell phone in the air. "Acting outside the scope of your employment or engaging in reckless conduct removes any protection you might have. You can't mock students and summarily dismiss parent concerns without consequences."

With that, Jerita tapped a number into her phone, held it to her ear a few seconds, then said, "Ms. Steiner, I'm through here and will be at the office shortly. Thank you for taking my case and for allowing me the time off."

Piper and Skye exchanged a look, then they watched Jerita march out of the office.

"Did I hear that right?" Homer sputtered.

"Is that woman talking to your sister-in-law?"

"Sounds that way." Skye smoothed a wrinkle from her black wool pants.

"I thought Loretta was about to pop a baby out any day now."

"She's got a couple weeks until her official due date." Skye didn't really think Loretta would make it that long, but it was fun to see Homer squirm.

"Well, a lawsuit would take more than a couple of weeks to get going." Homer blew a dismissive breath. "And no other shyster in town will touch that woman's case."

"Probably not." Skye shrugged. "But knowing my sister-in-law, not only will she get the suit in motion before she goes into labor, if necessary she'll follow up from the delivery room."

Homer swung his gigantic head in Skye's direction. "You're just saying that."

"Why would I do that?" Skye kept her expression completely innocent. "Loretta will love this case. And if you doubt she can do it before having the baby, did you know that she's hired a new paralegal?"

"Who?" Homer thundered.

"From what we just overheard, my guess is that Loretta's new employee is our contentious parent."

53

Skye closed the files. If she couldn't come up with a compromise, this would get ugly fast.

"Fine. Test her little brat." Homer's face turned an alarming shade of purple. "I am not losing my house and life savings over it."

"I plan to evaluate her child." Skye stared coolly at Homer. "But after what you said to her, I doubt that will stop Mrs. Quinn from suing you."

"You're so smart." Homer shook his finger at Skye. "You make this right."

"As the Zen proverb says, knowledge is learning something every day. Wisdom is letting go of something every day. And I'm putting this matter right back in your lap where it belongs."

Homer loomed over Skye. "I liked you better before you married into all that money. I even defended you when Pru called you a gold digger."

Willing her face to remain expressionless, Skye said calmly, "In order for you to insult me, I'd have to value your opinion." Skye shrugged. "Nice try though."

CHAPTER 4
TAKE ME HOME, COUNTRY ROADS

After dropping off Skye at the elementary school, Wally returned to the police station and checked in with Thea Jones, the day shift dispatcher. She reported that things were quiet in town and there was no news on the missing woman, so he grabbed his lunch from the break room fridge and retreated to his office.

As he ate his turkey and Swiss on rye, he made notes in the Edie Baker file and considered what the best next move would be in locating her. The city council would have a hissy fit when they saw that he'd called in Anthony and Martinez. But with as small a work force as the Scumble River PD employed, there was no getting around giving officers extra shifts. When they complained, Wally planned to point out that if they would hire two more officers, as he'd been suggesting, they could avoid paying the overtime.

Finished with his sandwich, Wally made a list of people he needed to telephone. He could only come up with two names and he chewed the end of his pen trying to think of someone else who might have information about Edie Baker's whereabouts.

A few seconds later, he reluctantly added another person to his list, but before picking up the phone, he opened the water bottle Skye had tucked in his lunch bag. She'd packed it along with his grapes and the banana oatmeal squares she'd managed to bake during one of the twins' naps.

Taking a long swallow of the cool liquid, he thought of how grateful he was that she'd taken over the chore of preparing his lunch. He usually forgot to do it himself and ended up eating fast food or nothing at all. He really was the luckiest guy in the world. How had he ever persuaded her to marry him and have his children?

Noticing how warm it was in the station, Wally took another gulp of water. He really needed to have a talk with Thea about her habit of kicking up the heat. The temperature was supposed to be set at seventy, but the dispatcher was always cold and usually nudged the dial to seventy-eight. And since heat rises, that put Wally's second-story office close to eighty.

Before he got started on the telephone, he ran downstairs, readjusted the thermostat, and grabbed the whiteboard from the inter-rogation room a.k.a. break room. He carried the dry-erase easel upstairs and placed it next to his desk, then sketched a rough map of Bord du Lac.

If Edie Baker wasn't found by the end of the day, Wally would create a grid of the outlying area and call in volunteers to expand their search. Then if there were no results from that, he'd have to request the fire department try a water search.

As Wally finished the bottle of water and tossed it into the recycle bin, he caught a glimpse of his watch and frowned. It was nearly two o'clock. Skye would be texting him for a ride soon and he wanted to have completed his calls before that time.

Number one on his list was the son and number two was the health aide. But before lifting the receiver, Wally turned to his computer and did a Google search on Ford Grogan. It was always a good policy to research persons of interest before speaking to them. And he definitely wanted to get some information about the man who advised his stepfather to abandon the search for his mother.

There were only two hits for Grogan and

one was to a social media page that he was denied access to when he tried to click on it. The other was a short piece about the man's early retirement from the Bakersfield public works department. According to the article, his departure was due to a job-related injury. Evidently, Grogan had been shot while removing graffiti and the injury had resulted in the loss of his left leg.

A trickle of sympathy shot through Wally's chest. A duty-related, career-ending wound might be the reason for the man's harsh words regarding his mother. Something like that could certainly make a man bitter.

Picking up the handset, Wally dialed Grogan's number. The phone rang and rang, and Wally was about to hang up when he was finally greeted by a gruff voice.

"This is Chief Walter Boyd of the Scumble River Police Department," Wally said smoothly, having uttered a similar statement a thousand times. "I'd like to speak to Ford Grogan, please."

"You got him," Ford snapped. "If this is about Edie, I don't have any information and don't give a shit what happened to her."

"That's a shame," Wally said, then ignoring the man's hostility asked, "When's the last time you saw or talked to your mother?"

Ford snarled, "She called a year ago, but I

didn't pick up. Some idiot notified her when I was shot and she wanted to know if I was okay."

"You never spoke to her?" Wally asked, wondering what had happened between the mother and son that resulted in this kind of hostility.

"Why would I? If I'd wanted to talk to her, I would have answered my phone." Ford's tone was hard to read, but Wally thought it might have held a hint of sadness or maybe self-pity. "I haven't seen her since I left Illinois thirty-six years ago."

"No visits?" Wally thought he knew the answer but had to ask.

"After I knocked the dust of that hellhole you people call a state off of my boots, I never went back."

"I see." Wally studied Ford Grogan's picture on his computer monitor, but it didn't give him any clues about the man.

"Listen," Ford snarled. "Don't call me again. She didn't give a damn about my well-being when I was younger, so I don't care about hers now."

Disconnecting, Wally made a note of the time and date of his conversation with Grogan, then googled the home health aide. There were no hits on the name Krissy Ficher and he frowned. Wondering if Baker had given him the correct spelling, he tried a few variations, but there was nothing that he could connect with the caregiver.

Unusual as it might be, it wasn't unheard of for someone to be completely offline, so Wally shrugged and dialed the woman's number. It was answered on the first ring and he identified himself, then asked to speak to Krissy Ficher.

"Speaking."

"I'm calling regarding Edie Baker," Wally explained.

"Did something happen to her?"

"Edie has been reported missing," Wally said and paused to gauge the aide's reaction.

"Oh my gosh!" Krissy squeaked. "I am so sorry to hear that. Is there anything I can do?"

"I was hoping you might have an idea of where she might go."

"Not really. We rarely leave the Bakers' property when I'm with Edie." There was a hesitation, then Krissy said, "I had a personal matter come up and couldn't make it to take care of her last weekend so I haven't seen her in over ten days. And I'll be out of state for at least another week."

"Please let me know if she contacts you. Also, as soon as you get back to Illinois, I'd like you to come to the police station for a more in-depth interview." Wally wrinkled his brow. His gut said that there was something he needed to find out from this woman but couldn't think of it. Finally it came to him and he asked, "Why didn't you let Mr. Baker know that you weren't going to be able to work your shift with his wife?"

"I did," Krissy said. "I texted him the minute I knew I wouldn't be able to make it."

After thanking Krissy for talking to him, Wally said goodbye and hung up, then cringed when he saw the last name on his list. Sadly, in good conscience, he had to make the call. She would probably know more about Gerald Baker, and possibly Edie, than anyone else.

Gritting his teeth, Wally punched in the number for the *Scumble River Star,* then took a deep breath, preparing himself to talk to the newspaper's owner.

"Kathryn Steele, how may I help you?" On the first ring, an attractive contralto voice that had made many people drop their guard and tell all answered.

"Wally Boyd here, Kathryn," Wally said pleasantly. "I'm hoping you can give me some background on Gerald and/or Edie Blake."

"Why?" Kathryn eagerly pounced. "Has something happened to him?"

"His wife is missing." Wally kept his tone level. "I understand she has dementia and may have just wandered off, but I wondered if you had information that might make me consider foul play."

Kathryn chuckled. "If Gerald was missing, I would say yes. He's a rigid jerk who has managed to alienate nearly the whole population of Bord du Lac. But Edie is a sweetie, so probably not."

"How did a sweet woman come to marry someone like Gerald?" Wally asked.

"Before I tell you anything more, I want the exclusive story," Kathryn demanded. "I can just get it into Wednesday's paper."

The *Star* was a weekly, and if it didn't make that edition, the news would be old by the next one. Not to mention that the Joliet, Kankakee, and Laurel papers would scoop her.

"Sure." Wally fidgeted in his chair, anxious to end the conversation, but knowing they'd want something in the paper about the missing woman anyway. "This morning, Baker called and . . ."

Once Wally had gone over Gerald Baker's call, the officers' current search, and the interview he and Skye had conducted with the husband, he said, "That's it so far, but I promise to keep you in the loop."

"I don't just want the 'official' party line," Kathryn said sharply.

"Of course not," Wally assured her, hanging on to his temper by a thread. "Calm down."

As soon as the words left his mouth, Wally tensed. He knew better than to say something like that. Skye would be so disappointed in him. Actually, if he were smart, he'd have asked Skye to deal with the newspaper owner.

After a moment of frozen silence, Kathryn said icily, "Telling a woman to calm down works about as well as baptizing a cat." She paused, then added, "And makes her about as angry."

"Sorry," Wally said. "It won't happen again."

"Good." Kathryn's satisfaction came through the phone line. "So you want to know the dirt on the Bakers."

"Yes, please." Wally kept his answer brief to lessen the likelihood of putting his foot back into his mouth.

"It's his second marriage, her third. All previous spouses are dead." Kathryn paused. "Maybe they both killed their other spouses and when they tried to do each other in, Edie ended up at the bottom of a lake."

"That might be possible," Wally said carefully, "but you just told me she was a sweet woman. And he's the one that called to report her missing."

"Still —"

"I'll keep it in mind," Wally hastily interrupted, running his fingers through his hair. "Anything more on the couple? Clubs? Friends? Habits?"

"Gerald's a member of the VFW and attends their meetings. He and Edie also show up for their fundraisers. I haven't heard that they were particularly friendly with anyone though." Kathryn took a breath. "Gerald's only hobby seems to be spying on his neighbors and reporting their misdemeanors to the Bord du Lac HOA." She paused. "Oh, the Bakers do eat at the American Legion's pancake breakfast every other Sunday and the Lions fish fries on Fridays."

"How in the world do you know that?" Wally was amazed at the breadth of Kathryn's knowledge about the citizens of Scumble River.

"Because he regularly posts a complaint about either the service or the food." She chuckled. "I once asked him why he keeps going back and he said that he had as much right to cheap meals as anyone else."

Once Wally thanked Kathryn — although he wasn't sure for what since her information hadn't sparked any ideas of where to search for Edie Baker — he disconnected the landline and took his cell phone from the case attached to his duty belt. Swiping the screen, he saw that he had missed a couple of texts and a voicemail.

He tapped the icon with his thumb and read the message from Skye first. Meeting is over, but I need to confer with my intern. Probably another hour.

The second text was from Beilin Quinn: Sorry I wasn't at the house this morning. I'll be there by one. I won't leave until the kitchen is ready for the cabinets tomorrow.

Beilin's voicemail repeated the same message.

Returning his phone to its holder, Wally stared into space, considering his next move. He'd told Skye that he'd let his father handle the general contractor, but it might be a good idea to run over to the work site and talk to the man face-to-face. If Beilin couldn't handle the job, they needed to find someone else to finish up the house ASAP.

Wally notified Thea that he was going 10-7 for an hour, but if there were any news about the missing woman, she should call

65

his cell phone. Then he closed the Baker file, straightened his desk, and stepped into the corridor.

Shooting the mayor's office a dirty look, Wally ran down the stairs. He hadn't been at all happy when Hizzoner had harangued Skye earlier. If he hadn't been a hundred percent sure she could handle her uncle, he would have stepped in to set the man straight. However, knowing Skye preferred to fight her own battles, he'd hung back and kept an eye on the situation. But one of these days, Dante was going to go too far.

Wally smiled meanly. He'd already bested the mayor a few times, including getting his authorization to bring Anthony on full-time to replace an officer Wally had had to fire. His smile slipped. Now if he could only find someone to take the part-time position.

Shaking his head — he hated the administrative portion of his job — Wally marched into the garage, slid behind the wheel of his personal vehicle, and backed out. He'd never admit it to his father, but he loved the modified Hummer that his dad had presented him with after his Thunderbird had been destroyed by the tornado.

Heading for home on autopilot, Wally's mind turned to their childcare situation. Skye teased him about wanting her available, and to a certain extent it was true, but he knew his wife, and he knew she'd never be happy without a life outside of raising their twins.

He thought that they'd lucked into hiring a great nanny, but the woman's sudden resignation made him wonder if they could find someone they trusted and who was willing to put up with their unusual families. He hadn't had the heart to share his concern with Skye yet, but he thought finding a nanny might be trickier the second time around.

Wally hoped he was wrong, but he needed to talk to Skye about his suspicions pretty soon so they could come up with an alternative solution before she had to return to work. Although they could afford for her to be a stay-at-home mom, that wasn't a role she'd be happy occupying for too long.

And even if she did decide to take a hiatus from her position, she'd never leave the district in a lurch by quitting without giving them time to find a replacement — an event that was about as likely to occur as the next Chicago mayor's election being unopposed.

Skye's mother had hinted that she'd be more than willing to quit her dispatcher job and become a granny nanny, but having May that involved in their lives would be a disaster. The woman was already way too obsessed with her children and grand-children.

Hmm! An idea flashed through Wally's head and he straightened in his seat. Maybe the answer was Dorothy Snyder. She'd worked as their part-time housekeeper before the tornado. Would she be willing to work for them exclusively and include childcare in her duties?

Skye wouldn't like the idea of a full-time housekeeper, but it would be the ideal solution. They both had demanding professions, which left them with little energy to do double duty at home.

Wally vowed to discuss the possibility with Skye the next time he saw a good opening. Deep in thought as to how to bring up the subject, he nearly missed his turn.

He forced himself to concentrate on his driving, and shortly afterward, he swung into his driveway. Continuing past the RV, he approached the construction site and pulled the Hummer next to Beilin's pickup.

Wally studied the structure. From here the new house looked move-in ready. He jumped out of the Hummer and strolled around the perimeter. The landscaping wouldn't go in until the spring, so he had to avoid the large clods of dirt and chunks of debris, but the view was worth it.

He and Skye had decided to build their new home closer to the river than where the previous one had been located, and they had told the architect to include a deck running the entire length of the rear wall facing the water. Their property included several acres, which had allowed them to choose a sprawling Prairie-style ranch with a welcoming front porch and a screened-in gazebo in the back, as well as a full basement.

Having made it through one tornado, neither of them would ever consider living anywhere without a basement. The one in their old place had saved both their lives and the lives of two of Skye's former students who had been visiting her at the time of the twister.

Returning to the front of the house, Wally took out his cell and turned up the ringer so that he'd hear Skye or his officers if they tried to contact him. Then after slipping the phone into his shirt pocket, he ran up the front steps and opened the mahogany, Craftsman-style door.

They had opted for an open floor plan that had a master suite on one side and the other four bedrooms in the opposite wing. The kitchen, great room, and dining room occupied the center of the house and there was a huge bonus room over the three-car garage that they'd initially planned to make into a home gym.

Later, the home gym had been downsized and relocated to one of the spare bedrooms. Instead, they'd decided to add a kitchenette and bathroom to the bonus space and make it an in-law suite. None of their parents were getting any younger, and with the twins, Wally suspected that once his dad returned to Texas, he would be a frequent visitor.

Stepping inside, Wally spotted the general contractor working in the kitchen and walked toward him. Beilin was a muscular man in his late forties. Usually good-natured, today he wore a frown as he and another scrawny-looking guy applied the grayish-tan paint Skye had selected.

The tile floor, covered with what looked like butcher paper, bore an assortment of splatters, and as Wally carefully stepped over them, he said, "Mr. Quinn, I'd like a word with you."

At the sound of Wally's voice, the contractor startled and drops of paints flew from his brush. He let loose with a stream of curses that made Wally raise his eyebrows.

Evidently seeing Wally's expression, Beilin shrugged. "Some people call those swear words. I think of them as sentence enhancers."

"But not around Skye or my kids," Wally stated, unamused.

"Of course not." Beilin told the other man to keep painting, then followed Wally outside to where the vehicles were parked and apologized. "I'm really sorry about this morning."

"What delayed you this time?" Wally didn't bother to hide his irritation.

"It's the wife." Beilin stuck his hand in one of his pockets and pulled out a pack of cigarettes. "She's got some bee in her bonnet about our daughter being a genius and needing special attention at school."

"And?" Wally made a mental note to ask Skye if she was aware of Beilin's daughter.

"And I think she's just a bright kid who should be able to enjoy kindergarten without a lot of overblown expectations." Beilin shrugged. "I think it's because we had such a hard time having her that Jerita wants everything about her life to be perfect."

"That's understandable." Wally nodded but kept his tone firm. "Unfortunately, I have my own family to consider and if you can't get the job done in the time you promised, we'll need to replace you."

"Don't worry, Chief." Beilin slid a cigarette from the pack, then must have noticed Wally's frown and put it back. "I told Jerita to do what she wants but that I wouldn't be a part of it."

"Okay." Wally blew out a breath. "Just make sure you remember that and show up on time tomorrow."

CHAPTER 5
DON'T COME HOME A-DRINKIN'

Skye slid a steaming bowl of creamy chicken and wild rice soup in front of Wally as he sat at their tiny kitchen table. Opening the oven door, she took out a pan of rolls, dumped them in a basket, then fetched her own bowl of soup and took the seat opposite Wally.

They hadn't had a chance to catch up on either his case or her meeting because Wally had been on the radio with Zelda Martinez when he'd picked Skye up from the elementary school. And he'd still been being briefed by Zelda when he'd dropped Skye at her SUV.

Then when Wally had gotten home from work, he and Skye were too busy feeding the twins and getting them to sleep to talk about anything important. Now as they ate dinner they finally had the time to discuss their respective afternoons.

Blowing out a tired sigh, Skye shook out

her napkin.

Wally stopped eating, tilted his head, and asked, "Hard afternoon?"

"Eva and CJ were all hyped up after being with Grandma." Skye swallowed a spoonful of soup. "On the bright side, Mom had the soup and rolls for us." She pushed the large wooden bowl in his direction. "All I had to do was throw together a salad for our dinner."

"How was your meeting?" Wally helped himself to the lettuce, tomatoes, and shaved carrots lightly dressed with a balsamic vinaigrette. "Did your intern really need you to be there?"

"Definitely." Skye selected a golden-brown roll and broke it open. "Did you hear that Caroline Greer was rushed to the hospital with appendicitis?"

"No." Wally frowned. "Did that happen during the parent conference?"

"I wish," Skye muttered, then realized how that sounded and added, "I meant I wouldn't want it to happen at all, but unfortunately it happened early enough for Caroline to call in another administrator. One who is totally inept."

"Homer?" Wally's eyebrows rose. "But why would she choose him? She thinks he's a buffoon and should retire."

"Process of elimination." Skye explained how Homer ended up being the only admin available. "We would have been much, much better on our own. Homer insulted the parent, even though he knew she was recording him, and she immediately headed to her attorney to file a lawsuit."

"Well, crap." Wally ate a bite of salad, then said, "Tell me her lawyer isn't Loretta."

"Of course it is." Skye tried to figure out if it would be a breach of confidentiality to mention that the woman was their contractor's wife and that she was likely Loretta's new paralegal.

Yep. It probably was against best practices and Skye couldn't see any acceptable reason to disclose that information to Wally.

"Was that why the meeting took so long?" Wally asked, buttering his roll.

"That, and afterward I needed to ask Piper about a statement that Homer made during the whole fiasco." Skye took a sip of her water before explaining. "He said something about matters piling up that my intern couldn't handle alone. Naturally I wanted to know what he was talking about."

"And?" Wally waved for her to go on, his mouth full of bread.

"Dooziers."

At Skye's single-word answer, Wally

75

choked and started coughing.

Earl Doozier was the alpha male of the Red Raggers pack. Although they weren't werewolves — as far as Skye knew anyway — when riled up, they were almost as dangerous. They were a clan of loosely related troublemakers who lived along the river in the part of town mothers warned their children to avoid.

They were the folks the upright citizens of Scumble River gossiped about during their church socials and in the stands at their kids' sporting events. But before they said a word, they made certain that none of the Red Raggers were around because no one was foolish enough to get the RRs sore at them on purpose.

The Dooziers and their kin didn't have family trees as much as they had bonsai bushes of hereditary mutations. They may not be the smartest or the strongest, but they were like cockroaches. They'd survive the next ice age wearing only a light jacket.

The reason Homer wanted Skye to handle Earl was her special relationship with the Dooziers. She acted as both their translator and advocate. And in turn, they made sure that anyone who messed with her was very, very sorry.

Finally Wally took a sip of water, regained

his voice, and asked, "What has Earl done now?"

"Evidently, Cletus, Earl's nephew and ward" — Skye checked to see if Wally was following and when he nodded she continued — "was caught making out with Iris Allen." When Wally didn't react, Skye elaborated, "Ginger's daughter. You know, the cousin who doesn't like me."

Wally whistled.

Skye wished she wasn't still breastfeeding because she really needed a glass of wine to deal with this mess. Now she was doubly glad that they'd made the decision to begin weaning the twins so they'd be completely on formula before she returned to work. She couldn't handle her duties as school psychologist without merlot and a massive amount of caffeine. The one cup of coffee a day she was currently allowed wouldn't cut it once she was back on the job.

"Anyway, Homer, living up to his title of idiot extraordinaire, suspended Cletus, but not Iris." Skye shook her head. "That usually wouldn't be a problem because Earl's not exactly big on education and wouldn't mind or maybe even notice that his nephew was off of school for a few days."

"But?" Wally raised an eyebrow.

"But Ginger threw a royal fit and demanded that Cletus be expelled." Skye finished her roll and wiped her fingers on her napkin.

"Why?" Wally continued to eat, but kept his attention on Skye.

"Even though Iris denies it and says she's in love with Cletus, Ginger claimed that he forced himself on her daughter." As Skye thought about the messed-up situation, she ate the rest of her soup. Finally, she said, "Ginger wanted to call the police and file charges, but since Iris is adamant that one, they're a couple, and two, they were only kissing, evidently even my crazy cousin decided that wouldn't fly."

"Thank goodness." Wally pretended to brush sweat from his brow.

"But Ginger wasn't letting the matter go. She's like a squirrel with an ear of corn. She was determined to keep at it until there wasn't a kernel left on the cob." Skye drained her water glass. "In response to my cousin's nagging, Homer tried to bring in Ginger and Earl to discuss the matter. However, from what Piper tells me, he was clearly on Ginger's side and even suggested that Cletus was old enough to drop out of school."

"Seriously?" Wally emptied the rest of the salad bowl onto his dish.

"Apparently he hasn't read the handbook, which plainly states that school personnel aren't allowed to advise or encourage students to drop out of school voluntarily due to behavioral or academic difficulties."

"Did your intern point that out to him?" Wally asked with a smirk.

"Of course she did. And in front of Earl, who promptly declared that he would be suing Homer." Skye blew out a breath. "That's why I suspect that Homer was trying to get Piper in trouble today."

"So that makes two lawsuits pending against Homer?" Wally chuckled as he finished his second helping of salad. "At this rate, the parents should just band together and make it a class action suit."

"Bite your tongue!" Skye yelped, then couldn't help but giggle.

"I'd rather bite into that pumpkin cake your mom sent over." Wally rose and cleared the table, then asked, "Shall we have dessert in the living room?"

"Sure." Skye got up and went into the bedroom to check on the twins, who were sleeping peacefully.

When she returned, Wally had pieces of cake and cups of decaf on the coffee table. She settled next to him on the couch and enjoyed a bite of the decadent dessert.

After sucking every speck of the cream cheese frosting from her fork, Skye asked, "How was your afternoon?"

"Nothing new on Edie Baker." Wally took a sip of his coffee. "Martinez thought she had something when they found a woman's tennis shoe wedged between the door and frame of a storage shed by the Bord du Lac clubhouse, but Gerald said it wasn't Edie's."

"So you'll enlarge the perimeter, right?" Skye asked.

"Yep. Just before I came home, I called to arrange for a water search for Wednesday if the expanded search tomorrow doesn't yield any results."

"It's good to have them prepped and ready." Skye's chest tightened, knowing that Wally was saying he thought Edie was dead.

"On a better note . . ." Wally put his arm around Skye's shoulder and hugged her to his side. "Beilin showed up at the new house around noon and was getting the kitchen painted when I stopped by to see him."

"Yeah!" Skye clapped, then asked, "How was the color?"

"It looks great," Wally assured her. "We can take a walk over later if you want."

"I want to see the paint in the sunlight."

"Then we'll go in the morning." Wally smiled and added, "I had a talk with Beilin,

80

and he swore that he'd settled things with his wife and would be on time from now on."

"Awesome." Skye wondered if things were still settled now that Jerita was intent on suing Homer and the school district.

The next week flew by, and once again it was Monday morning. And like the previous Monday, there was no sign of Beilin Quinn's truck at the construction site.

He'd been on time and on top of things since Wally's talk with him. Cabinets and counters had been installed and the backsplash was up. But today, of all days, Beilin hadn't showed up yet and the painter, who had finished the kitchen, then gone off to another job, was back, and looking for the contractor. He had knocked on Skye's door a few minutes ago saying that he was supposed to start on the rest of the rooms but couldn't do anything until the GC arrived.

When Skye had suggested he start without Beilin, the man had refused. It seems that the contractor had to approve each color before any work could begin. Evidently, Skye's okay wasn't enough.

Now she stood on the small metal porch in front of the RV, staring across their property at the construction site near the river, willing Beilin to appear. When her thoughts failed to conjure up the man, she sighed and took her cell phone from the pocket of her jeans.

Scrolling until she found Beilin's number on her contact list, she was about to hit dial when the contractor's silver pickup made a sharp turn into the driveway and zoomed past the RV. It came to a skidding stop in front of the new house and he jumped out of the cab.

Immediately, the painter marched up to him and put his hands on his hips. Skye couldn't hear what was being said between the two men, but their debate appeared heated.

Thrilled the contractor had shown up and unwilling to get pulled into their argument, Skye stepped inside. She had been keeping an eye on the twins through the glass door and had been happy to see them contentedly sitting in their bouncy seats batting at the soft toys attached to the bar in front of them. Every few seconds they would coo at each other as if in a deep discussion.

When Skye knelt between CJ and Eva, they waved their arms and legs and babbled at her excitedly. Evidently, they were including her in their conversation.

As she played with her babies, she thought

of the previous week. Edie Baker was still missing. Volunteers had looked for her via foot, horseback, and ATV but there had been no sign of the woman. A sonar search of the water surrounding her home hadn't turned up anything nor had dragging the lake.

Today, Wally and his officers were questioning people who claimed to have seen Mrs. Baker since her disappearance. The police had already talked via telephone to dozens of folks who alleged to have information, but they reserved these face-to-face interviews for the few who seemed to be the most credible.

On the school front, Caroline's appendectomy had had complications and she was still unavailable for consultation regarding the Jenna Quinn case. Skye had continued attempting to find another solution for the matter, but with Caroline out of action, things were at a standstill.

Jerita was indeed Loretta's new paralegal, and with the help of her boss, she had already filed a lawsuit against Homer. Usually filing a lawsuit would take longer, but Loretta was already cognizant of the full story and facts.

Added to her prior knowledge was the fact that she had cleaned up her caseload in anticipation of having her baby, so she had all her time and attention available. Then there was Jerita, who was more than motivated to do her part for the case.

Shaking her head, Skye noticed the twins were getting drowsy, so she quickly changed them and put them in their bassinets.

When her cell vibrated in her pocket, Skye was expecting it to be either Homer or Piper, both of whom had taken to calling her several times a day since being notified of Jerita's lawsuit. But when Skye swiped at the device's screen she frowned. Why was Earl Doozier calling her?

Curious, and more than a bit concerned, Skye hurried out of the bedroom, closed the door, and said, "Hi, Earl. What's up?"

"Miz Skye?" The connection was poor and Earl's voice crackled. "Are you by yourself?"

"Except for CJ and Eva in the next room." Skye found herself glancing around as if someone might have snuck inside the RV while she was putting the twins to sleep. "Why?"

"I needs you to come get me, right now," Earl panted. "I cain't be found here."

"Where?" Skye's heart thudded. "What's wrong?"

What had Earl done now? And why would he call Skye and not one of his kinfolk for a ride? Maybe he'd been in a wreck. But in that case, one of his relatives would still have been a better choice.

"Miz Skye." Earl started to sob. "I'm in real bad trouble and you're the only one that can help."

"But I don't have a sitter." As soon as the words left her mouth, Skye wondered how many times in the future she'd be saying that. "I guess I could bring the babies."

"No!" Earl yelped. "Cain't your ma watch 'em, or the chief's pa?"

"I'll try to find someone." Skye remembered that Carson had mentioned stopping by sometime that morning to see the progress on the new house. "Where are you?"

Earl named an address in one of the swankier areas of Scumble River. The houses were all built on two-acre wooded lots and cost close to a million.

Earl's voice squawked in Skye's ear. "I ain't got no car, so I'll be hiding." Then before she could ask him any more questions, he disconnected.

Skye immediately called her father-in-law and explained the situation. He wasn't thrilled that she was going out to rescue Earl, and downright unhappy she was doing it on her own. But after she explained how often Earl had saved her, Carson acquiesced

85

on the condition that Skye agree to his security detail accompanying her and promise to press the app on her cell if she needed help from them.

She gave in with the caveat that they kept their distance. With negotiations completed, Carson said he'd be there as soon as he could.

Her father-in-law arrived fifteen minutes later. An older version of Wally, he strode inside the RV and swept Skye into a hug, then hung his coat in the foyer closet.

"I still don't like you going to rescue Earl Doozier," Carson grumbled.

"I'll be fine. Your bodyguards will be with me." Skye rushed to the door, adding over her shoulder, "Thanks for babysitting!"

Dashing to her SUV before Carson could follow her and continue his objections, Skye unlocked the door and threw her tote bag on the seat. As she headed toward the ritzy subdivision, she used the hands-free feature in the Mercedes to phone Earl.

The call kept going to voicemail, and by the time Skye approached the house number that Earl had given her, her pulse was racing. Would she find the man hurt — or worse — when she got there?

As Skye turned into the driveway and got out of the SUV something moved near the side of the large two-story house, and from the shadows an Earl-like voice whispered, "Psst. Miz Skye. Over yonder."

Skye stepped off the pavement and onto the grass, then blinked when she got a look at the man speaking to her. Why in the world was Earl wearing a turkey costume?

Before Skye could fully grasp the sight in front of her, Earl grabbed her hand and started pulling her toward the backyard.

"Wait a minute!" Skye tried to drag her heels, but for a skinny little guy with a potbelly, Earl was stronger than she figured.

He yanked her into a metal shed and closed the door. Dim light poured through dirty windows and Skye was concerned to see sweat dripping from under the bright red turkey head perched on top of Earl's own cranium. The yellow plastic beak bobbed as he spoke.

"Miz Skye, you gots to get me out of here." He clutched the orange feathers over his chest and said, "I'm a cooked goose if anyone sees me."

Skye didn't correct his choice of fowl, but instead asked, "Why are you dressed that way?"

"It's my new business." Earl grinned, his tail feathers wagging. "I's selling Turkeygrams." He strutted around the small space on his yellow foam turkey feet. "Folks order a turkey cake for their friends and kinfolk."

"Turkey cake?" Skye wrinkled her forehead, hoping he meant a cake shaped like a turkey, not a cake made out of turkey.

"Yep." Earl continued to swagger in front of her on scrawny legs that Skye had to admit went well with his costume. "The cake has chocolate, vanilla, and our secret flavor, and one of my Turkettes deliver it."

"Turkettes?"

"All the Doozier women" — Earl scratched under his wing — " 'cept for MeMa, who's bakin' the cakes, dress in sexy turkey costumes to make the deliveries."

"Sexy turkey costumes?" Skye couldn't stop herself from repeating what Earl said.

"Yous know." Earl thumped Skye's arm. "Short little feather skirts and those busty things."

"Bustiers?"

"Uh. Huh."

Feeling dazed, Skye tried to clarify. "So you're going door-to-door to sell these Turkeygrams that your MeMa is baking, and the rest of your female relatives are delivering dressed as turkey strippers?"

"Yep." Earl beamed, then frowned. "It was goin' real good until I got to this house." He pointed through the shed's tiny window.

Skye squinted, but as far as she could see everything looked normal. In fact, the yard looked as if it were ready for a photo shoot in *Better Homes and Gardens.*

There was an enclosed in-ground pool, a lavish deck containing expensive-looking outdoor furniture, and a huge princess castle playhouse surrounded by a pink picket fence.

However, clearly since a man dressed like Thanksgiving dinner had her hiding in a toolshed, something was wrong. But did she really want to know what it was?

Giving in to the inevitable, Skye asked, "What happened?"

"No one answered the door, but there was a car in the driveway and I heared somethin' back yonder so's I walked around the house and poked around a mite, then I saw her."

"Saw who?" Skye asked, once again not sure she really wanted to know.

"I's guessin' the lady of the house." Earl's Adam's apple bobbled.

"What was she doing?" Skye asked, hoping it wasn't something risqué.

"Nothin'." Earl's gaze searched Skye's face. "She's deader than a revenuer trying to close down a still."

She fought to keep her expression neutral.

"Could you have had too much to drink and imagined it?"

"In dog beers, I only had one." Earl laughed hysterically at his joke.

"So you're positive?"

"I's pretty durn sure," Earl said, the red turkey head wobbling in time with his nods. "There's a butcher knife stickin' out of the side of her head, so even iffen she's a zombie, she's dead."

CHAPTER 6
LEAVING HOME AIN'T EASY

"Did you see anyone else around?" Skye slid her cell phone from her jean's pocket, ready to call for help, but Earl grabbed her wrist.

"There ain't been nary a creature stirrin' since I was back here."

"Are you sure?" Skye asked, looking over her shoulder as if she expected someone swinging a machete to spring out from behind the huge riding mower behind her. "Maybe they're hiding in the house."

"The back door was unlocked so I moseyed around in there afore I called you." Earl shrugged at Skye's gasp. "Don't worry none about me, Miz Skye. I'm always packin' and I didn't touch nothing."

He pulled up the bottom of his costume and Skye saw a handgun tucked into Earl's camo boxer shorts. Thank goodness that was all she saw before he dropped the turkey suit back into place.

91

Skye still held her phone ready to call Wally, but just in case Earl was having a psychotic break she asked, "Where's the woman you saw?"

"By the castle." Earl jerked his thumb upward toward the playhouse.

"Why didn't you call 911 instead of me?" Skye asked, then answered herself. "Because you don't trust the police and figured they'd blame you."

"A course they would." Earl scowled. "They 'uns been tryin' to pin somethin' on me for years. 'Specially that sergeant. He's a mean one."

Skye barely kept from rolling her eyes. "Sergeant Quirk would never try to frame an innocent man." She was sure of that, even if he did have some anger management issues. "And he's not mean."

"Not to you." Earl crossed his wings. "But that ain't true for the rest of us."

"Really?" Skye made a mental note to relay that information to Wally. Quirk seemed to have been doing better with his temper, but maybe once he wasn't being observed by his chief he didn't try as hard. "Well, I'll call and make sure Wally comes and not the sergeant."

"Maybe you oughta take a look first." Earl's face turned a deep shade of red and he grabbed Skye's hand, towing her outside the shed and toward the castle.

"Why?" Skye asked as he half dragged her toward the pink picket fence.

Instead of answering, he pushed open the gate with his hip and Skye took an involuntary step forward. Earl was right. Lying across the threshold of a custom-built playhouse was a dead woman with a knife sticking out of the side of her head. But what he had failed to mention was that the woman was Jerita Quinn.

Blinking, Skye backed away until she was on the other side of the little fence. In an effort to remain calm, she scanned the rest of the yard. A thick band of trees framed three sides and she knew that the neighbors wouldn't have been able to see a thing back there.

Skye glanced at Earl, who was hopping from one turkey foot to the other as if he had to go to the bathroom, and said, "I'm calling Wally."

Skye realized that she still held her cell and tapped the icon for her contact list, but before she could swipe Wally's picture, Earl said, "Wait."

"For what?" Skye asked.

"Couldn't I just leave and you tell your hubby you found her?" Earl took a step away, but this time it was Skye's turn to grab his wrist.

"No." Skye's nails dug into his skin as he struggled to free himself.

"Why not?" Earl squeaked. "I didn't do it and I didn't see nothin' so I'm not a witness."

"I'm sorry." Skye's voice softened. "Truly, I understand not wanting to be involved. But you might know something you don't even realize."

Something flickered behind Earl's eyes and he said, "I is more confused than a chameleon in a bag of jelly beans." With that, he wrenched himself free and ran toward the trees.

Well, shoot! Skye hesitated.

Should she try to catch him? It wasn't as if she didn't know where he lived. Before she could decide, two large men dressed in black jeans and long-sleeved black T-shirts and wearing headsets stepped out of the trees. Each held the runaway Doozier by an arm and Earl's bright yellow feet dangled several inches off the ground.

So much for Carson's promise that his security team would remain in their vehicle unless Skye hit the panic button. The two men must have circled around as soon as Skye left their field of vision.

94

Skye raised a censuring eyebrow at them and said, "I wasn't in trouble."

"No, ma'am." Both men responded but didn't elaborate even when she glared.

Giving up, Skye jerked her chin at Earl. "Put him in the shed while I call Wally."

"Yes, ma'am." Both guards nodded, carried Earl into the toolshed, and stood with their backs against the door and their arms crossed.

"Where are your coats?" Skye asked.

"No need for them, ma'am."

"Fine." A part of Skye wanted to scold the men for being overprotective, but another part of her was a little relieved. With her penchant for finding bodies, having backup probably wasn't a bad thing.

Skye tapped the Send button on her phone and frowned when Wally's cell went directly to voicemail, as did his private number at the station. Sighing, Skye dialed the nonemergency police number. As she listened to the phone ring, she checked her watch. Earl had called her less than an hour ago. Somehow it seemed longer.

When Thea answered, Skye identified herself and said, "I need to talk to Wally."

"He's in the mayor's office," Thea said, then demanded, "Is something wrong with the babies?"

"No," Skye answered quickly before the daytime dispatcher could sound an alarm. "But we do have an issue, so please get him on the line."

"What's wrong?" Thea's voiced oozed with suspicion. "Are you positive the babies are okay? You can tell me. I won't call May."

Skye repeated her assurances and her request to speak to Wally.

Finally, Thea told her to wait and put her on hold. Immediately Muzak blared in Skye's ear. But before she could identify the song, Wally was on the line.

Sounding out of sorts, he asked, "Are you and the twins okay?"

Skye assured him she and the babies were fine, then said, "I'm with Earl Doozier at Jerita and Beilin Quinn's house." Skye rattled off the address.

"Our contractor?" Wally asked, sounding bemused. "Why are you there? And why is Earl Doozier with you?"

Skye filled him in on the phone call that she'd received from Earl, then said, "I had no idea the address he gave me was the Quinn residence." She sighed. "Anyway, Earl was going door-to-door selling Turkey-grams — I'll explain that later — and found Jerita Quinn dead in the backyard."

"I take it you don't believe it was natural

causes," Wally groaned.

"There's a knife in the side of her head," Skye said, then added, "So no."

"Son of a bi . . . bison!" Wally bellowed. "Are you sure the killer's not still around?"

"Earl searched the house and didn't find anyone." Interrupting Wally's non-swearing version of cursing, she added, "I wasn't here when he did it, the back door was unlocked, and you know darn well that Earl was armed and able to take care of himself."

"I'll be right there," Wally said. "Get into your car, lock the doors, and wait."

"Relax." Skye chuckled. "Your father's security team is here so I'm pretty darn sure not even Genghis Khan could get to me."

"What —" Wally cut himself off and said, "Never mind. I'll be there in five. You can tell me everything then. Call my cell if anything happens."

Turning to the men guarding Earl, Skye said, "Chief Boyd says hi."

They grunted, then leaned against the door, ignoring Earl's complaints and threats. While she waited, Skye walked to the front yard and called Carson to tell him she'd be a little longer than she thought. He told her to take as much time as she needed. He, Eva, and CJ were having fun together. When he didn't ask her any questions about the situation, she suspected his security guys had already reported in.

Seconds later, Wally's cruiser, with lights flashing and sirens wailing, raced down the street. He pulled the squad car across the driveway, effectively blocking anyone from entering or leaving, and leaped from the vehicle.

Skye met him halfway and he enveloped her in a hug and rained kisses on her face. Finally, he held her away from him and examined her for injuries.

Once he was convinced she was okay, he said, "Where's Earl?"

Taking him by the hand, she led him around the house, watched as he took in the two men guarding the toolshed, then said, "Earl may not be the most cooperative witness."

"Like he ever is." Wally gave her fingers one last squeeze, then released her and said, "Where's the body?"

"Behind the pink picket fence." Skye gestured to the castle.

Wally marched over to the playhouse, looked over the gate, and said, "I'll check the house, then call the coroner and techs."

"Shouldn't you have backup?" Skye glanced at the security guards and explained, "I mean other officers." When Wally raised an eyebrow, she shrugged. "I know I said Earl searched the premises, but what if . . ."

"How long have you been here?" Wally asked, but didn't wait for her answer before adding, "Either the murderer was already long gone before either of you arrived, or, unless he or she is a moron, the killer escaped out the front while you guys were in the backyard."

"Right." Skye knew she wasn't being logical. She knew that the murderer would have attacked Earl or her rather than wait for an armed police officer. But now that she and Wally had kids, some protective instinct had kicked into high gear and she worried about everyone even more than she had before becoming a mother.

Wally kissed her on the cheek and told her to wait with the security team. Returning a few minutes later, his expression was grim as he made his calls. Then he tucked his cell phone into his shirt pocket and rubbed the back of his neck.

Skye hurried up to him and asked, "Did you see anything inside?"

"Nothing seems disturbed." Wally glanced in the direction of the body. "The county crime techs in Laurel will be here in about forty minutes and Reid is on his way. For once he was in town when we needed him instead of gallivanting somewhere in the city."

"Uh-huh." Skye murmured noncommittally, unwilling to comment.

Simon Reid, Skye's ex-boyfriend, was the coroner, as well as the owner of the local funeral parlor and Bunny Lanes. His mother managed the bowling alley he'd named for her, but she was currently out of a job until the damage from a bomb was repaired.

Skye and Simon had dated on and off for over two years, then she thought she caught him cheating on her. He'd been too stubborn to explain his actions and shortly afterward, Wally and Skye became an item. The three of them working together was always awkward.

Skye had hoped that when Simon started dating Emerald Jones, the tension would ease, but it hadn't. Emmy had arrived in Scumble River after getting into some kind of trouble in Las Vegas, promptly flirted with Wally at his gun club, and then ended up dating Skye's ex.

Although not exactly BFF material, Skye had tried to be cordial to her. However, every time they were in the same room, the outrageous woman managed to get on Skye's last nerve.

Shoving away all thoughts of Emmy and Simon, Skye thought about the crime scene. She concentrated on what she might have observed.

Wally had moved over to talk to the men guarding the toolshed and was taking notes when the thing that had been bothering Skye clicked into place and she snapped her fingers. She waited until Wally dismissed the security team, stuck his baton through the handles of the shed to keep Earl inside, then joined him by the shed.

"I just realized that Mrs. Quinn doesn't have on a coat." Skye pulled her own jacket tighter. "So she didn't expect to be outside very long."

"Hmm." Wally walked back over to the fence and peered over the pink pickets. "You're right. She's only wearing a blouse and slacks."

"I wonder if she heard something and came out to check." Skye took a deep breath. "I think people who move here from the city feel that they are safe from crime."

"Maybe." Wally sighed. "And although that's usually true, it isn't always the case." Skye nodded, and at the sound of a siren, Wally said, "That must be Quirk. I called him to report for duty."

Sergeant Roy Quirk was Wally's right hand

at the PD. He usually worked second shift, but with a murder, he was needed on days.

Wally headed to the front of the house with Skye trailing him. She watched as he and Roy began protecting the crime scene by stringing bright-yellow tape between sawhorses and her mind wandered to the twins and returning to work and a thousand other mundane thoughts.

Blinking back to reality, Skye realized that she was avoiding the real issue. Jerita Quinn was dead and her husband, Skye and Wally's contractor, would be a prime suspect. Especially since he'd confided to Wally that he and his wife had been fighting about their daughter.

Skye blanched. She'd forgotten all about Jenna. Where was the little girl? Skye checked her watch and blew out a relieved breath. Jenna would still be in school. Thank goodness Scumble River had begun all-day kindergarten this year.

Finished with securing the perimeter, Wally came back and said, "You have a strange look on your face." He stroked her arms and asked, "Do you feel all right? You can head home and we can go over everything later."

"I'm fine," Skye reassured him. "Just considering what I know about Jerita."

"Oh?" Wally stroked his chin. "You mean besides being married to our contractor."

"Uh-huh." Skye's cheeks reddened. Previously, she'd had to keep Jerita's lawsuit against Homer and the school from Wally because of confidentiality, but with her murder all constraints were gone. "Remember the parent meeting I attended after we talked to Mr. Baker?"

Wally nodded, then raised both his eyebrows and said, "It was with Jerita Quinn?"

"Yes." Skye tucked her suddenly cold hands into the pockets of her jacket. "And she is, I mean was, Loretta's new paralegal."

"Well, crap!" Wally started to say something else, but stopped when Simon pulled his shiny Lexus behind the cruiser blocking the driveway.

He jumped out of the car and jogged up to Wally and Skye carrying a black doctor's case that Skye knew contained a camera, stethoscope, flashlight, rubber gloves, and liver thermometer. The body bag would arrive with his assistant in the hearse.

Wally nodded a greeting and said, "Reid."

"Boyd." Simon jerked his chin in response, then asked, "Where's the body?"

Simon was the exact opposite of Wally. Where Skye's husband was muscular, Simon was built more like a male model. His auburn hair was never out of place, while the short black strands on Wally's head often stood up from his fingers combing through them. But the biggest difference was Simon's eyes. Skye had never seen them anything but cool and appraising, while Wally's were always warm when she looked into them.

"The vic's around back by the playhouse." Wally gestured over his shoulder. "We'll have to wait for the crime techs to get here before you can move her, but in the meantime, try to get a time of death."

Before Simon could move, the sound of wood splintering ripped through the air. Wally took off toward the backyard with Roy, Skye, and Simon on his heels.

As they rounded the corner, Skye's mouth dropped open. A riding lawn mower continued to roll over what remained of the toolshed's door, and once it cleared the debris, it picked up speed until Earl Doozier's tail feathers disappeared into the trees. She had no idea that a lawn mower could go that fast. It had to be doing thirty miles an hour. Had Beilin souped-up his mower? But why?

CHAPTER 7
HOME AIN'T WHERE HIS HEART IS ANYMORE

While Wally and Quirk took off in pursuit of Earl and Simon examined Jerita Quinn's body, Skye returned to the front of the house. She'd seen enough of that particular backyard to last her a lifetime. She was cold, her feet hurt from standing so long, and she wanted to be somewhere else. Preferably someplace warm, but she'd settle for somewhere she could at least sit down.

Spotting a wicker chair on the front porch, Skye sank gratefully into its brightly colored cushions and looked around. All the homes in this development were located on their own slight rises, and from her perch she could observe two of the houses across the street, as well the ones on either side of her.

With it being a Monday morning, Skye figured most of Jerita and Beilin's neighbors were probably at work. Still, there was always somebody who was home. And even with the large secluded lots separating the homes, a few people had responded to the sound of the sirens and come outside, doubtlessly determined to find out what was disturbing the peace in their exclusive subdivision.

From her comfy chair, Skye observed a couple of thirtysomething women, one blond and one brunette, dressed in designer tracksuits and standing at the end of one of their driveways. A redheaded woman in yoga pants holding a toddler's hand was a little to their side as if she weren't quite part of the group.

All three women wore those puffer vests that were so popular. Skye couldn't understand the appeal of the garment. Not only did it seem as if it wouldn't do much to keep you warm, but its bulkiness added the illusion of inches to their midriffs. And Skye was pretty darn sure most people didn't want to look like the Michelin Man.

Oh well. Skye smoothed her navy fleece jacket. *To each their own.*

The women were staring at her and Skye figured she should really put her time to good use. As she got to her feet, a groan escaped from her lips and she scrubbed her tired eyes. It was tough to be alert on so little sleep.

With a genial expression on her face, Skye

skirted the squad car blocking her way and crossed the street.

Strolling toward the lookie-loos, Skye waved and said, "Hi, I'm Skye Denison-Boyd. I work with the police department as a psychological consultant."

The trio returned her greeting, then the blond, the one Skye had immediately pegged as the leader of the group, said, "My name's Stacy Carter. What's going on at the Quinns'?"

"I'm afraid Mrs. Quinn has passed away," Skye answered carefully.

Considering the police call had gone out over the radio and the hearse was about to arrive any minute, she was pretty sure Wally wouldn't mind her revealing that Jerita was dead, but she would have to keep the details to herself. Especially the part about the murder.

The brunette introduced herself as Liz Semkiu and asked, "What happened to Jerita?"

"Cause of death hasn't been determined yet," Skye answered. Which was true. COD wouldn't be official until the medical examiner's report arrived on Wally's desk and it *was* possible that she'd been stabbed in the temple with a knife after she died.

"Maybe it was a heart attack. She was an

older mom after all." The woman with the toddler shook her head sadly, then added, "By the way, I'm Marla Ainsley, and this is Leo."

"Nice to meet you." Skye smiled at the boy, then focused on the mother. "Do you know Mrs. Quinn's age?"

"I think she was fortyish?" Marla looked at the other two women.

"She was forty-eight," Stacy said with certainty. "Jerita told me they had been trying for a baby for a long time and when she turned forty-two they decided to give it one more chance."

"Right." Liz nodded. "And little Jenna was five the end of October." She looked at the other two women. "Do you remember that over-the-top party Jerita had for her birthday?" Glancing at Skye she said, "Jenna is really into the whole princess thing, and Jerita not only had an actor playing Prince Charming, she came up with a live unicorn." At Skye's doubtful expression she shrugged. "Well, she rented a white horse dyed like a rainbow with a glittering horn somehow attached to his forehead."

"Wow!" Skye hoped May never heard about that party or heaven knew what she'd do to top it for Eva and CJ's first birthdays.

"You can say that again." Stacy *tsked.* "I

108

thought poor Beilin was going to stroke out when he saw what Jerita had done. He was always afraid she would spoil their daughter and make her into a brat."

"Hmm." Skye paused a second to tuck that info away, then said, "Were you three home all morning?" Skye hoped she hadn't been too abrupt. When the three women nodded without reacting to the sudden change of subject, she asked, "Have you seen any strangers hanging around the neighborhood?"

"Just the weird guy in the turkey suit." Stacy wrinkled her nose. "I glanced out my window and saw some woman with big hair and boobs ready to pop out of her shirt driving a rusty car drop him off about an hour ago."

Marla stooped to wipe her son's runny nose, then said, "I think it was more like ninety minutes. Leo was watching *Snickerdoo*."

"Whatever, Marla." Stacy rolled her eyes. "That turkey guy is the only nonresident I've seen. But of course, I don't just stare out the window so . . ."

"We have had an occasional hunter come through our woods. I live there." Liz pointed to the house next to the Quinns'. "All of us on that side of the street have property lines that back up to cornfields, and sometimes those guys ignore the 'no trespassing' sign."

Before Skye could respond, Stacy grabbed her hand and asked, "Has Beilin been notified?" When Skye shook her head, she *tsked* again. "That poor, poor man. He's such a sweetheart." She licked her glossy lips. "Handsome too." Smiling she added, "And not to mention successful."

"Seriously, Stacy?" Liz put her hands on her hips. "I doubt Jerita is even cold yet and you're planning on going after Beilin?"

"Well, your husband didn't run off with a slut he met online." Stacy glared at Liz, then smiled meanly. "At least not yet."

Marla looked at Skye, jerked her chin at the two other women, and winked. "Mr. Rogers didn't exactly prepare me for these neighbors."

Skye laughed and Stacy said, "It's just that Jerita was always yelling at Beilin and he really is a nice guy."

"The police will be notifying him soon," Skye assured the blond, then had an inspiration. "Do you know where he might be?"

Stacy narrowed her eyes at Skye, paused, then as something seemed to click, she said, "Are you married to the police chief?"

"I am," Skye admitted.

"Then you know where Beilin is," Stacy

110

accused. "He's working on your house. According to Jerita, he's there from dawn to dusk."

"Really?" Skye added that piece of info to her mental folder on Beilin and Jerita's relationship. He might be at their house now, but he sure hadn't been there every single day from sunup to sundown. "I guess that's where we better check first then."

"Yes." Stacy crossed her arms. "And you should give that man a rest too."

"Uh-huh," Skye said noncommittally, then asked, "You mentioned that Jerita yelled at Beilin a lot? Do you know what they were fighting about?"

"It used to be just that they seemed to disagree about how to raise their daughter," Stacy answered. "But lately it was everything. She — Hey." Stacy interrupted herself. "Why are you asking about Beilin and Jerita's fighting?"

"Yeah." Liz moved until she was shoulder to shoulder with her friend. "And why did you want to know if we'd seen any strangers?"

"Jerita didn't have a heart attack, did she?" Marla put her hand to her mouth.

"As I said before, cause of death hasn't been established." Skye edged backward. It was clear she'd gotten as much info as possible from the women.

"If you're interested in the Quinns' marriage and people hanging around, that means something bad happened to Jerita." Stacy's lips formed a stubborn line. "You tell us what's going on right now."

"You'll be informed if there is any threat to your safety." As soon as the words left Skye's mouth she could have slapped herself.

All three women screamed. Marla grabbed Leo and hustled him across the road and into their house. Liz ran for her front door too.

Only Stacy stood her ground and said, "If someone hurt Jerita, it wasn't Beilin. That man bent over backward to give her everything she wanted. He would never harm a hair on her head."

"That's good to know." Skye eased farther away. "Thank you."

As she walked back up the Quinns' driveway, she noticed Wally and Roy coming around the side of the house. Since they didn't have Earl in tow, Skye guessed that the Doozier had gotten away.

Skye bit her lips in a struggle to contain an inappropriate giggle at the image of Earl wearing a turkey suit as he rode a lawn mower down the center of Basin Street, and when Wally reached her he asked, "Everything okay?"

"Fine. I had a nice chat with the neighbors, which I'll tell you all about when you're ready," Skye said. Then she remembered Stacy's interest in Jerita's husband and continued, "But if you want to be the one to tell Beilin about his wife's death, and if you haven't already done it, you might want to send Roy over to pick him up." Skye quickly added, "Oh. And make sure he can't answer his cell phone."

"Why is that?" Wally asked.

But since he was already gesturing for Roy to come over, Skye waited until the sergeant had joined them before she explained, "One of the neighbors, a woman named Stacy Carter, seemed very fond of Beilin. I'm guessing that if she hasn't already contacted him, she's going to try to call him soon, and tell him that something's going on at his place."

"Go . . . sh darn it!" Wally jerked his chin at Roy. "Go scoop him up right now and try to get ahold of his phone without violating any of his rights." When the sergeant hesitated, Wally thumped him on the shoulder, "He's our builder and is probably at our new house."

Once the sergeant roared off, Skye looked

around and asked, "Where's the hearse?"

"Xavier was on a pickup at Laurel Hospital when I called Reid." Wally's jaw twitched. "He should be here with it any minute."

"Did Simon figure out the time of Jerita's death yet?"

"Let's hold off on that right now." Wally patted her shoulder. "Tonight, over dinner, we'll exchange all the information we've gathered."

"Oh goody." Skye's tone was less than enthusiastic. "My favorite kind of date. We haven't had Suspects and Supper in at least a month."

Wally looked at her quizzically, but before he could respond, the county's crime tech van pulled behind the remaining squad car.

"Finally." Wally kissed Skye's cheek. "I'll get the techs started."

While he was gone, Skye dug out her cell phone and called Piper. She explained the situation and instructed the intern to pull Jenna from her kindergarten class before rumors started to fly around the school. They couldn't let the little girl find out about her mother's death by overhearing teachers talking about it on the playground. She also told Piper that until she heard from Beilin she couldn't inform Jenna about Jerita's passing.

After hanging up, Skye thought about the issue and decided she'd have to hang around until Roy came back with Beilin, then once Wally told him about his wife's death she'd ask if he wanted Piper to break the news to his daughter.

Lost in thought, Skye didn't see the crime tech approach and let out a startled yelp when the woman cleared her throat and said, "Mrs. Boyd?"

"Yes?" Skye wasn't sure if she was asking her identity or had a question.

"Hmm." The tech pursed her lips, then plainly coming to a decision, nodded. "We'd like to process you now if you're ready?"

"Process me? Why?" Skye frowned. "I didn't touch the body or anything around it."

"The chief told me to do it." The woman's shrug conveyed that hers was not to reason why, and when she spoke her tone brooked no argument. "I believe you were in close contact with a suspect."

"Okay then." Skye stood and looked around. "How do we do this?"

"Would you have any other clothing you could change into?" the tech asked. "If so, we can use the garage since it's been cleared."

"I have a pair of yoga pants and a sweatshirt in my car." Skye scowled. "But no other coat, so I'll need to get that back right away."

She didn't mind giving up her jeans and top, but since she hadn't had time to replace many of the clothes she'd lost in the tornado, she was wearing her only jacket. If she gave it up she'd have to go shopping ASAP. Which would be just peachy with the twins.

"Sorry, I can't do that." The woman's face was blank of expression. "With only two of us, we only process what we can't collect."

Even though the tech's unit covered the entire county, Skye wondered if the woman was just being a pain. Surely it wouldn't take that long to press some tape, or whatever they did, on her coat.

She opened her mouth to protest, but before she could form the words, the tech said, "I'll meet you in the garage. Please hurry."

"Terrific." Skye headed for her car, muttering under her breath.

After retrieving the extra set of clothes she kept for emergencies such as baby poop and liquid burps, Skye trotted up the driveway and into the now open garage. She noticed that although there were three spaces, only one vehicle, a Volvo XC90, was parked inside.

The crime tech closed the overhead door, then had Skye stand on a large sheet of white paper and take off her jeans, shirt, and coat. The clothes were packaged separately and tagged. Then the tech scraped under Skye's nails, combed her hair into a bag, and ran what looked like a lint brush over her exposed skin.

The whole process took less than fifteen minutes, and as Skye exited the garage, Wally came around the corner from the Quinns' backyard. He took one look at her unhappy expression, removed his jacket, and slipped it over her shoulders. As she snuggled into the coat's warmth, she raised a questioning eyebrow.

"Sorry about that, but since you said Earl was pressed against you in the shed, we needed to collect any evidence that might have passed from him onto you," Wally explained, as he fetched a windbreaker from the squad car's trunk. It had *Scumble River Police* stenciled across the back in large white letters. "Any chance the turkey killed her?"

"I didn't see any blood on him." Skye threw up her hands. "And why would he call me to come here instead of just leaving if he murdered her?"

"Who knows how that man's mind works."
Wally tapped his chin. "I mean, running
away when it's not exactly a secret where he
lives doesn't seem logical either."

"If he's really scared, he'll disappear into
Doozier territory until we catch the murderer."

"Probably. Earl ditched the lawn mower
at the edge of the field and disappeared into
the corn." Wally looked around. "Hasn't
Quirk come back with Beilin yet?"

"No." Skye wrinkled her brow. "And it's
only a five-minute drive from here to our
house."

"Great!" Wally snarled. "Another missing
suspect."

CHAPTER 8
HONEY, I'M HOME

Wally watched Skye's Mercedes speed away down the street. A few minutes ago, Carson had called to say that Eva felt warm and wouldn't stop crying. Skye had immediately run for her SUV, impatiently waiting for him to move the squad car so she could get out of the driveway.

He'd wanted to go with her, but Quirk had just returned with Beilin Quinn and he'd had to be content with calling after Skye to keep him posted about their daughter's health. Her distracted wave was the only acknowledgment that she'd heard him.

As his wife's vehicle disappeared from sight, Wally refocused, turned to Quirk, and snapped, "What took you so long?"

Before the sergeant could answer, Beilin rushed up to Wally and demanded, "What's going on?"

Beilin was a big guy and Wally immediately put some distance between them, unsnapped his holster, and rested his hand on his weapon. Quirk followed suit.

"Whoa!" Beilin held up his hands. "There's no need for weapons."

"Step back and don't move," Wally ordered, then looked at Quirk and said, "Report."

"I arrived at the construction site, found Mr. Quinn inside, and told him that he was needed at home." The sergeant's expression was stoic. "We walked out to the squad car and found that it had a flat. After changing the tire, we drove directly here. There was no other exchange of information with Mr. Quinn."

"Yeah." Beilin scowled. "The sergeant here wouldn't answer any of my questions and I'm getting fed up with both of your attitudes."

Wally ignored the man. All the cruisers had recently been rotated through their monthly maintained schedule and that flat seemed awfully convenient in delaying Quirk.

His cop instinct kicked into high gear, Wally made eye contact with Quirk and said, "As soon as we're finished here, drop the tire off at Black Bear Repairs and have Grizzly examine it for signs of vandalism before he fixes it."

"Yes, sir." Quirk nodded.

"Look." Beilin wrinkled his face. "Clearly something's wrong here. Did we have another break-in?" He ran his fingers through his hair. "Thank God, this time of day Jerita's at work and Jenna's at school."

"I don't recall hearing about the previous incident." As the chief, he read all the officers' logs. "When did it occur and what was stolen?"

"It was about ten days ago and I didn't bother to file a police report. It looked as if the lock had been picked because there was no damage to the door." Beilin shrugged. "Nothing valuable was taken. There was just a bit of vandalism. I upgraded the deadbolts on both the front and French doors and figured that would stop any casual thief."

"Hmm." Wally pulled out his memo pad and made a note to question Beilin more about that later, then keeping his voice casual and Jerita in the present tense, he said, "You mentioned that your wife is at work. What are her hours?"

"She drops off Jenna at school around eight fifteen, then heads to the office. She works until she picks Jenna up at three thirty," Beilin answered, then asked, "Do you want me to call her to come home?"

121

He patted his pockets, then frowned. "Oh. I forgot the sergeant borrowed my cell phone. I need to get it back from him."

Wally was impressed that Quirk had managed to get Beilin's phone away from him. He couldn't legally confiscate it, but he certainly could ask to use it and forget to return it to its owner.

Disregarding Beilin's comment about getting his phone back, Wally asked, "Is there any reason that your wife might be home rather than at work?"

"If she didn't feel well or Jenna got sick," Beilin said slowly. "Why? Was she here when the break-in happened? Is she all right?"

"I'm afraid she was here." Wally carefully watched the man's reaction as he continued, "And I am very sorry to inform you that your wife is dead."

"No!" Beilin screamed and Wally grabbed his arms to stop him from falling, but he sank to his knees. "What happened? Was it her heart?"

Wally blinked. Skye had mentioned the neighbor had asked about a heart attack too.

"Did she have a medical condition?"

"She had a congenital heart problem, but she was real careful to follow the doc's orders and had been doing well on the meds for years."

"I see." Wally rubbed his chin. "While we won't know for sure until after the medical examiner submits his report, we currently believe that she was murdered."

Beilin tried to rise his feet. "I want to see her."

"I'm sorry, but your wife's body is on the way to the medical examiner at Laurel Hospital." Wally took Beilin's elbow and helped him get up. "You can head over there and see her as soon as he finishes."

"But . . ." Beilin tried to pull away. "Then I need to get my daughter from school."

"She's with the acting school psychologist," Wally said, then asked, "Would you like Ms. Townsend to break the news to Jenna or would you rather do that yourself?"

"Maybe together?" Beilin sounded completely at a loss.

Wally felt sorry for the man. He tried to imagine raising CJ and Eva without Skye and shuddered, then quickly pushed away that horrific thought.

"I'm sure Ms. Townsend would be happy to help you." Wally led Beilin toward the house. "I'll let her know, and she'll keep Jenna occupied until you get there."

"Thank you." The contractor's voice cracked.

While Beilin stared into space, Wally made

the call, then while he was at it, checked in with Skye. She assured him that Eva didn't have a fever and seemed fine. She'd stopped crying shortly after Skye arrived home.

Returning his attention to Beilin, Wally asked, "Did your wife have any enemies?"

"Of course not!" Beilin snapped. "She was a good woman who was devoted to me and our daughter."

"How about her job?" Wally probed. "She worked for a lawyer. That kind of job could expose her to some people who might harbor hard feelings."

"She'd only been employed there a few weeks and her boss was wrapping up cases to go on maternity leave." Beilin shook his head. "Jerita said the most exciting thing she'd been doing was finishing up the paperwork for a will and a couple of real estate closings."

Wally nodded, keeping his expression neutral. It was odd that Beilin hadn't mentioned his wife's issue with the school. Hadn't he known that she'd had a meeting about their daughter's placement?

"Okay. One last thing." Wally turned to Beilin. "Before you go to pick up your daughter, it would be very helpful if you could walk through the house and backyard and tell me if you see anything out of place or missing. We need as much info as possible to figure out who killed your wife and the motive behind the crime."

The crime scene techs had completed their work and Reid had accompanied the body to the morgue, so Wally sent Quirk to deliver the tire to the repair shop. The sergeant was under orders to return to the station and hold down the fort until Wally got there or called with other instructions.

After Quirk was gone, Wally escorted Beilin into the house. It took a while and the contractor had broken down more than once, but he eventually managed to get through the residence and outside property.

With the exception of the busted door on the toolshed and the missing lawn mower, Beilin couldn't find anything different from when he left that morning. He did mention that he'd been working on the mower to enter the annual Christmas Day Stanley County lawn mower race, but Wally was deliberately vague about what happened with it or the shed. And Beilin seemed too overcome with the situation to press for details.

Finally, Wally gave the man a ride back to his truck at the construction site. Once the contractor left to go pick up his daughter,

Wally decided that he would stop in at the RV to see how his own daughter was doing. Despite Skye's assurances, he wanted to see Eva for himself.

While Wally drove the short distance to the motor home, he radioed Thea and asked, "Has Martinez been able to locate the suspect?"

Knowing that there were too many people listening to their scanners who would gladly join the hunt, he didn't use Earl's name. He didn't want to declare open season on Dooziers. At least not yet.

"Negative," Thea responded. "No sign of him at his residence."

"How about the rest of the family's properties?" Wally asked.

By family properties, he meant the territory, which included a good stretch of land beside the Scumble River. Two groups of people dwelled in an uneasy alliance along that parcel. There were the upstanding citizens, who either had inherited the acreage or bought it for their retirement homes, and the others who the locals disparagingly called the Red Raggers.

The Red Raggers consisted mostly of a clan that Wally likened to a pack of wild dogs. They were extremely loyal to their own kinfolk, but everyone else was prey. They were proof that evolution can go in reverse and took survival of the sneakiest to new heights.

"Nothing around that area either," Thea answered. "She's headed over to do a backward search from the suspect's last-known location."

"Fine." Wally braked behind Skye's SUV and said, "Have her take a look in the local bars and the park camping areas too."

"Will do," Thea responded, then added, "Ms. Ficher called to say she would be back in Illinois this afternoon and asked if you still needed to talk to her. I told her that Mrs. Baker hadn't been found so you probably did, and Ms. Ficher said she'd come by tomorrow afternoon."

"Excellent." Wally smiled. If anything happened to him, they should name Thea as chief. She could certainly handle the administrative part of the job. "I'll be 10-7, but call my cell if anything urgent comes up. Oh, and call in Anthony to patrol for the remainder of my shift."

"Got it." Thea paused, then added with a smile in her voice, "Kiss those babies for me, and give your sweet wife some sugar too."

"Always," Wally answered, then gazed out the squad car's windshield, staring at the empty field opposite their property while he tried to figure out if there was anything else he should be doing. With one woman missing and another murdered, he felt like there should be something.

But they'd run out of places to look for Mrs. Baker, and until the reports from the ME and crime techs started to come in or they found Earl Doozier, he couldn't think of what else to do about the murder. He'd already tried calling Loretta to see why Jerita wasn't at work, but she didn't answer her cell and he'd left her a message to get back to him ASAP.

Skye had reported that the neighbors hadn't noticed anyone except Earl around the Quinns' house. And Beilin hadn't been able to come up with any enemies, which left Wally at a loss as to who to talk to about Jerita.

Sighing, he exited the cruiser. Maybe Skye would have some ideas.

Eager to see his family, Wally ran up the RV's metal steps and opened the door. CJ and Eva were in their bouncy chairs with Skye sitting between them dangling various brightly colored toys for them to bat around. Bingo was curled up at her feet. He was also taking a turn at whacking the toys. Wally beamed. This was exactly the picture he needed in his head to wipe away the horror of Jerita's murder.

Skye looked up and said, "Your daughter is fine. I think Carson just got flustered with her crying. Both of these cuties are usually so good, he was thrown off by Miss Eva's little hissy fit."

Wally scooped up the little girl and kissed her neck. "You nearly gave Daddy a stroke, princess."

"Princess?" Skye arched an eyebrow.

"Yes." Wally grinned. "It clearly states princess on her birth certificate." As CJ made a noise, he looked over and said, "Don't worry, buddy. Yours says prince." Glancing back at Eva he admonished, "Don't ever scare me like that again."

"Right." Skye giggled. "I'm sure they'll never worry us in the future."

"Of course they won't." Wally kissed Eva's head, then asked, "Have they been fed?" When Skye nodded, he questioned, "Have you eaten?"

"Not yet." She tilted her head. "I bet you haven't had anything either."

"You're right." Wally held out his free hand to help Skye up from the floor. "I was hoping my sweet wife would have lunch with me."

"Oh." Skye looked around. "Did you pick

up something for us?"

"Uh . . . no." Wally's ears reddened. "But I could make a McDonald's run."

"Just kidding." Skye laughed. "How does toasted cheese and tomato soup sound?"

"Great." Wally headed toward the bedroom with his drowsing daughter. "I'll get the twins changed and into their bassinets."

"Terrific." Skye moved into the kitchen. "The food should be ready by the time you're done."

When he finished getting the babies settled, Wally returned to the kitchen. As soon as he sat at the table, Skye slid a steaming bowl of soup in front of him and a plate with a sandwich and chips.

After getting her own meal, she took the chair opposite him, and with a teasing grin said, "Not that I'm not thrilled with your company, but I'm surprised you're here with a fresh murder case."

"Martinez and Quirk are looking for Earl and I called Anthony in to patrol." Wally spooned soup into his mouth. "The earliest that there will be anything from the crime techs or ME is tomorrow."

"Hmm!" Skye bit into her toasted cheese, chewed, and swallowed, then asked, "Was Simon able to estimate a time of death?"

"Between eight and eleven." Wally ate half

his sandwich before adding, "And if Jerita dropped off Jenna at her usual time of eight fifteen, we can probably narrow it down to eight thirty."

"Beilin was late getting to the house this morning," Skye said thoughtfully. "The painter was looking for him and I think it was about a quarter to nine before he showed up." She took a sip of water. "I suppose it's possible he could have stuck a knife in his wife's head at eight thirty and made it here in fifteen minutes."

"Yep." Wally pursed his lips. "I know they'd been having some disagreements, but is that enough of a motive for him to kill her?"

"Anything is possible." Skye shrugged. "The neighbors said they were fighting a lot." She paused. "But those women all seemed to think Jerita was the aggressor and Beilin was the one who was innocent. But he was worried about her turning Jenna into a brat." She snapped her fingers. "I almost forgot. They also said that Beilin claims he's been working on our house from sunup to sundown, which is obviously untrue."

"Maybe he was having an affair," Wally said slowly. "But if Beilin did it, he's a damn good actor. He looked poleaxed when I told him."

"It's amazing how good people are at denial," Skye warned. "He might have been able to block the whole incident from his mind."

"That's true." Wally ate a few potato chips, then said, "Didn't you tell me about a mother who watched a video of her son doing something and refused to believe it was her child?"

"Uh-huh." Skye was silent, then asked, "But if Beilin is the killer, what did Earl hear that got him to look in the backyard? Beilin was already here by that time."

"Who knows?" Wally wiped his fingers on his napkin. "It could have been an animal or maybe Earl lied because he didn't want to get in trouble for trespassing."

"Seriously?" Skye snickered. "A Doozier afraid to get into trouble for anything less than murder?"

Wally chuckled his agreement, then said, "Tell me more about the neighbors."

"They seem affluent and nosy." Skye twitched her shoulders. "But the lots are big and wooded and it'd be pretty easy to keep out of sight." She fiddled with her spoon. "The blond, Stacy Carter, seemed to be the leader of the group, and she has the hots for Beilin."

"Enough to kill his wife to get him?" Wally

brightened. Maybe this was the lead he needed.

"Probably not." Skye shook her head. "I can't see someone like that getting her hands dirty. Unless she hired a hitman."

"Anything else you can think of that was suspicious?" Wally asked.

"Not off the top of my head." Skye got up and cleared the table. "Did the crime scene tech mention finding anything unusual? Were there prints on the knife?"

"No. It was from a set in the Quinns' kitchen and it was wiped clean." Wally rose to his feet and started to fill the sink. "Evidently Jerita has an amazing house-keeper because the tech said there wasn't even any dust." Wally squirted in dish soap. "Which was why he found it odd that there were pumpkin seed hulls on the floor near the trash can in the kitchen."

"Why does that ring a bell?" Skye asked as she picked up a dish towel. A second later, her beautiful green eyes widened and she said, "Oh. My. Gosh! It's Homer!"

"Homer?" Wally repeated stunned.

"Yes." Skye nodded. "His newest food addiction is pumpkin seeds."

"But why would he kill Jerita?" Wally asked, but didn't wait for an answer before he added, "Because she threatened to sue him personally."

Skye nodded. "Exactly."

CHAPTER 9
MAMA, I'M COMING HOME

"When are you going to interview Homer?" Skye asked, as they finished the dishes. She checked the microwave clock and saw that it was 2:48. "He doesn't stay very long after the bell rings at three, so he'll be leaving school soon."

"I'll have to handle this matter carefully." Wally scowled at his phone. "As soon as you told me about Homer's pumpkin seed habit, I texted the city attorney to get a warrant for his DNA. He just answered that a judge will say that Homer isn't the only one who consumes that type of snack, and he won't issue a warrant without more probable cause."

"I could probably . . ." Skye hesitated before offering her help.

If Homer wasn't the murderer and/or didn't go to jail, she would have to continue working with him. He was tough enough to deal with when he wasn't holding a grudge.

135

What would he be like if he blamed her for the police investigating him?

"You could probably what?" Wally asked, gazing at her expectantly.

"Grab a used paper cup or something from his trash can." She tilted her head. "Is that legal?"

"Anything that is thrown in the trash is considered intentionally relinquished and is free for anyone to take." Wally walked over to the bedroom and peeked in at the sleeping twins, then headed for the front door. "It's called abandoned DNA. However, we might have a problem with the chain of evidence."

Seeing Wally was about to leave, Skye quickly said, "I'll be at the school tomorrow morning for the PPS meeting, and I can try to get something from his garbage either before we start or after we finish."

Skye had arranged with her mother to watch the twins for a couple of hours so she could attend the Pupil Personnel Services conference. The teachers had been trying to slip a lot of evaluation referrals past Piper that they knew wouldn't make it through the process without significant prior interventions once Skye got back from maternity leave.

"That would be great. Worse comes to

136

worst, if whatever you get has DNA that matches the pumpkin seed hulls from the crime scene, we can use that evidence as probable cause," Wally said. Then he paused with his hand on the knob and added, "Just be careful and don't let him know that he's a suspect."

"Absolutely." Skye wasn't about to take any chances with Homer. First of all, he was huge. And second of all, he had a terrible temper.

"Good." Wally glanced at his cell again and frowned. "Still no word from Loretta. Do you think she might be having the baby?"

"Mom would let me know," Skye said, then realized that her phone was set to vibrate and it was on the coffee table, not in her pocket. "Hold on a second. Let me check my cell and see if I missed something."

Wally followed her to the living room area of the RV and waited.

Skye saw that May had sent her a text a couple of hours ago. She quickly read the message, then looked up at Wally and grinned. "Wow! You must be clairvoyant. Loretta and Vince headed to the hospital a little past noon. Mom has April, but will bring her up to meet her new baby brother as soon as Vince calls and gives her the green light."

"Shoot!" Wally sighed, then grinned. "I supposed it would be tacky to interview Loretta about Jerita while she's giving birth."

"Probably." Skye smiled, then groaned. "Heck! This means Mom will be busy with April and won't be able to take care of the twins tomorrow." She bit her lip. "And your dad is flying out in the morning to attend a business meeting."

Although Carson Boyd was a majority shareholder and the CEO of a major Texas-based oil company, he'd put his nephew in charge in order to spend time with his new grandchildren. But every once in a while, there was something he needed to handle personally.

"You know, I have an idea for a nanny," Wally said casually.

"You do?" Skye asked, surprised. "I take it this person is someone other than the women we have lined up to interview?"

"Uh-huh. Someone we actually know," Wally said carefully. "Someone who could do more than just watch the kids."

"Oh." Skye nodded, studying Wally's expression. It was bland, but she still thought there was more to this than what he was saying. "Who?"

138

"Dorothy Snyder." Wally sat on the sofa and motioned for Skye to sit next to him.

"But Dorothy wouldn't have time." Skye happily snuggled next to Wally. She'd take any alone time she could get with her handsome husband. "She cleans for several people and has a full schedule to keep."

"I had a thought about that too." Wally tightened his arm around Skye and nuzzled her neck. "What if we hired her full-time just for us? We have that guest suite over the garage and she could live in as a combo nanny and housekeeper."

"We don't need a housekeeper," Skye automatically objected.

"Think about it." Wally ran his lips down her cheek. "You're exhausted taking care of two babies, this tiny RV, and working a few hours a week."

"It's not that bad," Skye protested. "You do your share of the chores."

"I try to be a team player, but I'm tired too." Wally's warm brown eyes gazed into hers. "And it's only going to get more overwhelming when your maternity leave is up and we move into a place five times the size of this motor home."

"Hmm." Skye had to admit that he had a point, but she still wasn't convinced. "But having a live-in housekeeper seems so pretentious. Like we're hitting people over the head with our wealth." Her chest tightened. "That's why we agreed to keep the size of the house reasonable. I don't want people to think of us that way."

"Sugar." Wally's soothing baritone usually calmed her, but not this time. "Since we came clean in *The Star,* there's really no hiding anymore that we have money."

"But we don't have to parade the fact we're rich in front of everyone." Skye chewed on her bottom lip until she drew blood.

"As much as Scumble River is a rural community," Wally said as he gently used his thumb to stop her from biting her lip, "there are several wealthy families who own big houses and drive expensive cars."

"Intellectually, I know that's true," Skye said softly. "But . . ."

She glanced at Wally, who was patiently waiting. She knew her real problem was wrapping her head around the fact that eight years ago, a few months before her thirtieth birthday, she'd arrived back in Scumble River with her tail between her legs.

She'd been fired from her job for trying to protect a child from being abused, jilted by her dirtbag fiancé, and had maxed out her credit cards trying to keep said dirtbag happy. She had no references, very little cash, and, at best, a bleak future.

Having prepared herself for an austere reality in which she might never find her soul mate, never have a family of her own, and always have to scrimp to make ends meet on a school psychologist's salary, she wasn't prepared for how quickly her life had turned around. In what had seemed like the blink of an eye, she was married, had twins, and could suddenly afford to buy anything her heart desired.

There were times, like these, that she still couldn't believe it was true. She still half expected to wake up alone, destitute, and unemployed.

It occurred to her that she was terrified that it all would be taken away. That if she made one wrong decision, Wally and the babies might vanish into thin air. And flaunting their wealth by hiring full-time help might be the poor choice that caused her to lose everything.

But in her heart, Skye knew they needed the help. Taking a deep breath, she said, "You're right about hiring Dorothy."

"Of course I am," Wally agreed with a wink.

Skye brightened. "You know, Vince mentioned that he and Loretta were going to look into hiring someone to take care of April and the new baby, as well as help with the house. And if they do that, we won't seem like we're showing off so much."

"True."

"We can see how their search is going when we go meet the newest member of the family."

"Have they decided on a name?" Wally got to his feet and helped Skye to hers.

"They're keeping to the months of the year theme and going with August." Skye followed Wally to the tiny foyer. "As it happens, it's Loretta's grandfather's name."

"How's your mom taking that?" Wally turned the knob.

"She's okay with it." Skye smiled. "But only because they're using Alberto, which is her father's name, for the baby's middle name."

"Smart." Wally opened that door. "I'd better get back to the station and see if there's been any progress on either the murder or the disappearance."

"Do you think there's any chance they're connected?" Skye asked.

"I don't see how." Wally shook his head. "But I also don't believe in coincidences so

I'll certainly being looking for a connection."

"I'll keep my ears open too." Skye kissed his cheek. "And I'll call Dorothy to see if she's interested in working for us full-time."

"Offer her whatever salary you think will get her onboard." Wally waved as he ran down the metal steps, then hopped into his squad car and sped away.

It was only after Wally left and she was changing the twins, who had woken up from their nap in dire need of fresh diapers, that Skye realized that they hadn't asked if Beilin would be continuing on as their general contractor. And if not, what was their alternative?

Immediately, Skye felt guilty. The man had just lost his wife in a horrific manner and all she cared about was getting her house finished. Glancing down at her babies, who now were clean and indicating rather loudly they'd like to be fed, she offered a quick prayer for Jerita's soul and for the woman's family.

As Skye gave Eva and CJ their bottles of formula mixed in with the breast milk she'd pumped earlier, she contemplated who would want to kill Jerita Quinn. Her husband was the obvious suspect. Beilin had been witnessed fighting with his wife, and he had been late for work the day she was murdered, not to mention all his other unexplained absences. That gave him both motive and opportunity.

But Skye just couldn't see him driving a blade into Jerita's skull. Although Beilin was a huge man, certainly strong enough, he didn't seem to have the kind of temper to do something so gruesome. Stabbing a knife into someone's head took a hatred-driven type of fury.

Skye finished feeding her babies and decided to take a ride over to her mother's. She wanted to sound out May on the subject of Dorothy's availability. However, she'd have to be careful not to let on why she was interested in her mom's friend or May would be applying for the job herself.

She also wanted to see if her mother had any hint as to how Jerita Quinn and Edie Baker might be connected. If anyone would, it would be Skye's mother. May was plugged into the gossip line for several of Scumble River's cliques.

Bundling the twins into their coats, Skye packed them all into the SUV and drove to her parents' house. As she pulled into her mom and dad's driveway, she didn't see May's car and it dawned on her that she should have called to make sure her mother hadn't left to take April to the hospital to meet her new brother.

Oh well. She was there now, so she crossed her fingers, got out of the Mercedes, and checked the garage. There, in all its pristine white glory, was her mom's Oldsmobile. It may be older than the hills, but Jed kept it waxed to a high shine and there wasn't a dent or scratch anywhere on the vehicle.

Relieved her mom was home, Skye unfastened Eva and CJ from their car seats and carried them up the front steps. Fumbling with the knob, she wasn't surprised that it turned easily. May wasn't a fan of locked doors.

As she stepped inside the utility room, Skye's nose twitched at the distinctive odor hitting her nose. Her mom firmly believed that a dirty window was a portal to hell and May certainly didn't intend to invite the devil into her house. Skye and her brother joked that their mother went through a bottle of Windex a week. More if they'd had a lot of rain or snow.

Walking into the empty kitchen, Skye raised her voice and called out, "It's me and the babies, Mom. Is there any news on Loretta yet?"

"Shh!" May rounded the corner from the living room, the distinctive blue liquid–filled container in one hand and a rag in the other. Putting her cleaning supplies on the floor, she said, "April is napping in your bedroom. She's been really cranky today. I sure hope she isn't coming down with anything. That would be all Loretta and Vince needed with a newborn."

"Sorry." Skye handed Eva to May and situated CJ into the bouncy chair, then asked, "I take it that Loretta is still in labor?"

"Yes. And what are you doing here? Is everything okay? Why didn't you answer my text?" May commanded, "Tell me you weren't at that murder."

"Everything's fine." Skye knew that her mother's go-to response to anything unexpected was to fear the worse had happened.

"But you did go to the crime scene." Suspicion glimmered in May's emerald-green eyes. She pointed her finger at Skye and demanded, "You didn't take the babies, did you?"

"I went, but I called Carson to come watch Eva and CJ." Skye folded her arms. "I suppose you heard about it on the scanner."

May nodded. "Then Thea called me and filled me in on the details." She narrowed her eyes. "And where's your coat? It's thirty-five degrees out there and the wind makes it feel colder than that."

Skye explained that her jacket had been confiscated as evidence, then sighed. "I guess I'll have to find time tonight or tomorrow to run to Kankakee and buy another one."

"Wait here." May disappeared for a few seconds and came back holding a forest-green jacket. "I bought this for you for Christmas, but . . ."

"Oh. My. Gosh." Skye slipped the coat on and twirled around. "It fits perfectly." She hugged her mom, then warned, "Don't even think of buying me anything else for Christmas or I'll return it."

"Of course I won't. Well, stuff for your stocking, but nothing else." May adjusted the crease in her perfectly ironed jeans, then said, "So what brings you here?"

"I just came over to visit. You always say that I never stop by to talk," Skye said, then seeing the doubt in her mom's expression, she added, "And to pick your brain about the victim."

"Oh." May nudged her daughter toward the sofa. "Why don't you sit down and I'll go get you a glass of milk and some brown-butter butterscotch oatmeal cookies. They're fresh from the oven."

"Diet Coke would be better," Skye called

at her mother's retreating back. May had it in her head that her daughter needed to drink more milk, and nothing Skye could say could convince her mom that she was consuming the amount recommended by her ob-gyn.

A few minutes later, May returned with Skye's snack and a stack of napkins. She placed everything on the coffee table and took a seat.

"So you want to know about Jerita Quinn." May reached for a cookie.

"Yes." Skye nodded. "Have you heard anything?"

"According to Carson, the Quinns moved here from Chicago after the tornado." May picked up the glass of milk and handed it to Skye, gesturing for her to drink. Once she complied, May continued, "Carson had met Beilin because of some business deal and knew he wanted to move out of the city, which was how your father-in-law persuaded Beilin to come to Scumble River to build your house."

Skye took another sip of milk, then put down her glass and selected a cookie. "How did the Quinns find a home here to buy?" After the tornado destroyed most of the town, intact houses for sale were few and far between. "Did Carson do something to nudge the seller?"

"I have no idea," May said. Then, not meeting her daughter's eyes, she added, "You'll have to ask your father-in-law how it all happened."

"Fine." Skye was pretty darn sure Carson had pulled some strings. "But why did the Quinns want to leave Chicago in the first place?"

"Because of their daughter." May wiped her fingers on a napkin. "Although they lived in a nice area of the city, Jerita was adamantly opposed to Jenna attending a school in Chicago, even a private one."

"That seems odd." Skye wondered if the woman had regretted that decision after her run-in with Homer. "How did Loretta come to hire Jerita?"

"When Loretta said she was looking for help, Carson may have mentioned that Jerita had been a paralegal in the city."

"My father-in-law has been a busy little bee, hasn't he?" Skye bit into the chewy cookie and moaned at the delicious hit of butterscotch. "I wonder if he knows the Bakers."

"I don't see how he would." May's voice was firm. "He wouldn't have anything to do with Bord du Lac people. They weren't affected by the tornado and certainly don't move in his circle of friends."

"Are you sure of that?" Skye teased. "After all, he is dating Bunny Reid."

May lips formed a hard line and she glared at her daughter. "I'm not discussing that woman, so drop it."

"You're awfully bossy today." Skye could have said her mother was bossy every day, but she didn't want to risk May taking the cookies away.

"I'm not bossy. I just know what everyone should do," May said without a shred of humor.

Understanding that the subject of Carson's love life was closed, Skye asked casually, "How's Dorothy doing? Has she been able to replace the clients she lost due to the tornado?"

"No." May sighed. "Having one of her regulars murdered put off some folks, and a lot of people are hurting financially because the insurance companies haven't agreed to payments for their damages yet." May brightened. "But that is getting better since the new adjuster took over."

"That's good." Skye crossed her leg. "How's Dorothy managing?"

"She's struggling." May crumpled up her napkin. "She mentioned trying to get on at a factory, but at her age that's going to be

150

hard." She gathered up the empty glasses as she headed to the kitchen, then asked, "Are you planning on having her back once the house is finished?"

Before Skye could answer, the telephone rang and May answered it.

A second later, she returned and said, "The baby's here and Vince gave me the okay to come to the hospital." Rushing down the hallway, she emerged from the spare bedroom with a drowsy April. Then as she jogged out the back door she yelled, "Talk to you later."

Skye slowly gathered Eva and CJ and headed to her car. It was time to have a chat with Carson, but first she needed to make a pit stop at the RV. She'd been so intent on quizzing her mom she'd forgotten the twins' diaper bag. And from the smell, one, or both, of the babies was in urgent need of a change.

CHAPTER 10
ANYPLACE I HANG MY HAT IS HOME

Turning into her driveway, Skye spotted the tricked-out F-150 Platinum SuperCrew Cab parked by the RV. When Wally's father had decided to stay in Scumble River for an extended period of time, he'd had his truck brought up from Texas. The Ford's distinctive metallic ruby exterior made the luxury vehicle easy to distinguish from any of the other pickups in the area.

As soon as Skye pulled to a stop behind the truck, Carson hopped out of the cab and hurried over to the SUV. Although in his early seventies, he was still trim and heartbreakingly handsome. His dark hair was mostly silver, but he had the same warm brown eyes as his son.

The minute Skye stepped out of the Mercedes, Carson asked, "Everything okay with you and my grandbabies?"

"We're all finer than frogs' hair." Skye liked to try out down-home sayings on her

father-in-law and grinned when he chuckled.

"Glad to hear it." Carson opened the door
to the back seat and began unbuckling Eva.
"How's your ma?"

"On her way to the hospital to see her new
grandson." Skye walked to the SUV's other
side and went to work freeing CJ from his
car seat.

She didn't bother to ask how her father-
in-law knew she'd been visiting May. When
he'd arrived at the RV and she wasn't home,
he'd doubtlessly called the babies' security
team to find out their location and demand
a safety check.

"That's great." Carson followed Skye up
the metal stairs. "I know Miss Loretta was
getting mighty tired of being pregnant."

Entering the RV, Skye almost stepped on
Bingo. Prior to the tornado, whenever she'd
arrived home, the black cat would be in the
foyer demanding petting and chin scratches
before allowing her past him down the hall.
But since the storm, the relocation to the
motor home, and the birth of the babies,
he'd spent most of his time on one of the
living room chairs or guarding the twins
while they slept in the bedroom.

At Bingo's age, the changes had been hard
on him and he'd seemed lethargic. His vet,

153

Dr. Quillen, had assured Skye that he was fine, but she'd still been worried. He was the last thing she had of Grandma Leofanti, and she wasn't ready to lose him like she'd lost the rest of her keepsakes from her grandmother in the tornado. Which was why she was thrilled to have him greet her with his previous affectionate rub against her ankles.

Once Bingo was sure he had her attention, he strolled toward the kitchen. Sitting in front of the cupboard that held his food, he glanced back at Skye, and she could swear he raised imaginary eyebrows as if to ask *What's taking you so long? I'm starving.*

Quickly handing CJ to Carson, who nestled the baby in his free arm, Skye complied with Bingo's implicit demand. Flinging open the cabinet door, she grabbed the bright-yellow bag containing the cat's favorite treat.

Dr. Quillen had warned her about Bingo's weight and told her not to feed him between meals, but she wanted to encourage his return to normal behavior so she hurriedly tore off the top strip off the package. At the loud crinkling sound, the cat's purr echoed off the RV's walls. Glancing down at Bingo, she smiled at his enthusiasm for the square brown tidbits.

He paced back and forth in front of her, his green eyes mere slits as he stared at the shiny bag as if to say *Hurry.*

"Just a second, sweetie," Skye cooed as she poured a handful out onto the floor and bargained, "We'll be in our new house soon, and your routine will be almost back to normal." She looked over her shoulder and saw that Carson had settled the babies in their swings. "I know you love CJ and Eva so they won't bother you, right?"

Bingo ignored her, demolished the treats, and licked his chops, then strolled to his water dish, sniffed the full bowl, and gave a disdainful meow.

"I take it you'd like your beverage up-graded?" Skye asked, emptying the bowl, then grabbing a bottle from the fridge and showing it to the finicky feline as if it were a fine wine. "Perhaps some Dasani?"

Wally had been the one to fill Bingo's dish that morning and he claimed there was no way the cat could tell the difference between what came from the faucet and the expen-sive stuff. Skye knew differently.

"Remember our policy," Skye cautioned. "Don't tell Daddy about this."

Bingo purred his agreement. Once Skye put down the refilled bowl, he touched the liquid with his nose, licked off the droplets,

155

then contentedly lapped up the purified water.

The sound of Carson's chuckles reminded Skye that she had an audience, and instead of explaining her behavior, she said, "You must have read my mind. You're just the person I wanted to see, Dad."

"I didn't get a chance to talk to you when you came back from the Quinns' because I'd just gotten a text from Bunny to pick her up so we could head over to Walmart." He took off his oilskin rancher jacket and laid it over the back of the sofa. "They're almost done repairing her apartment and she was over there making a list of what we'd need to buy to move back in."

"That was fast. But I heard the damage wasn't as bad as they first thought," Skye commented. "How much longer for the bowling alley to reopen?"

"Probably another month." Carson rubbed his chin. "They had to gut the area where the bomb went off, as well as most of the bar and grill."

"I bet you two will be glad to get out of that tiny cabin." Skye chuckled to herself at the picture of her billionaire father-in-law living with his ex-Las-Vegas-showgirl lady friend at the Up A Lazy River Motor Court in accommodations that hadn't been refurbished since the fifties. Heck! She could probably sell that image as an idea for a reality television show.

Skye took off her coat, hung it up, then walked over to CJ and sniffed. *Nope.* It wasn't him. She took a whiff of her daughter. *Yep.* It was Eva with the full load.

Carson trailed Skye as she took the baby into the bedroom to change her, and while she cleaned up the little girl, he said, "Yeah. I can't wait to get back to where we can cook our own food again."

"Would you like to stay for supper tonight? I've got a southwest stew in the slow cooker and I'll make those biscuits you like."

"Wish I could, Sugar." Carson took his freshly diapered granddaughter back to her swing. "But I promised Bunny a night out." He muttered, "She's not too happy I'm not taking her with me tomorrow."

"Oh?" Skye followed her father-in-law into the living room and sat on the couch. "Any particular reason you don't want her with you?"

"Well . . ." Carson's ears reddened, indicating either guilt or embarrassment, a tell he shared with his son. "This is sort of a delicate meeting. It seems some folks are upset about a certain Christmas carol that's playing in our holiday ads." He rolled his eyes. "Evidently, Rudolph the Red-Nosed Reindeer's line about all the other reindeers calling him names is a trigger for individuals who were bullying victims."

"Seriously?" Skye tried to be sensitive to others' feelings and she often worked with students who were bullied, but that someone would be triggered by a carol about a reindeer was ridiculous. Sometimes she just had to wonder if people had too much time on their hands. "What's the company's response going to be?"

Carson smirked. "What I'd really like to do is put up a billboard that says *Hello, Everyone! What are you offended by today?*" He made a face. "But in reality, we'll probably vote to remove the music from the ad. And that's going to annoy a lot of the board of directors, which isn't exactly the best time for them to meet Bunny."

"She might surprise you." Skye smiled, then said, "Anyway, I'm glad to see you before you left because I was hoping you could give me a little insight on the Quinns and their marriage."

"Let me think." Carson sat on a chair kitty-corner to the sofa, held his Stetson in his hand, and ran the brim between his fingers. "Beilin worked as a general contractor for a construction company that built an office building for me in Chicago. He'd been a residential GC previously and was looking to get back into that game."

"So you contacted him after the tornado?" Skye asked. She couldn't quite recall how everything got settled once she and Wally decided to build a new house rather than try to fix their old one.

"Yes." Carson crossed his legs. "Wally mentioned that all the contractors you and he had approached had waiting lists of more than a year before they could even get started on your place."

"Right." Skye shuddered. "I thought we'd be living in this RV until the kids were in preschool." She patted Carson's hand. "Not that we don't appreciate you providing it for us. Otherwise we'd probably be living with my parents, and you know how that would end up."

"May's a force of nature all right." Carson chuckled and said, "Anyway, I went through my files to see which firms my company had used, and that led me to Beilin. I recalled him talking about his experience in residential construction, and when I contacted him, he was thrilled to put in a bid for the job. His price was reasonable, and he could start right away."

"That was a stroke of luck." Skye wondered if Carson had somehow stacked the deck to make Beilin both available and interested.

"Yep. His only caveat was being able to find a home to buy in the area since he wanted to move his family here and make a fresh start," Carson explained. "Beilin felt that there'd be plenty of work for him what with all the tornado damage, and that your house would be a great advertisement for his new company."

"Besides the work, did he say why he wanted to leave the city?"

Carson pursed his lips. "As I recall, it had something to do with his daughter."

"Mom said it was because his wife didn't want her in Chicago schools," Skye commented. "That seems sort of silly. In addition to private ones, there are a lot of good public schools in the city."

"I'm trying to remember, but I don't believe it was the quality of the education." Carson closed his eyes for several seconds, then shook his head and opened them. "Nope. Beilin never said exactly why, but I got the feeling that it was something else."

"Hmm. I wonder what." Skye made a mental note to tell Wally they should find out the real reason Jerita didn't want Jenna to attend school in the city. Then she lifted

160

a brow at her father-in-law and said, "So along with everything else, you hooked up Jerita and Loretta?"

"Not really." Carson ducked his head. "I just told them about each other. I let Jerita know that Loretta was looking for someone to hire and I informed Loretta that Jerita was a paralegal."

"You're quite the matchmaker." Skye couldn't help but smile at her father-in-law's delight in helping people. He was one of a kind.

"For some reason, I've become the local employment agency." Carson shrugged. "I've met a lot of folks volunteering and some of them tell me they're in need of a job, and I tell 'em who's hiring."

"Do you get the info on who's hiring from working on the cleanup crews and serving at the shelters?" Skye smiled fondly at Carson. He had such a heart of gold it was difficult to remember that he was the CEO of a multibillion-dollar company.

"No. I just pick up things here and there around town." Carson twitched his shoulders. "Mostly at the American Legion. Bunny likes to go there for their bingo games, so I hang out at the bar while she plays."

Skye blinked at the thought of Bunny

elbow-to-elbow with all the little old ladies but didn't comment.

Carson checked his watch and stood. "I need to mosey on. Bunny doesn't like to be kept waiting."

"That's sort of surprising since she's rarely on time for anything herself." Skye snickered at how much that trait annoyed her son.

"True." Carson laughed. "Her motto is that it's better to be late than to be ugly."

Skye giggled. "You have your hands full with that one."

"That I do." Carson kissed CJ and Eva, then turned to Skye. "I almost forgot the reason that I stopped by was to tell you not to worry about the house. I spoke to Beilin and he plans to keep working on it and have it finished when he promised, if not sooner."

"If he needs to take some time off . . ." Skye forced herself to offer.

"I asked if he wanted me to bring someone else in to tie up the loose ends and he said no. He'd rather keep busy than sit and brood."

"Understandable." Skye rose to her feet. "Everyone handles grief differently."

"That they do." Carson gave her hug. "And you're in the profession to know that."

They walked to the door, and when Car-

162

son reached for the knob Skye said, "I just remembered one other thing that I wanted to check with you about."

"Okay."

"Do you know of any kind of link between Jerita Quinn and our missing woman, Edie Baker?" Skye asked. "Have you ever seen them together?"

"No. And nothing comes to mind to connect them."

"Shoot!"

"You be careful when I'm gone." Carson kissed her cheek. "I won't try to talk you out of investigating this murder with Wally, but promise me you'll notify the security guys if you're going anywhere at all dicey, and call them for help if you get into any trouble. Remember, if you press the star on your cell phone, it will act as an alarm for the team. They might be assigned to the twins, but they know you're a priority too."

"I have no plans to do anything risky," Skye assured him. "My involvement will probably be talking to people in the controlled environment of the police station or with Wally by my side."

"Good." Carson ran down the steps, then shouted from the bottom of the stairs. "When I get back, I'm buying you a Smith & Wesson Model 66, teaching you to shoot, and enrolling you in concealed carry classes."

"No thanks!" Skye waved and shut the door, knowing she hadn't heard the last of that subject, but determined not to let her father-in-law turn her into Annie Oakley. Until the apocalypse hit, she'd stick to pepper spray.

After checking on the babies, and finding them happily occupied with their toys, Skye tapped her chin. Who should she talk to next?

Skye paced the short distance between the front door and the entrance to the bedroom. Loretta was unavailable. Wally wouldn't want her talking to Homer until they determined if he was the pumpkin seed spitter. And there was no way Earl would answer his phone.

She'd like to quiz Piper to see if the intern had picked up on anything while she was working with Jenna. But that was better done in person, and Skye would have an opportunity to do it tomorrow.

Hmm. She needed to call Dorothy about the job offer, but maybe a visit would be better. May might be the head of the Scumble River rumor mill, but Dorothy was definitely her next in command.

Skye glanced at the microwave clock.

Since they'd eaten such a late lunch, Wally wouldn't want dinner until seven, so she had a couple of hours. If Dorothy were like most Scumble Riverites, she would be afraid of interrupting supper, but the woman lived alone and had confided in Skye that she rarely sat down to a meal. She preferred to graze all day.

After feeding the twins and leaving Wally a note just in case he came home early, Skye bundled the babies into their jackets, put them in the SUV, and headed out to Dorothy's place. It would be nice to have a chance to catch up with her mom's friend. She'd hardly seen her since the tornado and missed their chats.

Dorothy lived on one of the state routes leading into Kankakee. As Skye approached the park, she slowed. Dorothy's house was the last one on the right before the speed limit went down to forty-five, and it was easy to miss because it sat so far back from the road.

Spotting the long narrow driveway, Skye turned into it and parked on a concrete pad off to the side beside an older model Cadillac. The Catera indicated that Dorothy was home and Skye hopped out of her Mercedes, got the base of the stroller from the rear of the SUV, then settled Eva's car seat into the frame.

Repeating the procedure with CJ, she was wondering why she'd bothered with a coat when baby wrangling kept her toasty warm.

She made her way to a side entrance, then waved at the tall, solidly built woman in her early sixties who was waiting for them in the open doorway of the breezeway.

"Little mama. How the heck are you?" Dorothy hurried down the concrete stairs and swept Skye into a hug. "I saw the car pull in. It's sure spiffy. Is that the new Mercedes Wally bought you?"

"That's the one." Skye hugged her back and stepped away. "Are we interrupting anything?"

"Not at all." Dorothy grinned. "Come on inside. I was just thinking about you and these two cuties." She helped Skye lift the double stroller up the steps and ushered them down a short hallway into the kitchen. "I haven't seen them since your baby shower."

"That was quite a party." Skye took a seat at a glass-topped table and started the process of freeing CJ from his jacket.

"It was." Dorothy took off Eva's coat and said, "I had an interesting dream last night."

"Oh?" Skye said cautiously, surprised at Dorothy's statement. The older woman was one of the most down-to-earth people she knew. "Was it good or bad?"

"I think it was a message from your Grandma Leofanti." Dorothy's usual genial expression was serious. "You know I was over at your mom's house so much as a teenager, Antonia felt like my own mother."

"What was the dream about?" Skye trembled as a chill ran up her spine.

"I was in your new house when a monster broke in. I couldn't find you, but the monster hit Wally over the head and put him in its car. The monster was trying to take Eva, and I was fighting it off with a butcher knife." Dorothy shuddered. "I ended up stabbing it in the head."

"How awful." Skye's chest tightened. The butcher knife to the temple sounded too much like Jerita Quinn's murder. A detail that hadn't been released.

"It was." Dorothy straightened her shoulders. "I've been pondering the dream all day and I think I'm supposed to take care of these precious babies. You two have been so generous continuing my salary even though I'm not cleaning for you anymore that I feel like there's some force pushing me to return the favor."

"Actually, that's why I stopped by." Skye took a breath to calm her racing pulse.

"How would you like to be our live-in housekeeper and nanny?"

"I'd love it. And it will work out perfectly since Tammy is looking for a place to rent. Her apartment building has gone to no pets and she certainly isn't giving up her dog. Now she can move here and I'll stay with you."

"Terrific." Skye smiled. "That suite above the garage should be just right for you. It has a private outside entrance as well as a bedroom, sitting room, and bathroom. Do you want to bring your own furniture or shall I furnish it?"

"You go ahead. Tammy's stuff is in bad shape so I'll leave my slightly better crap for her."

"It sounds as if this will work out perfectly."

"Which is a good thing." Dorothy shivered. "Because I don't think I have a choice."

CHAPTER 11
PICTURES OF HOME

Wally's Hummer was parked in the driveway when Skye got home. From the sound of Bruce Springsteen's "Born to Run" pouring out of the RV's open front windows, Skye deduced that her husband was working out.

After getting the twins from their car seats, she climbed the steps and found him lying flat on the weight bench he kept stored in the shed outside. He was wearing low-riding nylon shorts and not much else.

Leaning against the doorjamb, Skye observed his chest and shoulder muscles flexing as he repeatedly lifted a barbell with a hundred-pound plate attached to each end. She admired the way the silver at his temples emphasized the midnight blackness of the rest of his hair and how his smooth olive skin stretched over his high cheekbones.

Wally was such a handsome man that when her insecurities surfaced she wondered why he was with her. Happily, those times were occurring less and less, and she was able to push aside her self-doubt faster and faster.

When he sat up, wiped his face with a towel, and grabbed a Dasani from the floor, Skye watched the strong column of his throat as he swallowed nearly half the water in one swig. Then chugged the rest before putting down the plastic bottle.

He got to his feet, closed the window, and turned the heat back on, then came toward her and fingered the fabric of her jacket. "Where'd you get the new coat?"

"Mom bought it for me for Christmas."

"That was lucky." Wally kissed her cheek. "How was your visit with her?"

"Good." Skye's grin was bemused. "She and your father are two of a kind."

"Oh?" Wally took CJ from Skye and nuzzled his son's head. "In what way?"

"They both have their fingers on the pulse of Scumble River." With only one baby in her arms, Skye could take off her jacket and hang it in the tiny foyer closet. "I don't know if you realize it or not, but that's a pretty amazing accomplishment for a new-comer like your father. It usually takes years to fit in."

"I can't see Dad as a gossip." Wally tested CJ's diaper and headed into the bedroom.

"Not exactly." Skye followed with Eva. It had been a couple of hours so both babies would probably need a change. "But he does seem to be the center of a lot of information. For instance, did you know he was the one who hooked Loretta up with Jerita Quinn?"

"No." Wally finished with CJ and watched Skye redress Eva. "Anything else?"

"He joked with me that he's become the town employment agency."

Skye examined the twins. They seemed drowsy so she settled them into their bassinets.

"Seriously?" Wally raised an eyebrow. "How would he do that?"

"It appears that people tell him about needing a job and he steers them toward folks who are hiring." Skye went into the adjoining bathroom and washed her hands. "Are you ready to eat dinner?"

"I'd like to clean up the living room and then grab a shower." He shot her a seductive gaze. "Would you like to join me?"

"I'll take a rain check until we have our big walk-in at the new house." Skye giggled. "This one's so small that I don't think we'd both fit into it."

"Trying is half the fun."

"Yeah. Unless we get stuck and have to be

rescued by the fire department. Then someone snaps a picture and posts it on Open Book."

"You win." Wally raised his hands in surrender.

"Of course I do." Skye smirked, then offered, "How about while you wash, I make some cheesy biscuits to go with the stew?"

"You know I'll never say no to cheesy biscuits." Wally grinned at her, then strolled into the living room and picked up the water bottle and dirty towel. Once he'd deposited the bottle in the recycle bin and put the towel in the hamper, he began to dismantle the weights and bench.

Skye watched him haul the equipment out the front door, then went into the kitchen and started to assemble the ingredients for the biscuits.

When Wally returned from outside, he paused by the counter and asked, "Did you get a chance to talk to Dorothy?"

"Yes." Skye waved him away. "Go shower." She hated eating so late and it was already past seven. "I'll tell you all about it while we have supper."

By the time Wally came back into the kitchen dressed in navy sweats, a Scumble River Police Department T-shirt, and flip-flops, Skye had their salads on the table and the biscuits were baking in the oven. He poured a can of Caffeine-Free Diet Coke over ice for Skye, uncapped a Sam Adams for himself, and took a seat.

Once Skye was in her chair, Wally picked up his fork, but paused as he lifted it to his mouth. "So what did Dorothy have to say?"

As they ate, Skye summarized her visit, then asked, "What do you think of her dream?"

"It's interesting that the knife in the monster's head matches Jerita's murder," Wally said cautiously. "We didn't release that information, and besides the authorities, only Earl saw it."

"I'm pretty darn sure Earl did not stop by to discuss the murder with Dorothy before he went into hiding."

Skye got to her feet, took the biscuits from the oven, put them in a basket, and placed them on the table along with the bowl of stew.

"So that leaves us with coincidence." Wally stood and grabbed bowls from the cupboard. "And I really hate coincidences. Too bad between the murder and the missing woman we are just full of them."

"Yep." Skye passed the biscuits to Wally, then said cautiously, "I know you don't believe in stuff that can't be proved, but I

173

do wonder if Dorothy's dream isn't some kind of warning."

"After the whole Mrs. Griggs/Fairy Godmother thing" — Wally took a drink of beer — "I'm willing to be a little more open-minded."

Skye had inherited a house from Mrs. Griggs, whose spirit had haunted Skye from the time she'd moved into the place until her wedding night — a fact that Wally had previously always denied, despite fires, explosions, and burst water pipes whenever they'd tried to get intimate before their marriage.

Once Skye and Wally returned from their honeymoon, the old woman's ghost had only made a few subtle appearances, leaving them rose petals and baby gifts. Then, after the house had been destroyed by the tornado, Skye had wondered what would happen to the spirit.

A month ago, a woman claiming to be a fairy godmother had passed on a message from Mrs. Griggs. There had been enough unexplainable facts that even Wally had had a hard time dismissing it.

"Good." Skye smiled. "Then I hope that by having Dorothy move in we'll be okay."

"When can she start with the kids?" Wally took a huge bite of stew.

174

"Thank goodness she's free tomorrow and agreed to come over for a practice run while I attend that meeting at school." Skye broke open a biscuit. "Otherwise I was down to Uncle Charlie or Bunny."

Wally choked on his food, then sputtered, "Not Bunny. Ever!"

"Everyone else is working. Your father's gone. And Mom's busy with April."

"Well, if it happens that there are ever no other options, you choose Charlie." Wally scowled. "Never Bunny."

"Seriously?" She couldn't hold back a snicker at the thought of her cigar-smoking, whiskey-drinking godfather trying to handle the twins.

"Yes. Better him than that unreliable woman." Before Wally went back to his supper, he asked, "Did your mom have anything else to say that might help with Jerita's murder investigation?"

"There was something." Skye tapped her spoon against her bowl.

"About Jerita? Or Beilin? Or?" Wally asked, continuing to eat.

"Let me think," Skye said, waving away his impatience while she flipped through her mental notes. Finding the right one, she exclaimed, "I know! Mom told me she'd heard that Beilin and Jerita moved here because they didn't want Jenna attending Chicago schools. And when I mentioned that to your father, he said he didn't think it was the quality of the education that drove the couple to avoid CPS."

"I'll bring that up to Beilin when I reinterview him." Wally was quiet as they finished their meal, but when they were doing the dishes he said, "I've been thinking that we really need to talk to Loretta. Along with everything else, she might know why Jerita didn't want Jenna to go to school in Chicago."

"So?"

"So tomorrow, we need to go see the newest addition to the family." Wally rinsed off the suds from the slow cooker, then handed it to Skye to dry. "And have a nice long chat with his mommy about her employee."

"Loretta will probably be home by late afternoon," Skye said thoughtfully. "I don't have a baby gift yet, but we could bring over supper for them."

"Let's plan on it." Wally hung the wet dishcloth over the faucet.

For the rest of the evening Skye and Wally managed to focus on their own lives — the new house, the babies, and the upcoming holiday — but as they were getting ready for bed, Skye said, "Before I see Trixie tomorrow, I need to know what information you're releasing to the public and what you're keeping back about the murder."

Trixie Frayne was the high school librarian and Skye's best friend. She'd finally finished the mystery that she'd been writing for what seemed like forever and she'd recently begun querying agents. Now she was on the lookout for her next plot.

Trixie was particularly fascinated by Skye's involvement in real-life cases. She was persistent and clever and often had better sources than the police when it came to investigating Scumble River crimes.

"Can't you dodge her?" Wally asked. "She won't be at the PPS meeting, right?"

"Probably not." Skye finished washing her face and applied moisturizer. "But she knows that I'll be at the school and she'd be hurt if I didn't stop by the library to say hi and catch up a little."

"Well, make sure you avoid telling her about the knife in the temple," Wally mumbled around his toothbrush, then after rinsing his mouth said, "As long as you have to talk to her, see if she's heard anything about the missing woman or Jerita."

"Will do, Chief." Skye watched Wally strip off his shirt and sweats, then crawl into bed wearing only his boxer briefs. She changed into her nightshirt and followed him. "But my main mission tomorrow is to get Homer's DNA." Wally cleared his throat and she hastily added, "But only if I can do it in a completely safe way."

After Wally left for work, Skye tidied up the RV, then played with the twins until Dorothy arrived. The housekeeper was fifteen minutes early, which gave Skye plenty of time to show her where all the baby paraphernalia was before she had to leave.

At 10:50 a.m., with Dorothy's assurances ringing in her ears, Skye grabbed her tote bag and headed to work. The high school's PPS meeting had always been late afternoons on Tuesday, but at the beginning of the academic year Homer and Neva had decided to trade slots, so now it was at eleven thirty. Neither principal had consulted with Skye, the speech therapist, or the district nurse, all of whom were required to attend the meetings and had to rearrange their schedules due to the change.

Pushing through the high school's glass front doors, Skye turned to the counter separating the main office from the lobby. Lunch A was due to start in a few minutes and Opal Hill, the school secretary, was busy with students purchasing last-minute meal tickets.

Skye examined the sixty-something woman. She looked more and more exhausted each time Skye saw her. The secretary's mother was nearly a hundred and Opal was her only child. While she worked, a home health aide stayed with Mrs. Hill, but at all other times, Opal was her mom's sole caretaker.

Raising her voice over the teenage babble, Skye asked, "Is Mr. Knapik around?"

"He's with the superintendent." Opal glanced behind her as if the men might sneak up on her, then pointed across the lobby to C wing's hallway. "They're holding the PPS meeting in the art room."

"Okay." Skye smiled and said, "Thanks!"

She waited until Opal was distracted, then slipped down the short passageway leading toward the principal's office. Homer often left a trail of trash on the floor of the corridor, but threw a fit if anyone else dropped as much as a piece of lint.

Since no one but Homer was allowed to eat in the main office, anything Skye found would be his and likely contain his DNA. She was hoping for an empty soda can or a discarded candy wrapper, but was disappointed to find the linoleum sparkling clean.

The custodian must have just been by. The

poor man swept this area three or four times a day trying to keep up with Homer's mess.

Skye checked her watch. She'd have to wait until Homer left his office to go through his trash can, but she didn't have time to hang around. The PPS meeting would be starting soon and she really needed to confer with Piper before everyone else arrived.

Turning to leave, Skye stopped in her tracks when she heard a sarcastic male voice say from behind Homer's partially open door, "You've really screwed the pooch this time."

Uh-oh. That was the superintendent and he sounded ticked. Usually Dr. Wraige and Homer were buddy-buddy, but something must have caused that to change.

Dr. Wraige continued his tirade. "I think it's time you retired."

Homer Knapik had been the high school principal so long it was difficult to remember anyone else ever occupying the position. For the past several years, every spring he'd announced that he was stepping down. But like the cold weather, he had always returned in the fall.

"You know I can't," Homer whined. "My investments really tanked during the recession and —"

Dr. Wraige cut him off and said, "You have plenty of money."

"Right." Homer's voice reeked with sarcasm. "As long as I die before tomorrow morning, I have all the cash I'll ever need."

"I don't care!" Dr. Wraige thundered. "I can't look the other way anymore. You've put the entire district at risk because you can't keep your damn mouth shut."

"It wasn't my fault," Homer babbled. "It's that intern. That stupid bit—"

"Save it," Dr. Wraige snapped. "You're an idiot. How in the hell could you allow yourself to be recorded saying those unprofessional things to that woman?"

Skye glanced down the hall. She was afraid she would be caught eavesdropping, but she couldn't make herself leave.

"I forgot," Homer bleated. "Skye or that other one should have reminded me."

"They did!" Dr. Wraige bellowed.

"Anyway, it doesn't matter now." Homer seemed to gain confidence. "That Quinn woman is dead, so the lawsuits against me and the school will go away."

"You don't think her husband will pursue them?" Dr. Wraige sneered.

"Her husband?" Homer stuttered. "No one told me she had a husband."

"Didn't you even read the child's file?"

181

Dr. Wraige's tone dripped with disbelief. "I'm beginning to think that the wheels do not go round and round on your bus."

"There's no call to get insulting," Homer protested. "It wasn't even my kid. This whole thing should have been Carolyn's headache."

"How I wish she had been the one to handle it, but you were there, not her."

"I . . ." Homer's heavy breathing was audible. "Since the husband didn't care enough to show up at the meeting, I bet he'll let the whole matter go. I'm sure if I approach him man to man —"

"Absolutely not!" Dr. Wraige cut Homer off for the third time. "You will instruct Mrs. Boyd to personally meet with him and offer anything, and I do mean anything, he wants for his child in exchange for dropping the lawsuits. You will not speak to Mr. Quinn or anyone having to do with Jenna Quinn. Am I clear?"

"Fine," Homer griped. "I never wanted to be involved anyway."

"Then for once we're all on the same page."

As the door flew open, Skye only had time to jump back and pretend as if she were coming down the hallway before Dr. Wraige exited Homer's office.

"Mrs. Boyd." The superintendent's smile was all teeth and no sincerity. "Just who I need to see."

In his late fifties, Shamus Wraige was a solidly built two hundred pounds. His red hair had faded, giving it the appearance of a rusty steel wool pad. And his personality was about as warm. He towered over Skye, using his size and position to try to intimidate her.

"My name is Denison-Boyd," Skye said coolly.

If they wanted her to clean up their mess, they could treat her with a little respect.

Wraige's pale-brown eyes narrowed, but he acquiesced, "Sorry, Mrs. Denison-Boyd."

"Yes?" Skye bit her tongue to keep from grinning at the pain in his voice.

"Whenever you feel the time is appropriate, I would like you to meet with Mr. Quinn and assure him that whatever program he would like his daughter to attend is fine with the school district." Dr. Wraige tilted his head as if assessing Skye's knowledge of the situation, then added, "That of course is contingent upon him dropping those silly lawsuits his wife filed."

"I'm not sure we can legally require him to do that." Skye searched her mind regarding best practices, but although nothing specific came to mind, she was pretty sure blackmail was considered a no-no.

Dr. Wraige inched closer, and Skye found herself with her back literally to the wall. "It is perfectly legal to offer quid pro quo."

"Then maybe you should be the one to talk to Mr. Quinn." Skye injected a note of innocence into her voice.

"I believe it is best for a trained psychologist to handle this." Dr. Wraige's face flushed.

"Fine. I will discuss his daughter's education with him, but I won't threaten to withhold services if he continues to sue us."

"Fine." Dr. Wraige echoed her words. "Just make this all go away and I will personally guarantee you a reasonable-sized office in each school building and a budget for furnishings and equipment."

Skye blinked. He was offering her the school psychologist holy grail.

Before she could formulate a response, the superintendent abruptly turned and strode down the hallway. Pausing just before stepping into the main office, he said, "And if you don't, I'll make sure that the only space you have to work in is the boy's locker room."

CHAPTER 12
TAKE THE LONG WAY HOME

Skye glared at the superintendent's back as he disappeared from sight. Shaking her head at the nerve of the man, she checked her watch and saw that the PPS meeting would be starting in less than a minute.

Crap! She hurried down the hall and into the main office. Opal waved a sheaf of papers at her as she rushed past the woman, but Skye didn't have time to stop for them. She'd always emphasized to the team how important it was to be prompt and showing up late would set a bad example.

Instead, she called out, "I'll pick them up before I leave for home."

Skye jogged across the large lobby area and race-walked through the corridors heading for the art room. Of course it was in the farthest section of the building, sharing a wing with music, consumer science a.k.a. home ec, and industrial technology a.k.a. shop.

185

PPS meetings were held weekly in each school to assist students exhibiting academic, social, or physical needs. Skye, the principal, special education teacher, speech therapist, and nurse met to discuss pupils experiencing difficulties in those areas.

None of the team ever missed a PPS meeting without a really good excuse — like death — if for no other reason than to defend themselves from getting assigned the unpleasant duties.

Classroom teachers who had referred the children on the agenda were scheduled in fifteen-minute slots, which nearly always ran over, causing the next person to have to wait. Skye had suggested that the appointments be lengthened to thirty or at least twenty minutes, but Homer refused, stating it would just make the teachers even more long-winded.

Skye was shaking her head at his reasoning when she entered the high school's art room and got a whiff of turpentine, clay, and glue. Scraps of brightly colored construction paper were scattered on the faded green linoleum from whatever lesson had been taught the previous period. The windows rattled as wind gusts pummeled them, and cold air seeped around the frames, causing the students' projects hanging from the ceiling to rustle.

The members of the PPS team sat silently at two long tables that had been pushed together to form a square. The only one missing after Skye entered the room was Homer.

Skye slid into an empty seat between Piper and Euphemia Cunningham, the latest special education teacher. Neither the junior high nor the high school seemed able to retain a special education teacher for longer than a year. From the time Skye had begun working for the district, there had been a new one every fall. For some reason — probably the low salary, poor working conditions, and/or lack of respect — it was difficult to keep good educators in Scumble River.

Euphemia had come from the St. Louis school system after teaching there for ten years. Short, barely over five feet, and stocky, so far she seemed to take whatever was thrown at her in stride.

When she was interviewed, Euphemia had said she was looking for a change of pace. And Skye had to admit Scumble River was certainly different from the mean streets of the area where the woman had been teaching.

Skye had been meaning to ask how Euphemia was doing. The teacher's caseload consisted of students with behavior disorders and severe learning disabilities who were mostly in regular classes. They were supported by the special education department, which consisted of Euphemia and six teacher assistants.

Since Skye's plans to go over the referred pupils with Piper before the meeting had been scuttled by her eavesdropping on Homer and the superintendent, she grabbed the agenda and quickly skimmed the names. None of the kids were frequent flyers and she scooted the pile of folders closer to her chair. She'd have to scan them as the students were being discussed.

Skye had just taken a glance at the first file when Homer stomped in, shot her an annoyed look, and said, "Sorry I'm late." He shrugged his massive shoulders. "But let's be real, I didn't want to be here, so make this quick."

"Okeydokey."

Sure that she'd remained expressionless, Skye was exasperated when Homer barked, "Wipe that smirk off your lips."

Skye had had it with Homer and retorted, "I can't be held responsible for what my face does when you talk."

There was a gasp from the others, then

Abby Fleming, the school nurse, drawled, "I agree. Homer, you test my patience too, and the results are not benign."

The principal's mouth flapped open and closed like a fish out of water, then ignoring his mutinying staff, he narrowed his eyes and turned his gaze to Piper. "You ready to get this thing going?"

"Yes, sir," the intern squeaked. "I see there are several students on the list, so I believe we will need the full hour."

Homer sulked as he took a seat and scowled at the paper in front of him.

Piper glanced at Skye, who nodded for her to continue.

Straightening her spine, Piper looked at the special education teacher and said, "Euphemia, please tell the team what you told me this morning."

The teacher cleared her throat and said, "One of the rewards available to my students is an after-school session in the weight room, which I supervise. Yesterday, I had three boys taking advantage of that reward and they were all strangely excited."

Skye watched Piper's expression darken and wondered what was coming.

Euphemia's face clouded. "I sit at a desk in the back of the room. It allows me to keep an eye on them, but also gives them a

189

chance to maintain their behavior without my instruction." She sighed. "But yesterday, they seemed unusually wired so I listened a lot closer to their conversation than I normally do."

Abby flipped her long blond hair over her shoulder and asked, "And what did you hear?"

"There's a new internet challenge called the invisibility prank." Euphemia's brown eyes were hard. "And it's just plain mean."

"What in the name of all that's holy is that?" Homer demanded.

"According to what I saw online," Euphemia answered, "the prank involves convincing a child, usually a younger sibling, that he or she is invisible."

"How in the heck do they do that?" Homer's furry eyebrows formed a single caterpillar.

"They start by pretending to do a magic trick," Euphemia explained. "They cover the child in a sheet, then they remove it and claim that the child is now invisible. They also Photoshop a picture to demonstrate to the child that he or she no longer shows up in snapshots. Many kids who have been the victims of this prank have become hysterical."

"That doesn't sound too bad. Just kids

190

having some fun," Homer sneered. "You all baby these kids too much. Stuff like this toughens them up." He shook his massive head. "You women all overthink everything. And overanalyzing is the art of creating problems that don't exist."

Ignoring Homer's pronouncement, Belle Whitney, the speech therapist, demanded, "Can you explain to me how making a child violently sob with a prank is funny? How can frightening the life out of a kid be cool with anyone?"

Abby shook her head. "And what if that child has asthma or decides since he or she is invisible they can do something dangerous?"

"Did you call their parents?" Skye asked, mentally running through Euphemia's class list, attempting to determine which moms and dads would be helpful and which wouldn't.

Before the teacher could respond, Piper answered, "I asked her to wait until this meeting. I thought that some of the mothers and fathers might need some guidance on how to handle the situation." Her voice dropped as she sneaked a peak at Homer. "And I was afraid that a few might think it was funny and not see the harm the prank could cause."

"Do you want me to talk to the parents with you?" Skye offered.

"I just want some help getting a handout together that outlines the danger of this prank and why it's a bad idea." Euphemia shook her head and the beads on her braids clicked softly together. "I think this is a good opportunity for me to get to know the parents better and allow them to see me as a part of their team."

"That's a great idea," Skye said. "And just off the top of my head, you can emphasize how causing children unnecessary distress isn't good for them, particularly the very young or very fragile kids." She thought for a moment and added, "Point out that there are a lot of other ways to provide a stimulating environment for their children and this type of prank doesn't provide any benefit to either cognitive or developmental function." She paused, then said, "And one more thing. Perhaps the most important issue is that something like this could ruin the relationship between the siblings involved."

Euphemia beamed at Skye. "Those are terrific starting points. Thanks!"

"You're very welcome." Skye smiled back and then said to Piper, "I bet you would have come up with the same suggestions if you thought about it."

"Maybe." Piper dipped her head. "But this was too important to fly solo."

Homer snorted and pushed back his chair. "Now that we've all had our feel-good moments, can we get on with the kids who are actually on the agenda?"

"Of course." Piper's cheeks reddened. "Although Ms. Cormorant has referred Liam Gooding, she refused to attend the meeting. She said that her time is too precious to waste on a subpar student. She feels that he is intellectually delayed."

Belle and Abby rolled their eyes. Like Homer, Pru Cormorant should have retired twenty years ago, or maybe she shouldn't have ever been a teacher. The woman had been a blister on Skye's big toe since Skye had first stepped foot in Scumble River High School. The sound of Pru's loud, whiney voice made Skye consider sticking pencils in her ears just to stop the painful noise.

Pru regularly mailed parents insulting notes. One she'd sent just before Skye went on maternity leave had said:

I noticed today that your daughter's lunch included four chocolate bars, a bag of gummy bears, soda crackers, and a pickle. Unless she is pregnant, in which

193

case she shouldn't be in school,
please see that she has a proper
lunch tomorrow.

The English teacher had also flat-out refused to have children with special needs in her classes. She preferred to deal only with intellectually gifted and extremely motivated pupils. At the first sign of laziness or a behavior issue, she complained until Homer transferred the student to another teacher.

Intent on setting a good example instead of commenting on Pru, Skye asked, "Did you review Liam's file?"

After her little lapse with Homer, Skye was determined to keep the tone of the meeting professional. She'd be a good role model for her intern if it killed her.

"Yes." Piper tapped the folder Skye held in her hands. "His group intellectual measures put him in the high average range, his achievement scores are all above grade level, and currently his lowest grade in any class is a B, and that's in Ms. Cormorant's class."

Homer grabbed the file from Skye's grip and slapped it down on the table. "Next."

Thirty minutes later, they'd made it through names three and four on the agenda. Each of the referring teachers had

194

come in and discussed her concerns. Piper gave the women suggestions and promised to observe the students in their classrooms.

When Skye noticed that the fifth student on the agenda was a boy whose mother had referred him with speech and language concerns, she realized that this might be her best chance to go through Homer's trash.

Before they began the discussion, she said, "Sorry. I need to go to the bathroom really quick. Go ahead without me."

"I thought now that you're finally not pregnant anymore you might be able to last an entire meeting without rushing off to the john," Homer sneered.

Ignoring him, Skye grabbed her tote bag and hurried out the classroom door. Luckily, it was between passing periods and she could jog down the hallway without any of the kids seeing her break the no-running rule. She slowed just before she reached the lobby and continued though it at a more sedate pace.

Opal was at the counter, and as Skye passed her, she picked up the stack of papers she'd tried to give her before and said, "Here are those special ed forms I wanted to give you."

"Great." Skye tucked them in her tote and explained, "I need to use the restroom, but the PPS is still going on so I have to be quick."

The main office was set up with an open area in front. Opal's desk and the staff mailboxes were behind the long counter that bisected it from the lobby. A short corridor led to the rear of the area. The nurse's office was on one side and a unisex bathroom was on the other. Homer's office was at the very back.

Thankful the secretary didn't ask why she hadn't gone to the bathroom in the art room's wing, Skye hurried away. She'd just started down the short hallway when a familiar voice from inside the nurse's office called out her name.

As the girl stepped into the doorway, Skye said, "Bambi, you scared the heck out of me."

Bambi Doozier was Earl's youngest child — at least as far as anyone knew. She was a sophomore, but extremely slender and petite, which made her seem a lot younger than her fifteen years. Unlike the rest of her kinfolk, Bambi was a good student and followed all the rules. She was a member of the high school's service club, Get Involved, Value Everyone, and had even won GIVE's first award.

Bambi and her aunt Yolanda were the only

two of the Doozier family, at least those whom Skye had met, who had ambitions beyond scamming Scumble River citizens. Both made it a point to speak Standard English instead of Doozierese, and both understood that doing well in school was their best chance to make something of their lives.

"Sorry, ma'am." Bambi twisted the end of her ponytail. "I was hoping you could help me with something so that I can get back to class in time for fifth period. Science is my worst subject and I need to be there from the beginning or I won't be able to understand it."

"Are you sick?" Skye asked. If the girl needed to see Abby, Skye would have to abort her mission to gather a sample from Homer's trash and go get the nurse.

"Just . . . you know . . ." Bambi's face blazed crimson. "That time of the month surprised me and I don't have any . . . uh . . . with me."

"Oh." Skye nodded. "That's something I can definitely handle." She moved into the nurse's office and headed toward the cabinet that held Abby's supplies. She opened the door and asked, "Tampon or pad or both?"

"May I have a few of each?" Bambi whispered. "I'm out at home and it might be a couple days before Ma will go get some for me at the store. She's really angry about Pa being gone and all, and I'm afraid to ask her."

"No problem." As Skye took a plastic sack from the shelf, filled it, and handed the supplies to Bambi, she wondered where Earl was hiding out. "Here you go, sweetie. Let Ms. Fleming know if you want more. Do you need fresh undies right now?"

Bambi nodded and Skye selected the smallest size available, gave the package to the girl, and said, "If you see your father, tell him to call me. Hiding is just making the situation worse."

"I sure will, ma'am." Bambi bobbed her head.

"Good. Now you clean up, then get back to class." Skye smiled. "We wouldn't want you getting a bad grade in science."

"Thank you, Ms. D." Bambi waved as she disappeared into the bathroom.

With Bambi taken care of, Skye left for Homer's office. She made a mental note to give Abby a twenty to cover the cost of what Skye had given the girl. All the female staff contributed to Abby's tampon, pad, and underwear fund since lots of girls ended up needing the supplies when their period caught them unawares.

Easing into the principal's office, Skye was thankful for the wall of windows behind his desk. They provided enough illumination that she didn't have to turn on the overhead lights. The last thing she needed was Opal glancing down the hallway and seeing the fluorescents on.

As usual, Homer's garbage can was overflowing with snack food packages and soda cans. Along with plastic gloves, Wally had given her an evidence bag and she fished both from her tote bag. She shook the bag open, put on the gloves, and selected a peanut butter cup wrapper and the lid of a pudding cup. She figured Homer was likely to have licked both of those.

After tucking those items safely inside the evidence bag, she removed the gloves and returned everything to her purse. Before she left, she scanned the room and noticed a crumpled ball of paper near the trash can.

Scooping it up, she hurried back to the PPS meeting. As she walked, she smoothed out the sheet and saw that it was the top page from Jerita's lawsuit. Slashed across it in red Sharpie, Homer had written *You lose, bitch!*

CHAPTER 13
SHE'S LEAVING HOME

Wally sat in the Mayor's office waiting for Dante to get off the telephone and reveal his newest "amazing" idea. The current police contract with the village of Scumble River was ending on December 31 and the two parties were nowhere near an agreement. Although Hizzoner claimed to have come up with the solution to all their problems, Wally was skeptical.

Still, he was willing to listen to the man's proposal. That is, if the guy ever hung up the phone and talked to him.

Among the most contested items were compensation, the need for additional officers, and the length of time the contract would cover. The last agreement had been for six years and Wally, as the bargaining representative for his department, wanted to shorten that span to three. In a pinch, he'd settle for four, but not a day longer.

Tuning in to Dante's conversation, Wally

heard the mayor say, "No. I told you we need those two parcels." He paused, then snapped, "For parking, you idiot! Basin Street is going to lose a quarter of its spots once the reconstruction starts. We can put meters in the lots and recoup our investment in no time."

Hmm! While Wally knew about the proposed Basin Street reconstruction project, this was the first he'd heard about buying land for parking lots. Any decent-sized footage along Scumble River's main drag would cost well over seventy-five thousand, which meant the village board would have to spend at the very least a hundred and fifty K. Maybe that was the reason that the trustees were nickel-and-diming the police department's contract negotiations.

It was odd that there was no scuttlebutt about such a major purchase. The board members must have taken a vow of silence and been plotting this in their closed-door session. Otherwise, May would have said something to Wally. His mother-in-law kept her ear to the grapevine, and she hadn't even mentioned hearing a hint of the board's plans to him.

As Wally squirmed trying to get comfortable on one of the pair of too-small chairs facing the mayor's enormous oak desk, he looked around. Something was different since his last visit to Hizzoner's lair.

Ah! He mentally snapped his fingers. *That was it.* The Zen fountain that Dante had installed, hoping to lower his sky-high blood pressure, was gone. Noticing the mayor's flushed face, Wally thought getting rid of the water feature had been a mistake. Because if anything, Hizzoner's hypertension seemed worse than ever.

Wally cleared his throat and Dante shot him an irritated look, then raised a finger indicating he'd be with him in a minute. Which, as Wally was distrustful of any promise made by the mayor, he seriously doubted.

After another attempt to get comfortable, Wally reached for his phone to check on the vibration that he felt a few seconds ago. Usually, he'd wait until he was alone to look at his messages. He believed it was rude to constantly be glued to a cell phone in the presence of others.

However, with Dante, Wally would make an exception. The mayor was the epitome of bad manners and needed a taste of his own medicine.

Wally's frown morphed into a smile when he saw a picture of Skye on the cell's screen, indicating that the text was from her. He gazed at her beautiful face for a moment before he swiped to see the message.

Skye had no idea that he had this particular photo, but he'd managed to snap it on their honeymoon. She was self-conscious about wearing the two-piece bathing suit he persuaded her to buy for the trip, but the sight of her luscious curves on display sent a jolt southward every time he looked at them.

Getting texts from his wife warmed his heart. Her updates on Eva and CJ were the highlight of his day and the best part was that she always signed her messages with hearts and kisses.

Wally glanced at Dante, but the mayor was still scowling at the telephone, so he thumbed his cell's screen and saw: There are now several items from Homer's trash and an extremely interesting piece of paper in my possession. We're wrapping up the PPS meeting, and after I help Piper talk to a teacher and say hi to Trixie, I'll head home. I just checked with Dorothy and she's doing fine with the twins.

Wally quickly tapped out a reply: If you have time, drop off the evidence at the PD before returning to the RV. I've arranged with the crime scene techs to rush the DNA tests on the pumpkin seed hulls. We can have it in

24–72 hours from when we deliver the comparison sample.

Dante's voice broke into Wally's concentration. "If you're done playing with your cell, maybe we can get this meeting started."

"Seriously?" Wally raised an eyebrow. "I've been waiting twenty minutes for you. Granted, it's less than your usual half an hour, but —"

"Judas Priest!" Dante yelled. "Doesn't anyone realize how busy I am?"

"About as busy as I am with a murder and a missing person." Wally allowed his exasperation to show in his voice.

"I told you to quit wasting resources on that Baker woman," Dante screeched like a buzzard thwarted from its afternoon snack of carrion. "She's either dead at the bottom of some lake or in Las Vegas spending her husband's money!"

"I've called off the searchers, but Mrs. Baker's disappearance is still an open case." Wally crossed his legs and drawled, "Now what's your grand plan?"

Dante scowled at Wally. "I should just let you and the police department end up with the scraps you deserve on your contract."

"Try that and you'll have no officers working as of New Year's Day." Wally tapped the arm of his chair. "Do you understand what it would look like without the police on duty when all the drunks start leaving the bars at three a.m.?"

"Yeah. Yeah. Yeah." Dante thrust out his chin. "Anyway, I've come up with a solution for both the salary issue and the additional staffing."

"And this idea is what?" Wally waved his hand at Dante to continue.

"Annual bonus payments — a thousand a year for rookies, two thousand for senior officers, and twenty-five hundred for sergeants and above," Dante announced, then hurriedly added, "By awarding bonuses versus increases in salary, we lessen the costs of pensions."

"You also decrease the pensions." Wally leaned back and crossed his legs.

"Only slightly," Dante wheedled. "But otherwise we would need to raise property taxes and all those citizens who supported keeping the police department rather than having the county deputies take over might reconsider."

Although the mayor was right, any sense of cooperation Wally had felt coming into the meeting immediately evaporated. The trustees would make sure that the Scumble Riverites never heard that the true reason for the tax hike was due to the property the board was trying to buy and not the police contract. Even if the information was made public, most people would never believe it. The trustees would manage to spin it so that the cops were the bad guys.

"I can take your idea of the bonuses to my officers." Wally threw Dante a warning look. "But how about the increase in uniform allowance and lifting the cap on how many hours the part-timers can work?"

"Done." Dante nodded. "We'll raise the allowance to fifteen hundred and do away with the limitations on the part-timers."

"That sounds fair." Wally narrowed his eyes. Dante didn't usually give anything away without a struggle. There was a catch here somewhere. "What about the increase in staff?"

"I saved the best for last." Dante laced his fingers over his beer belly, rocked back in his chair, and smiled smugly. "Through one of my good friend's generosity, we are being provided with a police dog at cost."

When Wally was silent, Dante continued, "You've stated that the main reason you want an additional cop is to have two officers on duty during the evening hours. A police dog can be that second officer. It can add a level of safety for the officer, help with drug busts, and track missing persons."

Wally fought to keep his voice neutral. "But officers need to be trained to work with a K-9 partner and we don't have the budget for that." He wasn't thrilled with the idea, but it might be workable if there was money for an officer's education in the budget.

"According to her résumé, that girl you hired had a dog handling course in college. We can start with that." Dante straightened a stack of files on his desk, then not looking up he said, "It's my best offer. You got Anthony full-time and we can't afford another salary right now. Maybe on the next contract."

"Which will come up when?" Wally stared until Dante met his gaze.

Dante fingered the gold chain that stretched across his vest. "We're willing to drop the time span from six to five years."

"Three," Wally stated, leveling a firm look at the mayor.

"Four," Dante countered.

"Let me talk to the other officers." Wally tapped his pen on his thigh.

"You know good and well they'll go along with your lead," Dante sneered.

"My officers think for themselves." Wally was about to say more when he felt his cell phone vibrate. "I'll get back to you as soon as there's a decision."

"Fine." The mayor turned away, snatched up the receiver, and began to dial.

Wally stood and walked back to his own office before checking his phone. When he saw that the missed call was from Thea, he punched in his password and listened to the dispatcher's voicemail. "Krissy Ficher is here for her one o'clock appointment with you."

Wally glanced at his watch. It was already five after one. He'd hoped to grab a bite to eat before the home health aide's interview, but as usual Dante had kept him cooling his heels too long.

Sighing, Wally headed downstairs. When he reached the station's lobby, he found an attractive woman who appeared to be in her mid- to late twenties leaning against the counter. She was dressed in a black skirt, white blouse, and a jean jacket that looked to be more for fashion than warmth.

The woman was chatting with Thea, but as soon as she spotted Wally, she turned and with a bright smile asked, "Chief Boyd?"

"Yes." Wally held out his hand. "And you must be Krissy Ficher."

"I am. I'm sorry I couldn't get here last week, but as I told you, I was dealing with a family situation." The woman shook Wally's hand. "I had my fingers crossed that Edie would be home by the time I got back."

"Unfortunately not." Wally watched the woman carefully. "I was hoping Mrs. Baker might have contacted you. Maybe sent you a note in the mail or something."

"No such luck. Besides, I don't think she had my postal address." Krissy wrinkled her brow. "I hadn't been taking care of her that long and I can't think of a reason that I would have given it to her."

"She might have seen it on your employment application since I'm sure Mr. Baker had you complete one." Moving toward the door, Wally said, "Come on back. We can use the break room to talk."

"Sure." Krissy cheerfully crossed the threshold, her ankle boots clicking on the linoleum.

As Wally held the door for her, he caught a whiff of her perfume. He wrinkled his nose at the overpowering fragrance. Why women bathed themselves in cologne was beyond him. He preferred a lighter scent or none at all.

Walking down the hall, Wally asked, "Would you like a cup of coffee?"

"Do you have any herbal tea? Coffee really isn't good for you." Krissy smiled. "I try to eat and drink only organic to stay in tiptop shape."

"That's an admirable goal. My wife just had twins a few months ago and as an older father, I'm doing my best to get healthier too."

Krissy nodded approvingly. "I think older fathers can be better than young, immature ones. They have so much wisdom to share."

Wally glanced at her. Her expression was open and she didn't seem to be flirting.

He led her into the break room, and when he flipped on the switch, the overhead lights sputtered to life. They cast a harsh fluorescent glow, which wasn't very restful for officers grabbing a cup of coffee but perfect for interviewing suspects.

Gesturing to the table, Wally said, "Have a seat and I'll see what kind of tea we have."

"Thanks." Krissy settled on one of the chairs and placed her large purse on the floor. Then she folded her hands on the tabletop in front of her and said, "If you don't have herbal, green tea would be okay."

Wally searched through the cabinets by the sink and found a Tupperware bowl containing assorted tea bags. After rifling through them, he held up a yellow packet and asked, "How's this?"

"Ah. Lemon Zinger." The tan fedora on

210

Krissy's brown curls bounced as she nodded. "That's fine."

Wally heated a mug of water in the microwave, then placed it and the tea bag in front of the young woman. He sat across from her and waited to see what she'd say. In his experience, people told you more when you allowed them to start the conversation.

As the silence lengthened, Krissy tore open the packet, dunked the bag in the water, and stared at the liquid in her cup, then finally said, "I was really surprised about Edie. Mr. Baker kept a close eye on her."

"I imagine watching someone with memory issues 24/7 is impossible." Wally pulled a legal pad toward himself and took a pen from his shirt pocket. "How is Mr. Baker as a boss?"

"You know." Krissy shrugged. "Kind of old school and strict, but at least he isn't a letch. I hate when old guys try to grab me when I'm taking care of their wives. My fiancé would kill them if he knew."

"I bet." Wally tapped his pen on the legal pad. "So you're engaged?"

He glanced at her bare finger and she quickly covered it, then said, "We're waiting until we can go shopping together to get the ring."

"Good idea." Wally smiled, then refocused the conversation. He didn't want to discuss emerald cut versus pear shapes. "Can you go through a typical day with Mrs. Baker? From when you arrived to when you left."

"I made her breakfast — Edie liked this puffy French toast and Mr. Baker couldn't get it right." Krissy played with the ends of her hair. "Then we'd do the dishes together and watch TV while Mr. Baker ran errands."

"Like what?" Wally asked.

"I don't really know, but I think he mostly stayed around Bord du Lac." Krissy sipped her tea. "We usually went with him if he went into town. Edie liked going to the supermarket or dollar store."

"What did you do with her the rest of the day?" Wally jotted down a note to check the security cameras at those places on the date Mrs. Baker had gone missing and a few days after that.

"Edie liked to do crafts so we generally worked on one of those." Krissy tilted her head as if in thought. "And she liked to play UNO."

"Did Mr. Baker join you?" Wally doubted it, but he had to ask.

"No." Krissy grimaced. "Mr. Baker mostly watched war movies or sat out on his deck keeping an eye on the lake to make sure people obeyed the rules." She giggled. "He had this huge megaphone that he'd use to yell at them if they were doing something wrong."

"Did you and Mrs. Baker ever go outside?" Wally asked, hoping for some kind of lead since crafts and UNO didn't give him any ideas.

"Once, we took a walk on the concrete pathway that circles the development." Krissy exhaled loudly. "But we never did that again."

"Why is that?" It felt as if he was onto something and Wally leaned forward.

"Well . . ." Krissy bit her lip. "The thing is, Edie slipped away from me when we stopped at the little park halfway through."

"Oh?" Wally made a note to look at that park again. "How did that happen?"

"I had to use the bathroom and I asked her to sit at the picnic table until I got back." Krissy clasped her hands around her mug as if she were suddenly cold. "And when I was finished she was gone."

"But you located her." Wally studied the young woman. She was harder to read than he expected. He should have had Skye here to help.

"Yes." Krissy stared over Wally's head. "She'd taken a golf cart from one of the neighbors' driveways and was almost to the main road by the time I found her."

Wally made a note to have Anthony check to see if any golf carts had been reported stolen, then asked a few more questions and rose from his seat.

As he walked Krissy to the lobby, Wally said, "Oh. One more thing before you leave. When I spoke to you the day she disappeared, why didn't you tell me that she'd gone missing previously?"

"Uh." Krissy studied her boots. "I never reported that incident to Mr. Baker, and I didn't want him to find out." She looked up with wide blue eyes. "When he loses his temper, he's sort of scary, you know?"

Wally watched the young woman exit the station, staring at her retreating figure. Just how scary was Gerald Baker when he was annoyed?

CHAPTER 14
I'LL COME HOME TO YOU

As Skye hurried down the high school hallway alongside her intern, she rubbed her temples. Homer had ordered Piper to inform Pru Cormorant that her referral had been rejected. Unfortunately, Skye hadn't felt as if she could send the young woman into the lion's den all alone, even if Pru was more a hyena than the king of beasts.

After the PPS meeting was over, Skye had called Dorothy. Once she heard that everything was fine at home, Skye had texted Wally, then told Piper she'd accompany her to confer with Pru. This year, the English teacher had sixth period free, and Skye was intent on getting to her before the end of fifth period. Otherwise she'd have to track her down, which would take more time than Skye had to spend.

"Ms. Cormorant sure lucked out with room assignments," Piper murmured, keeping pace with Skye. "Hers is one of the few in this school that has actual walls instead of those folding accordion partitions. And windows too!"

"Don't forget the exterior door. When the weather's nice, she usually spends her planning periods on a lawn chair outside her room tanning." Skye lowered her voice. "And unless she calls you Ms. Townsend, don't call her Ms. Cormorant. It puts you in a subservient position. As if you're one of her students instead of a colleague."

"Right." Piper's cheeks reddened. "I knew that, but she's so . . . so . . ."

"Intimidating?" Skye suggested.

"Yes." Piper nodded. "And it seemed to make her mad when I used her first name."

Skye slowed down and looked into Piper's eyes before she said, "If you want to make everyone happy, school psychology may not be the best choice for you." Skye winked. "Although the only profession I can think of that makes everyone happy is an ice cream truck driver."

Piper giggled, then turned serious and squared her shoulders. "You're right. I need to toughen up."

"Just remember, behind Pru's back most of the staff call her Corny. Not that I condone that kind of thing," Skye said, then added under her breath, "Even if she is a bully."

A few steps later, Piper and Skye arrived at Pru's door just as the bell rang. They waited while the students poured out of the room, and when the last one passed them, they entered and found the aggravating English teacher cooing sweet nothings into her cell phone.

Skye blinked at the affection in Pru's voice and studied her. There was something different about the woman. Her egg-shaped body and gaunt limbs were the same. Her head still seemed too small for the rest of her. And her skin still had an alligator-like quality after all her years chasing the perfect shade of bronze. So what was it?

Before Skye could decide, Pru noticed them, said something into her phone, then hung up and demanded, "What are you two doing here?"

Skye nudged Piper. She was there to support the intern, but the young woman had to learn how to deal with difficult faculty members.

"I . . . uh . . . I mean the PPS team discussed the student you referred and —"

"Speak up." Pru's watery blue eyes were malicious. "I don't know how you think you can do your job if you can't make a clear

217

statement."

Skye bit the inside of her cheek, then forced a pleasant expression on her face and said, "In our job, sometimes it's better to be less blunt."

"What are you doing here? I thought you were still home with your babies." Pru raised an overplucked eyebrow. "Tired of playing mommy already?"

"Of course not." Skye pasted a fake smile on her lips. "But supervising Piper's internship is my responsibility." She shot the teacher a hard look. "And making sure she learns how to handle all sorts of individuals, especially those who have strong opinions, is part of that."

"If you're implying that I go out of my way to offend people, go ahead and say it." Pru chuckled nastily. "But trust me. It's not at all out of my way."

"You know, Pru, that little thing in your head that keeps most people from saying things they shouldn't?" Skye crossed her arms. "It seems motherhood has destroyed mine. So watch it."

"Fine. Can we get on with this?" Pru glanced at the cell she still held in her hand. "Some of us have better things to do in our one free period."

Hmm! Skye was dying to know who the

teacher had been flirting with on the phone. At one time, she'd suspected that Pru and the superintendent were having an affair, but she'd found out that their parents were second cousins and they were raised like brother and sister. So he was out.

Skye nudged her intern again and Piper cleared her throat, then said, "After an extensive file review and a discussion of the student with the members of the PPS team, we have decided that Liam does not require any additional modifications or services."

"He isn't able to cope with the high standard to which I teach." Pru pursed her thin lips. "He isn't at the same level as the other students and needs to move into a different English class."

"He is on the college prep track." Piper lifted her chin. "And will remain in your section."

Skye's chest swelled with pride. Piper had faced the scary woman without flinching.

Pru *tsked.* "When I started at Scumble River High School, someone like Liam would have been guided into the trades or perhaps the military."

Skye dug her nails into her palms to stop herself from asking what it was like to teach during the age of dinosaurs.

Piper, having apparently found her courage, said, "Thank goodness children are now guided according to both their interests and abilities."

"Not in my opinion. We need to stop coddling these students and their helicopter parents. They need to be steered into some area they can earn a living and not become a drain on society."

Pru patted her hair and Skye figured out the difference. Not only was it now blond, it was freshly shampooed and had been cut into a more attractive style. How had she missed that when she first looked at the teacher?

Having heard the teacher's opinion on the subject before, Skye decided that it was time to put the brakes on her rant and said, "Be that as it may, Liam is staying put. Deal with it."

"We'll see about that." Pru waved her skeleton-like hand. "Wait until I speak to Homer."

"He was at the meeting and was the first one to say that Liam was fine." Skye held back a snicker as the woman's jaw dropped.

"That's . . . I mean . . ." Pru's voice rose. "Homer would never . . ."

"What was that about speaking clearly?" Skye murmured before she could stop herself.

"I beg your pardon?" The self-centered teacher wrinkled her brow, seeming not to understand the reference to her earlier jibe at Piper.

"Never mind." Skye shook her head and said, "We won't keep you any longer."

"Wait!" She looked at Skye through her sparse lashes and asked, "Do you still work as the psych consultant to the police department?"

"Yes." Skye had no idea where the teacher was headed but waited for her to go on.

"Have the police had any luck locating that missing woman?" Pru's pointy nose twitched, making her look like a rabbit on the trail of a tasty carrot. "I believe her name was Edie Baker?"

"Not so far." Now Skye was really confused. Pru rarely showed concern for another human being. "Wally is meeting with her home health aide today, so maybe that will result in a new lead."

"But don't you think the poor thing is probably dead?" Pru nibbled a ragged cuticle. "After all this time and in her mental condition?"

"It's certainly possible," Skye said carefully, again wondering why Pru cared.

"Do you know how long they keep the case open before they declare her deceased?" Pru's tongue snaked out and licked her lips, which Skye noticed had a coat of soft pink lipstick rather than her usual harsh dark red.

"I have no idea." Skye made a mental note to tell Wally about Pru's interest.

"It would be a blessing really." Pru's expression was hard to read. "For everyone concerned."

"Anyway." Skye shuffled her feet. "Piper and I need to get going."

"As do I." Pru's irritation with Skye was obvious. "You do not have thirty young minds to enlighten."

"Right." Skye herded Piper toward the doorway. "Have a good afternoon."

As soon as Skye and Piper were behind the closed doors of the psych office, Skye went to her desk and opened the drawer. After a bit of rummaging, she found her secret stash and selected a candy bar.

She presented the giant peanut butter cup to her intern and said, "You did an extremely good job handling a difficult faculty member."

"Thank you!" Piper tore off the wrapper and took a huge bite.

"I'm also impressed with how well you're working with Euphemia." Skye debated for a second, then grabbed a miniature Kit Kat for herself. "How do you feel you're doing with the rest of the staff?"

"Things seem to be going okay with almost everyone." Piper sighed. "But how do you stop from blurting out things when they're being ridiculous?"

"Actually, I've often thought that I should be given an award for keeping my mouth shut when there's so much that needs to be said."

"You're so funny!" Piper squeezed past Skye, took a seat behind the small desk, and flipped open her iPad. "Just a second while I find my notes."

As Skye waited, she considered Dr. Wraige's bribe. It would be nice to know that not only was this space hers for good, but that she'd have a budget to fix it up and buy new materials.

She'd only wrested the ten-by-ten windowless room away from the boys PE teacher/guidance counselor after pointing out that he already had a private office in the gym complex, while she had to beg, borrow, or steal a closet or cubbyhole to evaluate or counsel students. He hadn't been happy to relinquish the space and Skye was always on the alert for his counterattack.

It had taken a tornado to get the walls repainted, and while the new soothing blue

223

color helped a lot, the uncovered fluorescent tubes in the overhead lights still cast a sickening tinge over everything. And the furniture was all stuff that she'd managed to scavenge.

It was fun to think about actually ordering new things like a trapezoidal table that didn't have one leg shorter than the other two and student chairs that were actually comfy. She'd keep the wooden file cabinet. The vintage style appealed to her. But she really needed a cupboard that locked to keep her assessment kits safe.

Still, what she had at the high school was heaps better than the space or furnishings at the grade school or the junior high. There, the rooms barely fit Skye, a student, and the folding tray she used for testing.

Wait a minute! Skye straightened. She didn't have to depend on Dr. Wraige. Now that Wally's family wealth was public knowledge, she could just pay to redecorate all three offices herself. She couldn't do anything about their size, but she could make them more comfortable.

The insurance they'd collected on their previous cars and house had covered over half of what the Mercedes and the new place cost. And even with those expenses, they'd barely touched the interest that had been piling up from Wally's trust fund all those years that he had hidden the fact that he had money beyond his salary.

"Skye?" Piper's voice broke into her thoughts. "Are you okay?"

"Sorry, just daydreaming." Skye reluctantly quit mentally shopping, refocused on the issue at hand, and asked, "What did you say?"

Piper nodded. "I found my notes and I could use some suggestions with how best to interact with a couple of people in the district."

"Shoot." Skye settled into her old leather chair and folded her hands on top of her scratched wooden desk. "Homer is one, right?"

"Yes." Piper made a face. "And Ursula Nelson at the junior high."

"Homer is a lot like Pru Cormorant." Skye narrowed her eyes. "But he uses his size and position to intimidate his employees. Truly, I'm not sure I handle him all that well myself, but my best advice is to maintain a respectful demeanor, but don't allow him to push you around, which you seem to be doing."

"Okay." Piper jotted a note into her iPad, then asked, "And Ursula?"

"Another tough one." Skye thought about

the junior high secretary. "She's touchy and I suspect it's because she feels as if we all think we're better than her because of our education."

"So maybe try to make sure that I let her see that I value how much she does to keep the school running," Piper murmured. "Right?"

"Bingo." Skye held two thumbs up. "Oh. Also, she has a weakness for homemade chocolate chip cookies. But only give them to her, not anyone else. She needs to feel special."

"Got it." Piper smiled.

"I wanted to check with you about one other thing." Skye couldn't believe she'd nearly forgotten about poor Jenna Quinn. "How did it go when Beilin Quinn showed up and you helped him break the news about his wife to his daughter?"

"As well as could be expected." Piper sighed. "Mr. Quinn explained that Jenna's mom had gone to heaven and then I helped Jenna process the information and her feelings."

"It sounds as if you handled another tough situation very well." Skye smiled warmly. "A few weeks ago, when you were testing Jenna, did she mention anything about why her mom didn't want her in the

Chicago schools?"

"Nothing about that came up." Piper tilted her head. "The only thing that I got from our sessions that was even remotely related to that was Mrs. Quinn's excessive protectiveness of her daughter."

Skye had also gotten that impression and said, "Maybe Jerita felt that all city schools were dangerous, even though that clearly isn't true."

They spent another fifteen minutes talking over cases, then Piper left to do an observation. With the office to herself, Skye checked her phone.

When she saw the text from Wally asking her to drop off Homer's trash at the police station as soon as she could, she typed a hasty reply: Should be there in fifteen to twenty minutes. I just need to say a quick hello to Trixie.

As if Skye had conjured up her friend, the office door crashed open and Trixie Frayne burst into the room. While Skye wanted to spend time with her BFF, she also thought that Trixie might have some information on Jerita or the others involved in the case.

In addition to being the school librarian, Trixie was also the cheerleading coach, cosponsor of the student newspaper, and founder of the service club, so students often told her things that they'd overheard from their parents.

As Trixie rushed into the office, Skye examined her friend. It was hard to believe they were the same age. Trixie's elfin quality made her seem at least ten years younger. She had short cocoa-colored hair with matching brown eyes. And although she was less than five feet tall, and probably didn't weigh a hundred pounds after eating a big meal, her body was the only thing about Trixie that was tiny. Her personality and her heart were the size of the Statue of Liberty.

After plopping into one of the folding chairs, Trixie leaned forward and said, "Bambi told me you were at school today. Why haven't I seen you?"

"Let me count the whys," Skye teased. "PPS, a meeting with Pru —"

"Ugh." Trixie made a face. "What was Corny's problem this time?"

"She wanted a gifted student labeled intellectually challenged."

"Seriously?" Trixie blew out a long, disgusted breath. "When does old enough to know better start to kick in? What is wrong with that woman?"

"What isn't?" Skye asked dryly. "If only she and Homer would retire . . ."

"Dream on." Trixie glanced around and asked, "Where's Piper?"

"Observing a student for a reevaluation," Skye answered, then asked, "Speaking of Pru, she did seem different today. Have you heard anything?"

"Well . . ." Trixie crossed her legs and dangled her bright-pink high heel from her toe. "There is some chatter floating around, but you don't like gossip."

"Trixie," Skye warned.

"Okay. If you insist." Trixie smoothed her pink-and-black polka dot skirt over her thighs. "Rumor has it that Corny is in love."

"With who?" Skye asked, thinking how Pru had been cooing into her cell phone. Had there been a clue to the person's identity?

"No one knows." Trixie leaned forward. "Which is why I suspect whoever it is, he's married."

CHAPTER 15
2,000 LIGHT-YEARS FROM HOME

Skye discreetly checked her watch. This was Trixie's free period and it looked as if she planned to spend the entire forty minutes catching up.

Squirming in her seat, Skye waited for her friend to take a breath in her stream-of-consciousness chatter, then said, "Sorry to interrupt, but I need to get going."

"Of course." Trixie jumped up from her chair. "But before you go, I wanted to ask you about yesterday's murder. Is it true the vic was suing Homer?"

"I really can't say," Skye hedged, then asked, "Where did you hear about that?"

"It was the talk of the teacher's lounge." Trixie winked, then jerked her gaze to Skye and asked, "What's the chance he killed her?"

"What's that saying?" Skye stood. "Who knows what darkness lurks in the heart of men?"

"Hey. The principal as the murderer would be a great plot for my next book." Trixie's brown eyes lit up and she grabbed a notepad and pen from Skye's desk. As she wrote, she mumbled, "Maybe he's having an affair with an English teacher and the vic found out and was blackmailing him."

"That sounds like an interesting plot." Skye walked out of the office with Trixie trailing her. After locking the door, she headed toward the school's rear exit with her friend on her heels. "How's the querying going?"

Trixie had recently finished her book and was in the process of submitting it to agents. Skye hoped her friend would have some success before she got discouraged from the flood of rejections.

"I forgot to tell you!" Trixie squealed. "I just got two requests for the complete manuscript this morning. Both agents said the first three chapters showed a lot of promise and the writing was compelling."

"That is completely freaking awesome." Skye hugged her friend. "I bet they'll both offer to represent you and you'll get to choose the one you like best."

"Fingers crossed."

"Let me know as soon as you hear anything more from the agents." Skye waved goodbye as she hurried out to her car.

Happy for her friend, Skye grinned as she drove to the station. Then as she neared the PD she refocused on the case and considered what she'd learned during her time at the high school.

One, Earl was still in hiding. Two, Homer was in trouble about the lawsuit. And three, Pru was interested in Edie Baker's disappearance.

Still trying to come up with a reason that the irritating teacher might ask about the missing woman, Skye pulled her SUV into one of the open spots. As she hopped out, grabbed the bag with Homer's trash from her tote, and went into the garage, she considered what she knew about Pru.

After she used her key to enter the station, Skye concluded that the only reason the English teacher would care about Edie Baker was if the woman's disappearance somehow impacted Pru. And Skye couldn't see any connection between the two women.

Hurrying down the hallway, Skye slowed as she passed the break room. Zelda was sitting at the long rectangular table staring at a laptop and Skye squinted to see what the young officer was viewing so intently. It seemed to be security footage from what looked like the interior of the dollar store.

What was up with that?

Skye watched for a few minutes but didn't see anything interesting. Had there been a robbery at the store? Or did it have something to do with the murder?

With nothing happening on the screen, Skye quickly grew bored and continued to the stairs. She climbed the steps to the second floor, knocked on Wally's closed door, then opened it a crack and looked inside.

Wally was on the telephone, but he gestured Skye over to the visitor chair across from his desk. He smiled at her and put the phone on speaker.

From what Skye could make out, the medical examiner was in the middle of summarizing the preliminary results of Jerita Quinn's autopsy.

When the woman stopped speaking, Wally said, "So what you're saying, Doc, is that the vic was stabbed in the temple somewhere between nine and eleven?"

"Yes." The ME's voice was a rich alto. "I was able to narrow it down a bit from your coroner's estimate, but that's the best I can do."

Wally made a note in the file in front of him, then continued, "And your conclusion is that the victim was most likely unconscious when the stabbing occurred?"

"From the trauma to the back of her head, that would be my conclusion."

"How about drugs or alcohol?" Wally asked.

"Except for the prescription medication her husband said she took for her heart condition, our tests didn't detect anything unusual in her system."

"Is there anything else about the vic you can tell me?" Wally tapped his pen on the desktop.

"Not at this time," the ME answered. "I still have a few results I'm waiting on, but as of now, that's all I know for certain."

"Thanks, Doc," Wally said. "When can I expect the full report?"

"Twenty-four to forty-eight hours." The ME said goodbye and disconnected.

As soon as Wally hung up the phone, Skye asked, "Anything from the crime techs yet?"

"Nothing helpful." Wally gestured to the evidence bag Skye was holding. "Is that Homer's trash?" When she nodded, he slid a sheet of paper across the desktop along with a pen and said, "You'll need to fill out this form and attach it to the bag."

"Okay. And you probably want this as well." Skye tossed him the crumpled ball of paper she'd found on the floor by Homer's garbage.

After looking it over, Wally murmured, "Interesting. If the DNA on Homer's trash matches the pumpkin seed hulls at the murder scene, I'll use this to get a warrant to formally obtain his DNA and a sample of his handwriting."

"Right." Skye wrinkled her nose. "No use rocking the boat if the hulls aren't his."

While Skye completed the document Wally had given her, he made a call. "Martinez, stop what you're doing and get up to my office right now."

"That was rude." Skye finished writing and attached the paper to the bag.

"Martinez wouldn't appreciate it if I treated her any different from the other officers." Wally rubbed the stubble on his jaw. "She's been briefed on the importance of this evidence and has been waiting to take it to the crime scene techs in Laurel."

"Well, you could say please." Skye hid her smile. Her husband was generally the sweetest guy, but unsolved murders brought out the worst in him.

"I'll try to remember that in the future." Getting up, Wally walked around the desk and leaned down. "May I please have a kiss?"

"You may." Skye's lips brushed his and he

235

drew her into his arms.

Things were just getting interesting when the door burst open and Zelda Martinez rushed inside. She skidded to a stop and, with red cheeks, stuttered, "Uh . . . sorry, Chief. I should have knocked."

"No worries, Zelda," Skye giggled. "It's okay. We *are* married."

"Here." Wally released Skye, grabbed the bag on his desk, and thrust it at the young officer. "Tell them to let me know the minute they have the results."

"Will do, Chief." Zelda clutched the evidence to her chest and backed out of the office. "You can count on me, sir. I won't let you down."

As the door closed behind the young woman, Skye fanned herself. "Wow. She has a bad case of hero worship."

"What?" Wally frowned. "Not at all. She just wants to do a good job."

"Sure." Skye wiped the smirk from her face. "Anyway, I need to get home before Dorothy thinks I've abandoned her and the twins."

"Anything I should know before you leave?" Wally put his hand on the small of her back and guided her into the hallway and down the stairs.

"Earl's still hiding, but I asked Bambi to

have him call me if she sees him or he comes home." Skye walked toward the garage door, pausing with her hand on the knob. "Oh. One other thing. Pru Cormorant asked me about the Edie Baker case. I have no idea why she'd be interested."

"Could she know them from the VFW or American Legion or Lions Club?"

"Maybe." Skye frowned. "You know, it's odd. I don't remember ever hearing anything about Pru outside of school. The only other place I've ever seen her is church. No, wait a minute." Skye tapped the metal knob with her fingernails. "I've also run into her at the dollar store. She mentioned that they have a certain candy she likes that she can't get anywhere else."

"That could be it." Wally nodded. "Today when I talked to Mrs. Baker's home care worker, she said that Edie liked to go there."

Skye snapped her fingers. "Which was why you had Zelda viewing their security footage." She grinned. "Well, I'm sure glad to have both those mysteries solved. Pru and Edie must have struck up a conversation and Pru was curious when she heard Edie was missing." Skye kissed Wally's cheek, opened the door, and waved as she walked out. "See you later."

As she drove home, Skye realized that she

hadn't asked Wally if he'd found out any-thing in addition to the dollar store informa-tion from his interview with the home health aide or if he'd learned anything new about the murder. The fact that Jerita had been hit over the head and was probably unconscious when she was stabbed made Skye think that it had been a sneak attack. Had the killer lured her outside, then somehow gotten her to look away long enough to knock her out?

Arriving back at the RV, all thoughts of the murder and the missing woman were pushed aside as Skye thanked Dorothy. Then despite the woman's protest that her babysitting fee could be added to her sal-ary, she paid her and walked her to the door.

Once the housekeeper left, Skye fed the twins and changed both their diapers. After she had them settled in their swings, she called her mom.

When May answered and they exchanged the usual greetings and assurances that she, Wally, and the twins were fine, Skye asked, "Is Loretta out of the hospital?"

"Surprisingly she is," May answered. "She got home around noon and is doing great."

"That's wonderful." Skye cradled the phone between her ear and shoulder, tied on an apron, and grabbed a package of Italian sausage from the refrigerator. Then after selecting a large cast iron frying pan from the cupboard, she said, "Wally and I thought we'd bring them dinner and welcome the new addition to our family."

"I'm sure visiting them would be fine. But since Vince picked up April, and I'm off work, why don't you let me make the dinner? I could bring it to your place and you could take it over to their house?" May continued before Skye could respond. "I can stay with the twins for you."

"I'll accept the offer to watch CJ and Eva, but I already have the lasagna started." Skye had known her mom would want to cook, so she'd deliberately gotten the meat browning while they were talking.

"You could save it for you and Wally to eat tomorrow night."

"No thanks." Skye filled a pot with water and put it on a burner to bring to boiling. "I already have something for Wednesday, and then Thursday's Thanksgiving and you know you'll give us leftovers."

"There's always the freezer," May persisted. "You'll be happy to have some quick meals in there once you go back to work."

"That's still over five weeks away. Besides —" Skye cut herself off. She wasn't ready to tell May that they'd hired Dorothy to work as a full-time housekeeper yet. She wasn't sure how her mom would take it. "I don't like keeping food in there that long."

"How about a salad and garlic bread?" May countered quickly. "I could make you a nice green salad and I have some Italian bread just sitting here waiting to be slathered in garlic butter."

"I've got that covered." Skye crossed her fingers. She had the makings in the fridge, but she hadn't actually put them together yet.

"Dessert!" May's voice was triumphant. "I bet you don't have a dessert."

"Got me there, Mom." Skye smiled. Her mother was so predictable. "Any chance you could make that yummy fruit cocktail pudding?" She'd been hungry for that dessert and hers never tasted as good as May's. "And homemade whipped cream?"

"In my sleep." May's tone was smug. "What time do you want me?"

"Do Loretta and Vince still like to eat late?" Skye preferred to have dinner at five, but with Wally's schedule, they'd pushed dinnertime back an hour. She'd be starved by seven and would have to resist the urge to snack.

"Yes." May *tsked*.

"Then how about you come over here

about six thirty?" Skye suggested.

"Fine," May said, then added, "I've told Vince eating that late isn't good for them, but he just does whatever Loretta wants him to do."

"Kind of like Dad does with you?" Skye chuckled.

"And Wally with you," May pounced. "Which is how it should be."

"Mmm." Skye kind of agreed but wouldn't admit her mother was right. "See you at six thirty."

"I'll let Vince and Loretta know that you're bringing supper instead of me."

"Thanks!" Skye disconnected and glanced at the microwave clock.

It was already four thirty. Wally would be home in an hour and would want to shower before going over to Loretta and Vince's, which meant Skye really should freshen up now while the sink and mirror were free. She definitely missed having a second bathroom.

Once she slid the pan of lasagna into the preheated oven, Skye checked on Eva and CJ. Both were dozing and the lasagna needed to bake for an hour. This was Skye's chance for a quick sponge bath and to change out of her work clothes.

Leaving the bedroom door open so she

241

could keep an ear out for any sounds of distress from the twins, Skye stripped off her dress pants and tunic. After a hurried wash, she touched up her makeup and combed her hair.

She was zipping up a pair of dark jeans when there was a loud knock on the front door. She hastily pulled on a forest-green cowl-necked sweater, rushed from the bedroom, and put her eye to the peephole.

There was no one there. Confused, she moved to the window and looked out. Sitting behind her Mercedes was an old Buick Regal. Its light-blue paint was hard to see for the primer and Bondo, but there was only one person in town who drove a car like that one.

Skye rolled her eyes and returned to the foyer, grabbed her coat, and flung open the door. As she stepped out, she scanned the yard, but there was no one in sight.

Making a megaphone with her hands, she shouted, "Earl Doozier, get your skinny butt over here right now."

CHAPTER 16
A LONG WAY FROM HOME

Skye gave Earl five minutes to show his weaselly little face, but when the time was up and he still hadn't put in an appearance, she patted her pockets, searching for her phone. She had to call Wally. He would be none too happy to hear that the fugitive he had his officers searching high and low for was currently in his very own driveway.

Or at least his car was parked there. At the moment, Earl's location was anyone's guess.

When Skye didn't find her cell in her jeans' pocket, she remembered that when she went to change clothes she'd plugged the phone into its charger. As she opened the door to go get it, she heard a shout and turned around.

Shading her eyes with her hand, she scanned the area until she saw Beilin Quinn marching Earl across the lawn. They were about halfway between the motor home and the new house and Skye could clearly see Earl's face, which looked a lot like an over-ripe tomato getting ready to burst out of its skin. Beilin had a meaty forearm against Earl's throat, a nail gun to his temple, and eyes blazing with barely contained rage.

Earl waved both skinny tattooed arms in the air as if he were drowning and gurgled, "He's chokin' me to death. Save me, Miz Skye. Save me."

For a moment, Skye wondered why Earl wasn't wearing a coat. Beilin didn't have one on either, but he'd probably been working inside the new house where it was warm.

Blinking away her distracted thoughts regarding the men's outerwear, Skye shouted, "Let him breathe! I know this man!"

"So do I." Beilin continued to goose-step Earl toward her. "He's the guy who destroyed my shed, stole my lawn mower, and killed my wife."

Interesting that Jerita's murder had come last on Beilin's list of Earl's crimes. She tucked that fact into a corner of her mind to think about later.

"He's not the killer." Skye was only ninety-nine-point-nine percent sure she was telling the truth, but that was enough for this situation. "Yes. He did those other things." She glared at Earl. "And he shouldn't have left the scene of the crime when the police wanted to question him, but he only found her body. He had no motive to hurt her."

"Maybe he was trying to rape her and she fought back," Beilin countered.

Earl let out an affronted squawk as he and Beilin arrived at the bottom of the RV's metal steps.

"Definitely not." Skye glanced through the motor home's open door. She was thankful to see that CJ and Eva were still sleeping in their swings. Now if she only had her phone.

Beilin glared at Skye. "How do you know?" He loosened his choke hold on Earl, but kept a firm grip on the man.

"She was completely clothed, none of her garments were torn, and Earl was dressed in a turkey costume." Skye wondered if she should mention that Jerita had been hit on the back of the head, which implied she'd been turned away, but although she couldn't specifically remember Wally saying that he was keeping that information from the public, it was highly likely that he didn't want the information disclosed. "However, most importantly, the ME found no signs of sexual assault."

"Then he was trying to rob us," Beilin argued. "He could have been the one that vandalized our place before and came back to finish up."

"That's not the Doozier way." Skye was a hundred percent certain of that statement. "Scams and get-rich-quick schemes, but not breaking and entering. That would take too much physical labor."

Earl's voice cracked in outrage. "That ain't a nice thing to say about a friend, Miz Skye. I ain't lazy." He shook his finger at her and added, "I's just in power saver mode most ah the time."

"Shut up, Earl." Skye looked nervously at the contractor and said soothingly, "Beilin, how about you let me take him inside and call Wally. It's his job to figure this out, not yours."

The angry man didn't move.

"I promise you Earl isn't dangerous," Skye pledged, putting her hand to her heart. "He's just not the quickest rabbit in the forest."

"Miz Skye!" Earl bleated. "I ain't no kinda bunny. I's a wolf."

She ignored him. "Listen, you can stay right out here by the motor home's steps, and if he tries to run away before Wally gets here you can tackle him or shoot him in the butt with your nail gun."

"Shush, Miz Skye!" Earl clawed at the arm

246

around his neck. "What are you sayin'? This idjiot don't knows that you're joshin' him."

Before Beilin could react, an ancient Lincoln Town Car roared into the driveway. Seconds later, the queen of the Red Raggers flung open the driver's door and stepped out as quickly as her skintight jeans and high heels allowed. A lit cigarette hung from the corner of her mouth and smoke streamed from her nose like the dragon she resembled.

"Just what we needed." Skye closed her eyes and mumbled under her breath, "Ms. Train Wreck. This isn't your station."

How had Earl's wife, Glenda, known his location? Unless, of course, the moron had told her where he was going. Which, considering that Glenda hated Skye's guts, would have been the epitome of stupid even for a Doozier.

Glenda's bleached-blond hair was teased into a towering inferno and her Dolly Parton bust was barely contained by the low-cut sweater revealed by her unfastened faux-fur bolero jacket. She was dressed to kill, and with her wolverine personality, that wasn't just a trite saying, it was an actual fact.

Ignoring everyone else, she glared at her husband and screamed, "Earl Doozier, you disappear on me for days, and I get a call that your car is" — Glenda extended a bright-red talon toward Skye and hissed like a snake — "in this one's driveway!"

Earl shook his head and said, "Honey pie, I's told you and told you, you ain't got no reason to be jealous of Miz Skye. She's jus' my friend and I needed her help." He grinned, displaying picket-fence teeth the color of Dijon mustard. "She ain't my type." In a loud whisper he added, "She's way too chunky for me."

"Gee. Thanks, Earl," Skye muttered.

She contemplated going inside and leaving Earl to handle the situation on his own. No one could blame her for letting the freaky little man who had just called her fat get out of this mess without her help.

"She better be." Glenda put her hands on her hips and narrowed her eyes. "Get in your car and follow me home right now."

"I'd love to, Sugar Beet, but . . ." Earl shot a pointed look at Beilin.

Glenda turned her attention to the contractor. "You let my husband go."

"You just keep the hell back, lady," Beilin growled. "Your husband murdered my wife and the only place he's going is to jail."

"But . . ." Earl struggled to free himself.

The contractor snarled, "That's if I don't

kill him first."

"I'm countin' to three." Glenda dropped her cigarette to the ground, then crushed it out under a scarlet stiletto-shod foot. "And you better have your hands off my man and some distance between you and him, or I'll be forced to show you what it's like to be up close and personal with my shiny red high heel when I plant it where the sun don't shine."

Skye seized the moment to run down the steps, yank Earl away from Beilin, and tow him up the stairs. She didn't stop until she'd pulled the Doozier inside the RV with her and pushed him toward the sofa.

Glenda quickly followed at Skye's heels, but Beilin's reaction was a shade too slow, and the Red Ragger queen was able to slam the door before he could get inside. Smiling victoriously at Skye and Earl, Glenda tugged at the crotch of her jeans with one hand and triumphantly turned the deadbolt with the other.

Earl looked from his wife to Skye and back, chuckled like an insane clown, and said, "Ladies, not to be self-defecatin' or nothin', but there's no needs to fight over me."

Skye scowled at him and said, "You better not do that in my house." Then she translated his remark from Doozierese to English and realized he meant self-deprecating.

"Look how much your youngen has growed since the baptizin' party." Earl headed toward CJ.

Skye jumped in front of him and ordered, "You two sit on the couch and don't move or I'll let Beilin in to deal with you both."

When the Doozier king and queen obeyed, Skye grabbed her cell from its charger and dialed Wally. Keeping an eye on the couple as the phone rang, she shoved the device between her ear and shoulder, scooped up both twins, and headed toward the bedroom. She hated taking the chance that she'd wake them up, but with Earl and Glenda, she couldn't be certain that a fight wouldn't suddenly break out, and she didn't want her children in the line of fire.

Depositing the drowsy babies in their bassinets, Skye gently closed the bedroom door and prayed they would fall back to sleep rather than start screaming. She didn't want to leave them alone, but they were safer away from the Dooziers.

The instant Wally answered, Skye explained the situation, and before she even finished, he said he was on his way. He instructed her to stay on the line and she could hear running feet and him shouting instructions.

While she waited on the phone, Skye noticed that the kitchen timer was dinging. With a glance at the Dooziers, who were still where she'd put them, she took the lasagna out of the oven. Her mother's voice niggling in her head about hospitality, Skye grabbed two bottles of water from the fridge and offered them to her unwelcome guests.

Earl looked at the Dasani as if he had no idea what it was and whined, "Ain't you got nothin' else? I could use a Dew rights about now." He winked. "Or somethin' a bit stronger, if you knows what I mean." He sniffed the garlic-scented air. "And I wouldn't mind a piece o' that noodle pie."

"You fool. Those Eye-talian vittles will give you gas." Glenda elbowed her husband, took the water Skye offered her, and with an expression on her face somewhere between acceptance and aggravation muttered, "Much obliged."

Earl glanced around and asked, "Does you still gots your kitty?" Before Skye could answer, Earl crooned, "Here, critter, critter, critter."

"Don't waste your breath, Earl," Skye snickered. "Dogs may come when commanded, but cats check their phones first to see if there are any better offers."

Glenda shot Skye a puzzled look, then glared at Earl and said, "I told you not to go to that house. Was you drunk or somethin'?"

"A course not," Earl said, then cackled, "Ons the other hand, in my mind, drinkin' sensblee means I's doesn't spill it."

"What house?" Skye asked, trying to refocus the couple on the important part of Glenda's comment. "This one?" She blinked when she realized what Glenda meant, and she said, "No. You're referring to the Quinns' house."

Glenda ignored her and continued to lecture her husband. "When he called to give you that big tip" — she made exaggerated quotes in the air — "about where to sell the turkey cakes, I told you that somethin' was fishy and he'd be the last guy to help you."

"But, dumplin', I figured he was tryin' to get on my good side. Yous know, so that I don't sue him over Cletus." Earl scratched under his baseball cap. "Why else would he have called?"

"Don't be stupider than you already are." Glenda whacked him upside the head. "He was settin' you up and now you're the one in hot water and he's floatin' down the river on a pontoon made of gold."

Skye was still attempting to interpret Glenda's tirade when the front doorknob rattled and Wally yelled, "Why is this thing locked?"

Skye hurriedly let in her distraught husband and explained about Beilin, then asked, "Is he still standing in the driveway?"

"Yep." Wally marched over to the Dooziers, put his hands on his hips, and demanded, "Now what in the Sam Hill is going on here?"

Earl shrank into the sofa cushions and mumbled, "Bambi told me Miz Skye wanted to talk to me so I came over, but that crazy dill weed out there comes runnin' up and chases me and tackles me."

Suddenly exhausted, Skye sat in one of the chairs flanking the couch. Now that Wally was handling the Red Ragger couple, she had time to study Earl. The skinny little man was dressed in his usual camo and cowboy boots. He almost looked like a ten-year-old boy playing army. At least, until you noticed the dense tattoos up and down his forearms and exposed by his half-buttoned shirt.

"You shouldn't have run away the day of the murder." Wally scowled, then must have realized Earl wasn't going anywhere because he took a seat on the other chair facing Skye's.

"I meant to behave myself, but there were just too many other options." Earl nodded as if he had just imparted a great nugget of wisdom.

"You call bulldozing a door with a lawn mower an option?" Skye shook her head. And she had thought dealing with teenagers' logic was tough.

"I figured the cops would blame me for the lady with the knife in her head." Earl's nearly nonexistent chin dropped to his concave chest. "And" — his voice dropped — "I might have panicked a little bit. It was sceery being locked in that dark shed."

"Running just made you look guilty." Wally crossed his arms.

"But I ain't!" Earl brayed like an enraged donkey. "I never touched her."

"Well, in that case, you can come down to the station, make your official statement, and be fingerprinted." Wally glanced at Glenda. "You can come along if you want or you can get Earl an attorney."

"We ain't got money for no shyster." Glenda glared at Wally.

"We can get you a free one." Wally shrugged. "Or Earl has the right to remain silent. Anything he says will be used against him in a court of law. With that all in mind, are you willing to talk with me about what happened the day Mrs. Quinn was killed?"

Skye wondered if the Dooziers realized that Wally had just read them their rights.

"Yeah." Earl shrugged. "I guess. I ain't got nothin' to hide. But I wanna talk here. The police station gives me the heebie-jeebies. I'm a feared you'll keep me there and I want to sleep in my own bed tonight."

"It's been kinda restful without your snoring." Glenda looked at Earl out of the side of her eye. "And I don't wake up with no covers on."

"Baby, yous know I don't snore." Earl elbowed his wife and hooted, "I's jus dreams I's a motorcycle." He unwisely added, "And I only take the covers to save you when yous havin' a hot flash."

"Earl Doozier, you better not be implyin' that I'm old enough to be goin' through the change."

"What? No! Just that you're one hot mama." Earl's sense of self-preservation finally must have kicked in.

Wally got up, walked over to Skye, and asked in a low voice, "Do you have time to interview him here?"

"Sure," she whispered. "This might be our best bet at getting the whole story from him.

Who knows what will happen if you force him to go the PD. He might even lawyer up."

"Okay." Wally returned to his seat and fished his cell phone from his pocket. "But I'll have to record our conversation. And we'll still need to go to the station for your prints."

"Okeydokey." Earl took off his filthy baseball cap, revealing muddy brown hair that formed a horseshoe around a bald spot the size of a cantaloupe. "Where does you want me to start?"

Recalling what they'd been talking about just before Wally arrived, Skye said, "Why don't you begin with the telephone call you were discussing with Glenda. The one where the guy gave you the sales tip."

"That's a good place as any." Earl blew his lips in and out, then said, "I'd been going door-to-door in some of the neighborhoods in town tryin' to sell the Turkeygrams." He looked at Wally and explained, "They's homemade cakes shaped like turkeys."

"Right. Skye told me." Wally waved his hand and said, "Go on."

"Anyways, I wasn't havin' much luck so I took a break at McDonald's for lunch." Earl glanced uneasily at Glenda. "Sorry, Snookie

256

Bear. I was goin' to bring you a Happy Meal. Cross my heart."

"Just get on with it." Glenda seemed to have run out of steam and was slumped in the corner of the couch picking at her nail polish.

"Wells, I was halfways through my McRib . . ." Earl paused, then said, "That's one of the reasons I went there. It's McRib season."

"Yes. We all love McRibs." Frustration oozing from every pore, Wally's fingers dug in to his chair's leather armrest. "But what about the call?"

"Oh. Yeah." Earl scrunched his face and said, "My cell phone rang and when I answered it, you'll never guess who was callin' me."

"Not if you don't tell us." Wally ground the words out between clenched teeth.

"It was Homer Knapik." Earl shook his head in apparent disbelief.

"The principal?" Skye asked, knowing full well there was only one Homer Knapik in Scumble River. "Why would Homer be calling you?"

"He said his wife said that I's sellin' Turkeygrams and he found my entrism . . . enperl . . ."

"Entrepreneurialism," Skye offered.

257

"Yeah, that." Earl nodded. "Was admiral and wanted to help me out."

"Admirable," Skye translated for Wally, whose Doozierese was less developed than hers.

"Right." Wally looked at Earl and asked, "So how did he help you?"

"He said that I should try the snobby neighborhoods over by the cemetery." Earl frowned. "Then he gave me an address and told me that he knew for a fact that family wanted to buy a Turkeygram."

"And that address was the Quinns'," Skye guessed.

"Yessiree Bob." Earl frowned. "Cletus had my Regal so I had Glenda pick me up at the corner so as she wouldn't be mad about me eatin' at McDonald's. Then she drived me there and drop me off. But when I knocked, no one answered the door. Then, likes I told Miz Skye, there was a car in the driveway and I heared somethin' back yonder so's I figured someone was home. So's I walked around the house and poked around a mite, then I saw the dead woman."

"Did you see anything else?" Wally asked.

"No." Earl shook his head. "Just the lady with the knife in her head."

"What kind of noise did you hear before you went around back?" Wally asked.

"It sounded like an elephant trompin' in the forest."

"Or a man the size of Homer escaping through the trees once he was sure his patsy had shown up," Skye murmured.

"Yep." Wally's lips thinned. "That seems about right."

CHAPTER 17
HOMEWARD BOUND

Skye glanced at the clock on the bedside table. It was nearly six o'clock, and Wally had just returned from escorting the Dooziers to the police station where he'd fingerprinted Earl, then drove the couple back to their cars. Now Wally was hurriedly shedding his uniform as he rushed into the master bath, leaving the door between it and the bedroom open.

While he'd been gone, Skye had explained to Beilin Quinn what was happening. The contractor wasn't happy that Earl would not be arrested, but he perked up when Skye mentioned they had another suspect. Since Beilin was still a person of interest himself, she'd been vague about the details pertaining to Earl's statement, but the GC was still glad to hear they were making progress on the case.

"Knapik is an idiot," Wally yelled from the shower. "Did he really think Earl wouldn't tell anyone that he had called him and lured him over to the Quinns'?"

"He figured no one would believe a Doozier." Skye raised her voice as she selected a Henley waffle-knit shirt for Wally to wear. The rust color flattered his olive skin and made his brown eyes sparkle. "That man believes that everyone thinks exactly the way he does." She took a pair of dark wash jeans from the closet and laid them next to the shirt, then added a belt. "So what's our next move in regard to Homer?"

Skye couldn't make out Wally's answer above the sound of the water, so she stepped inside the bathroom. She was rewarded with a view of her naked husband exiting the shower. Droplets ran down his body, spotlighting the delineation of his chiseled muscles.

She unconsciously licked her lips. With the space limitations of the RV and the demands of the twins, they didn't get much time to enjoy each other anymore. Another reason she couldn't wait until the new house was finished.

An amused chuckle dragged her attention up to Wally's face and he drawled, "Sugar, you need to stop looking at me like that unless you want your mom to arrive to find us in a compromising position."

Grinning, Wally dried off, pulled on a pair of boxer briefs, then walked over to the vanity and picked up his razor.

"I don't know what you're talking about." Skye widened her eyes innocently and said, "I just didn't hear your answer about Homer."

Over the buzz of his electric shaver, Wally said, "Once we get the DNA results from the pumpkin seed hulls, I'll bring him in for questioning." He leaned closer to the mirror and added, "Until then, I want him to feel safe and think he got away with setting up Earl."

"He's pretty complacent." Skye frowned. "Except I did overhear the superintendent pressuring Homer to retire. It sounded as if Dr. Wraige had finally had enough of his incompetence."

"Good. Worrying about that will keep him busy until we're ready for him." Wally smoothed on some aftershave balm and Skye breathed in the crisp lime scent.

At the sound of knocking, Skye turned, and over her shoulder said, "That must be Mom. We should probably leave in ten minutes or so."

"Okay," Wally said as Skye closed the bathroom door and hurried away.

It was actually more like a quarter hour before they were ready. But finally the food was loaded into the SUV and May was ensconced on the sofa with a twin cradled in each arm.

After kissing Eva and CJ goodbye, and thanking May for babysitting, Skye and Wally left the RV, got into the Mercedes, and drove toward the other side of town. A year and a half ago, after being unable to find exactly the home they, or actually Loretta, wanted in the area, Skye's brother and sister-in-law had decided to build a house.

Jed and May had deeded a good-sized lot to Vince and Loretta from a forty-acre parcel that Jed had purchased several years ago to add to his farmland. It was located a couple of miles down the road from the Denison homestead on the Stanley side of County Line Road.

Loretta's perfectionism had almost guaranteed that she and Vince would need to have a custom home built, and Skye hadn't been at all surprised when Vince went along with the plan. For a man who had dated nearly every pretty girl in the surrounding three counties, he had turned into a shockingly devoted husband. And if Loretta wanted something, he moved heaven and earth to make sure she got it.

Loretta and Skye were alums of Alpha Sigma Alpha, so were both sorority sisters and sisters-in-law. In fact, that was how Loretta, a hotshot defense attorney in Chicago, had come to marry Vince.

Skye had reached out to her sorority sister several years ago to defend Vince on a murder charge. And then, despite Loretta's often-declared aversion to small towns and their citizens, she had fallen in love with Skye's brother, married him, and agreed to live in Scumble River.

Before her first pregnancy, Loretta had continued to work for her Chicago firm, but after April was born, she'd decided to quit trying to juggle a demanding career and long drive into the city. Instead, she'd opened her own practice in town. Handling real estate closings and estate planning wasn't as exciting as defending criminals, but it was a lot less stressful, as was a five-minute versus hour-and-a-half commute.

Vince and Loretta had been in their home nearly a year, and as Wally turned the SUV down the long lane leading to the house, Skye examined the oaks, pecans, and hickories interspersed with redbuds, hawthorns, pawpaws, yellowwoods, and crabapples that were planted along the driveway. Once the trees had grown and matured, the allée would make an elegant entrance to the spectacular residence.

Wally parked the Mercedes along the circular driveway, helped Skye from the car, and then they both gathered the food from the cargo area in back. Loaded down with containers, they carefully made their way up the cobblestone walkway leading to the double mahogany doors.

Skye managed to work a finger free and rang the bell, smiling when the percussion solo from Iron Butterfly's "In-A-Gadda-Da-Vida" filled the air. Although Vince had stopped performing with his band, the Plastic Santas, once he was married, he would always be a drummer at heart. The beauty salon he owned and operated was a way to make a living, but it wasn't his passion.

"We need one of those." Wally jerked his chin at the doorbell.

"Okay." Skye wrinkled her brow. Hers and Wally's tastes in music weren't exactly similar. "But what song would ours play?"

"Let me think about that and surprise you." Wally winked at her.

Before Skye could respond, Loretta threw open the door and said, "Hey, guys. Come on inside and take off your jackets. Let me take some of those goodies while you hang your coats in the hall closet. I'm starving!"

After Skye and Wally removed their jackets, they followed Loretta through the foyer and the family room, then into the kitchen.

As Skye placed the lasagna and dessert into the warming oven and stuck the pot holders in the tote bag dangling from her wrist by the straps, she asked, "How are you feeling?"

"Pretty much as if a semitruck just drove out of my V-J." Loretta raised an eyebrow. "Which I'm sure was how you felt after the twins were born."

"But I got to stay in the hospital and rest for a couple of days."

"You obviously have better health insurance than we do." Loretta took the salad bowl from Wally. "With us both being self-employed we have to pay our own premiums. And even the HMO policy we chose is expensive."

"Finally a good reason to work in the public sector," Skye teased.

"Right." Loretta winked, then asked, "When can we eat?"

"Fifteen minutes." Skye grabbed the foil-wrapped garlic bread from the counter where her sister-in-law had put it, then marched over to the second oven, and as per her texted instructions, it was preheated to 350 degrees.

When the sound of a crying baby ripped through the house, Wally looked over his shoulder and said, "How about I give Vince a hand with the kids?"

"He has . . ." Loretta trailed off as Wally hurried from the room.

"You look amazing." Skye fished in her tote bag for the lasagna spatula.

Loretta's dark-brown skin glowed with health and her coal-black braids were impeccably coifed. At six feet tall with a lean-muscled body, she didn't look at all as if she'd just had a baby.

"Sure." Loretta blew out a doubtful snicker. "No makeup, wearing a ratty track-suit, and leaking milk. I'm beautiful, all right."

"You look better than most women do who have spent three hours getting ready for a date." Then deciding to change the subject, Skye gazed around the mammoth space. Counting three sinks and two dish-washers, she said, "I hope I didn't make a mistake building a smaller kitchen. But the house already seemed so huge."

"Well." Loretta gingerly eased into a chair, the first indication she was still sore from giving birth. "The plans for this place did get a little out of hand. I'm sure yours is plenty big enough."

"Yeah." Skye took a seat next to her. "But you only build your dream house once and I probably should have listened to Wally."

"True." Loretta picked up the water glass to the right of the place setting and took a long drink. "Why didn't you?"

"I was afraid we'd look as if we were showing off," Skye admitted.

"Seriously?" Loretta tilted her head. "Now that people know about Wally's money, it's almost insulting to them if you try to act poor."

"Come on. Saying *that* is insulting to people who really are poor." Skye frowned. "I mean, even if we never spent a penny of Wally's trust fund, between his salary and mine, we have the means to live comfortably."

"That's what I'm trying to tell you." Loretta waved a finger in Skye's face. "You still act as if you're in the same circumstances as you were when you moved back to Scumble River broke and in hock to Visa."

"Hardly like that," Skye scoffed. "Wally and I are building a thirty-five-hundred-square-foot house and I'm driving a Mercedes SUV."

"Fine. You've dipped your toes in the

water, but you need to let go." Loretta tilted her head and stared at Skye. "I'll bet it hurts Wally and his dad that you treat their money as if it has cooties."

"Cooties?" Skye giggled, then sobered. "You're probably right. But, truthfully, I'm overwhelmed. You grew up with money. My folks struggled to send me to college and I struggled to pay for graduate school. I've always had to pinch pennies."

"Well, quit bruising Old Abe and enjoy what you have." Loretta crossed her arms. "If you feel guilty, you can always donate to the local food pantry or some other good cause in the area."

"I see your point." Skye nodded. "I'll try to ease up on the purse strings."

"Terrific! Before you go back to work, you and I are going shopping. I've been dying to have my personal shopper at Nordstrom dress you."

"That sounds fun." Skye grinned. She'd been waiting until she lost the baby weight to replace the clothes the tornado had destroyed, and she was almost back to her pre-pregnancy size. "Let's plan to go the week after Christmas. Everything will be on sale." Skye ducked as Loretta threw a balled-up napkin at her. "Seriously, why pay more than you have to?"

"Back to your house." Loretta pursed her lips. "I suppose it's too late now to make any changes."

"Yes, it is. We added the apartment over the garage after we'd already started construction, and that caused a good month's delay." Skye made a face, then smiled. "But I did get all the stuff inside I wanted. Fireplace. Huge closets with built-ins. Screened-in porch."

"Speaking of that suite over the garage . . ." Loretta's sudden interest in the zipper of her tracksuit jacket alerted Skye that her sister-in-law was uncomfortable with what she was about to say.

"Yes?" Skye prodded.

"Was that for the nanny that you had?" Loretta asked hesitantly.

"No." Skye shook her head. Not that Loretta could see her since she still appeared enthralled with the tab of her zipper. "Mrs. Winters wasn't going to be full-time. We were thinking more of Carson or Mom and Dad if they need to live with us at some point."

Skye studied her friend. Something was fishy. As she opened her mouth to ask, she heard a familiar voice say, "You two go eat. I'll just show the wee one to your sister, then put him in his bassinet and read Miss

April her story."

Loretta's head jerked up, and when her gaze collided with Skye's outraged stare, she stuttered, "This . . . this isn't what it seems."

"You stole my nanny!" Skye screeched. "How could you stoop so low?"

"I didn't." Loretta held up her hands, palms facing Skye. "I wouldn't."

Skye pointed at the woman who had just entered the kitchen holding a baby in her arms. "So you're telling me that isn't Mrs. Winters?"

Wally and Vince followed the nanny into the room; both took one look at Skye's face and retreated.

"No. It's her." Loretta got to her feet. "But I only approached her after she gave you her notice and left your employment."

"It's true, Mrs. Denison-Boyd." The nanny's expression was contrite. "Ms. Steiner didn't offer me this job until I was a free agent."

"But why?" Frustration almost drove Skye to tears. "You said it was because of my father-in-law and my mother. Carson might not be a factor here, but you do realize that Vince and I share a mother?"

"I promised her May would not drop in without an invitation." Loretta raised her

271

eyebrow. "Could you say the same thing?"

"Well . . ." Skye scowled. "No. I can't control my mother's actions."

"I can." Loretta walked over to stand shoulder to shoulder with the nanny. "First, I made sure May never got her hands on a key to this house. Second, when April was born, I made it clear that any interference and May would only see her at holidays and birthdays. And third, my father isn't a billionaire so there's no need for the kind of security Eva and CJ require for their safety."

"I understand." Skye narrowed her eyes. "But I still think you could have told me instead of being so sneaky about the whole thing."

"That's your brother's fault." Loretta nodded her head toward Vince and Wally, who had rejoined them. "You do know he's scared of you?"

"Good." Skye sent Vince a death glare. "How is it you aren't on Mom's naughty list with Loretta's rules about visiting?"

Vince's emerald-green eyes sparkled and he grinned. "I just tell her that Loretta's the boss and I do what she tells me to do."

"I don't suppose I could do the same and claim Wally's the boss?" Skye mused.

Both men broke out laughing.

"Fine." Skye looked between Loretta and

Vince. "But I'm only forgiving you because Wally came up with an even better solution." She glanced at Mrs. Winters and said, "No offense."

"None taken." The nanny smiled and handed Skye the baby. "Now, meet your nephew, Master August Alberto Steiner Denison."

"Gus for short." Vince leaned over and touched the baby's cheek.

Once Skye and Wally finished admiring the baby and Mrs. Winters whisked him away, Skye took the lasagna and garlic bread from the oven and the two couples sat down to eat.

They kept the conversation light until they finished dessert, but as they relaxed in the enormous family room enjoying the roaring fire, Wally said, "Loretta, I hope you don't mind if I ask you some questions about Jerita Quinn."

"Not at all." Loretta's expression hardened. "I want you to catch whoever killed her. We hadn't worked together long, but she was a strong, smart woman and I admired her devotion to keeping her family safe."

"Was she scared of anyone?" Wally asked. "Did she mention any enemies?"

"No." Loretta took a sip of coffee. "She

273

was angry at the school and Homer Knapik, but certainly not frightened of him."

"Did you have a good case for her lawsuit against him?" Wally asked.

"Fair." Loretta hesitated. "I'm uncomfortable discussing this because of lawyer-client privilege, but I can say that she wasn't interested in settling." Loretta shrugged. "I haven't talked to her husband yet, but from what she said, he probably won't want to pursue the matter."

Skye tucked that bit of info away. If Loretta was correct about Beilin, it would make Dr. Wraige's assignment to stop the lawsuit much easier.

"So Homer has a lot to gain from Jerita's death," Wally mused. After asking Loretta a few more questions about Jerita, Wally looked at Skye and said, "We should get going."

"Yep. Time to let Loretta get some rest and relieve Mom from twin duty." Skye rose to her feet, then paused when she thought of another question. "One more thing, Loretta. You said something about Jerita keeping her family safe. What did you mean by that?"

"Hmm." Loretta tapped her chin. "I guess I said that because Jerita told me she'd moved to Scumble River to make sure her daughter was protected."

"From the normal dangers of city life?" Wally asked.

"Jerita changed the subject when I asked about that." Loretta bit her lip. "But my feeling was that there was a specific threat she was trying to avoid."

Chapter 18
Follow You Home

"Sorry, Dante. I haven't had a chance to talk to the officers about the city's contract offer yet." Wally kept his voice pleasant, but he fidgeted in his chair, anxious to end the conversation. "I promise to get them together later today and discuss it."

The mayor had already contacted Wally three times about the issue and it hadn't even been twenty-four hours since he presented the compromise. Hizzoner was as intent on settling this matter as a buzzard determined to get every scrap of carrion from a roadkill carcass and a zealous Dante made Wally suspicious. What was he up to now?

"Later today, my good right eye," the mayor sneered, his voice cracking like a bullwhip. "You talk to them this morning. I want an answer by one."

Wally drew in a deep breath, then released it slowly. He hated waking Paul Tolman and asking him to return to the station. Tolman had covered the midnight shift and would have just gotten to sleep. The man had had an emergency appendectomy a few months ago and he still seemed a bit under the weather. His skin hadn't returned to his normal olive complexion and his movements seemed stiff and painful.

Tolman had always been one of those people who left the job with great gusto at quitting time. But now, even when the man was physically present, his spirit was in a galaxy far, far away. Wally was already worried that his distraction would result in harm to him or a fellow officer, and interrupting his rest wouldn't help matters.

"They really have no choice." Dante's grating cackle brought Wally back to the matter at hand. "Settle or —"

"Or you'll do away with the department, hire rent-a-cops from the county sheriff, yadda, yadda, yadda." Wally hung on to his temper by a thread. "Your threats have already been duly noted."

The twins had been fussy all night and their bad mood had continued that morning. It had taken both Wally and Skye's best efforts to get them fed, changed, and soothed, making him late getting to work.

He couldn't wait for the house to be

finished and Dorothy to move into the garage apartment. It would be such a relief to have some room to spread out and to have a helping hand when they were overwhelmed with the babies' needs.

"If I don't hear from you by one o'clock, I'm telling the city council you declined their offer and contacting the Stanley County sheriff." Dante paused, then sing-songed a warning. "And you do not want me talking to the sheriff. He'd love to get his hands on Scumble River."

"Make it two," Wally countered, running his fingers through his hair and noting how long it had gotten. He liked to keep it above his collar. Maybe he could swing by Great Expectations Salon after work for a trim. He'd have to give Vince a call to see if he had an opening. "I promise to have an answer for you by then."

Disconnecting the line, Wally stared at the stack of reports that he needed to study. They contained the summaries of what Martinez had viewed on the dollar store and supermarket security recordings.

But now, before he buckled down to read her findings, he had to ask Thea to get ahold of all the full- and part-time officers about the contract meeting. He'd hold it at eleven and provide lunch.

After making his call to Thea and giving her his instructions, he added, "When you're done contacting the officers, call County and request a deputy be assigned to our area between eleven and one. Tell them that all our people will be tied up in a meeting and not on the streets patrolling."

Once he finished with Thea, Wally glanced around his office. Skye had suggested making it more comfortable and he admitted that the space was utilitarian, but that was how he liked it. The large metal desk, two serviceable chairs for visitors, and a couple of file cabinets were all he needed.

His space was practical, with nothing to distract his thinking. The only personal items in the room were his wedding picture and a photograph of the twins the day they were baptized.

Wally reached for the matching silver frames and studied his beautiful family. He still couldn't believe that Skye was really his wife or that they had so easily had two precious children.

Their first anniversary was coming up in a little over a month, but the memory of standing next to her in her gorgeous dress at the church altar was as clear as if it had happened yesterday. At that moment, as they'd exchanged their vows, he'd realized how lucky he was to have gotten a second chance to marry the love of his life.

Then, after so many years thinking that he'd never be a father, the twins were born and he finally had the family of his dreams. He was almost afraid of how happy he felt and he said a prayer every day thanking God for giving him what he'd always wanted.

Once he'd put down the pictures and angled them so that he would see the beautiful faces of his wife and children every time he glanced up from his work, Wally took a gulp of tepid coffee. When he'd arrived at work, he'd poured himself a mug from the communal pot downstairs, but that was over forty-five minutes ago.

If things hadn't been so chaotic at home, he would have stopped at Tales and Treats for a decent cup of java in one of their special to-go cups that kept the liquid piping hot for hours. Still, the police station's bitter, lukewarm brew was better than nothing, and after a restless night he needed the hit of caffeine.

Giving in to his fatigue, Wally closed his eyes and rested his head on the back of his chair. Last night at Loretta and Vince's house had been interesting. Mrs. Winters's presence had certainly been a surprise. And for a bad moment, he'd thought Skye was about to blow her top at the perceived nanny poaching. It would have been a shame if her anger and hurt feelings had ended the years of friendship between her and her sister-in-law. He'd been relieved that Skye and Loretta had held onto their tempers and worked things out.

Then there'd been Loretta's impression of Jerita Quinn. Up until she had revealed that she thought Jerita had been fleeing Chicago to protect her daughter from a specific threat, Wally had had three top suspects in the murder. Now, he had to reconsider.

Earl Doozier continued to be a person of interest, and Beilin Quinn couldn't be ruled out, but they had both moved down the list. As crazy as Earl's description of the events had been, they made a kind of sense. At least for a Doozier. And unless Beilin's reaction to the news of his wife's death was Academy Award–winning acting, it was hard to believe he'd killed her.

Then there was Homer. While the devious principal could still be the perp, he wasn't the number one suspect anymore. Nevertheless, Homer had a lot of explaining to do before he was free from suspicion.

Wally had thought he had a good handle on Jerita's murder — at least some solid leads. But now there was this mysterious menace that had caused the Quinns to uproot themselves, to move from the city to a little town in the middle of nowhere. And if this danger was so serious, why hadn't Beilin mentioned it when he'd been questioned right after Jerita's body was found?

Sighing, Wally made a note to re-interview the contractor that afternoon. His conscience gave a bit of a twinge. Was he putting off talking to Beilin because he had a busy morning or was it to give the man a chance to work longer on Wally and Skye's new house?

No. He shook his head. He didn't have an ulterior motive. Reviewing Martinez's notes on the security recordings, contacting the crime lab about Homer's DNA, and holding the contract meeting were the priorities for the morning.

Finally settling in to get some work done, Wally grabbed a yellow highlighter, flipped open the file containing Martinez's reports, and started reading. He'd just finished studying the officer's notes on the supermarket's recordings when a sharp ring interrupted him.

He snatched the receiver from its cradle and his greeting was a terse "Yes?"

"Chief?" The tone was brisk.

He immediately recognized the feminine

voice and said, "Yeah. What's up, Dr. Norris?"

"I'll email you the final report later this afternoon, but I figured you'd want to know this sooner rather than wait for the official paperwork."

When the old medical examiner had retired a few months ago, Wally had been a little afraid that the person replacing the ME wouldn't be as good. However, although Wally hadn't met the new pathologist in person, they'd exchanged several phone calls and handled one successful closed case together already, allowing him to feel comfortable with the woman's competence.

"I appreciate that." Wally grabbed a pen, flipped to a clean page on his legal pad, and said, "What do you have for me?"

"The DNA results you requested from the crime lab were forwarded to me to include with my report." Dr. Norris's voice was somewhat bemused. "I'm not sure why they didn't send them to you directly, but I have to say that I'm impressed with the rapid turnaround."

"I am too. I was told it would take twenty-four to seventy-two hours and it's only been maybe eighteen. Not that I'm unhappy to have them early." Wally wouldn't look a gift lab result in the mouth.

Dr. Norris rustled some paper, cleared her throat, and announced, "The DNA on the pumpkin seed hulls found at the crime scene matches the DNA on the candy wrapper and pudding cup lid provided."

"Thanks." Wally had expected those results, but now that they were confirmed, he'd bring Homer in for questioning that afternoon. He'd schedule the principal's interrogation right after Beilin Quinn's. "That's very helpful."

"No problem," Dr. Norris said, then added, "And I'll let the crime lab know that in the future they can send you their results directly. I'm guessing the previous ME had control issues and ordered the lab to funnel all information through him."

"So it would seem." Wally had just thought that was the generally accepted protocol. Now he felt like a fool for not questioning it all those years. "Thanks for the call. Keep me in the loop."

After saying goodbye to Dr. Norris, Wally went back to the reports from Martinez. The young officer had diligently scanned and summarized hours of security recordings from the supermarket and the dollar store. Wally had instructed her to concentrate on the twenty-four-hour period from

10:00 p.m. the evening before Edie was reported missing to 10:00 p.m. the day of her disappearance because even when the dollar store and supermarket were closed, they both had security cameras aimed at the parking lots.

Although Martinez had painstakingly detailed the comings and goings at the supermarket, there wasn't anything Wally could see that suggested Edie Baker had been at the place since she'd gone missing. Only a few cars had entered the lot after closing, and those never stopped.

Wally figured it was just teenagers who were buzzing the gut, a.k.a. riding up and down Maryland and Basin Streets. The kids used the McDonald's on one end of town and the grocery at the other to turn around and repeat the route.

Pushing the supermarket pages aside, Wally ran his finger down the list for the dollar store. Again, nothing during the night, but Martinez had found a possibility the morning Mrs. Baker had been reported missing.

The young officer had attached a still shot of a woman about Edie's age wearing jeans and a blue sweater. She was turned away from the camera and only a quarter of her face was visible. The time stamp showed

7:02 a.m., just a couple minutes after the store opened for business that day.

Wally rubbed his jaw. He'd have to get Anthony to check with the dollar store to see if a golf cart had been abandoned anywhere nearby. No one in Bord du Lac had reported a stolen cart, but there were always residents who weren't home and didn't return the police's telephone calls.

Once Anthony was finished at the dollar store, he could run the picture out to Gerald Baker to see if the man could identify the woman in the shot. Dealing with a guy like Baker could be tough, but it would be good for the young officer to get some experience handling difficult witnesses.

After Wally had Thea radio Anthony to come in from patrol, he studied the security camera image of the possible Mrs. Baker. There was another woman in the shot, and as he looked closer, it appeared as if Edie was greeting her. Her hand was stretched toward the other woman and her body was leaning in her direction.

Most of that woman's image was obscured, but a sliver of her face was discernable. Half closing his eyes, Wally tried to figure out why she seemed familiar. He could swear he knew her. He'd have to have Anthony ask Gerald Baker and the employees of the dollar store if they recognized her. If that didn't come up with any results, he'd have his officers take a look during the contract meeting. And if all else failed, he'd ask Skye. She knew nearly everyone in town.

Giving up his own effort to identify the woman, Wally turned his attention to the murder. Earl's fingerprints had been emailed to the crime lab yesterday afternoon, but they hadn't responded yet and since Dr. Norris hadn't mentioned them, he assumed the results hadn't been forwarded to her either.

The murder weapon was wiped clean so Wally didn't expect the Doozier's prints to reveal much. But they might be able to document Earl's path at the crime scene and thus support his story.

It was frustrating that his key suspect, or witness — Wally wasn't sure which label to give Earl yet — was a man who was about as honest as a political ad. Getting Earl to tell the truth was like trying to fill a swimming pool with a slotted spoon.

Wally was about to call the crime lab and ask about Earl's prints when Anthony knocked on the partially open office door. Motioning the young officer inside, Wally gave him his instructions, handed him the security camera still shot, and told him to be back at the station by eleven.

Once Anthony left, Wally dialed the lab. As soon as they picked up, he identified himself and asked, "Did you have any hits on the Earl Doozier fingerprint we sent over to you yesterday?"

"Yeah, we did, Chief," the tech answered. "I was just about to send them to you. Dr. Norris said that from now on you were to get our results directly."

"Good."

"Anyway, Earl Doozier's prints were found on the front door knocker, the back doorknob, the fence around the playhouse, and all over the shed."

"Nowhere inside the residence or between the fence and the playhouse?"

"Nope."

"Okay." Wally sighed. "Thanks."

Next Wally contacted Homer and Beilin. The contractor quickly promised to be at the station by two, but the principal was less cooperative. Only after Wally threatened to go to the high school and lead Homer out in handcuffs did he agree to be at the PD by three thirty.

Wally quickly sent Skye a text to bring her up to speed and warn her that Homer was on the warpath. She wasn't scheduled to go to the school that day, but just in case there was some kind of emergency that she got called in to handle, he wanted her to know to avoid the principal.

Glancing at his watch, Wally texted Tales and Treats the sandwich order for the meeting, then let Thea know he was leaving the station for a bit. He'd head to the supermarket to buy the chips and soft drinks, then pick up the food at the combination bookstore and café on the way back.

An hour later, Wally had the sandwich trays and bowls of chips on the break room counter and was placing the drinks in the fridge when his officers started trickling through the door. They all grabbed a plate of food and a can of soda, then settled into chairs around the long table that ran down the center of the room.

Wally counted heads and said, "We'll give Anthony a chance to get back from Bord du Lac before we get started. In the meantime, there are copies of a security camera still shot on the table. Please take a look and let me know if you can identify either woman."

While the others studied the picture, Wally walked over to Martinez, patted her on the shoulder, and said, "Good job on finding that image."

"Thank you, sir." Martinez smiled, her

cheeks coloring. She quickly added, "And thank you for the opportunity to work on the missing person case."

Wally patted her shoulder again, then looked at the others and asked, "Anyone recognize either of the subjects in the photo?"

Everyone shook their heads and Quirk said, "I'm assuming you think that Blue Sweater might be Edie Baker, but there's not enough visible of the other woman to hazard a guess."

Anthony had walked into the break room just as Quirk was speaking and quickly said, "No need to guess." Beaming, he turned to Wally and asked, "Would you like a verbal report or do you want me to write it up?"

"Both." Wally stared at the young officer.

"Yes, sir." Anthony stood at attention and summarized, "No one at the dollar store could identify the women in the still shot, but an abandoned golf cart was found in their parking lot the day Mrs. Baker disappeared. There was an identification card attached to the steering column and the cart was dropped off at that address by one of the clerks who lives in Bord du Lac."

"And this clerk never thought to notify the police?" Wally ran his fingers through his hair. "Even after Mrs. Baker went missing?"

"She went on vacation the next day, and by the time she returned, she didn't hear about the missing woman." Anthony shrugged. "Apparently after a week, Mrs. Baker's disappearance was old news."

"Right." Wally gestured to the young officer and said, "Go on."

"Mr. Baker is sure that the woman in the blue sweater is his wife." Anthony paused, then said, "And he thinks the other woman might be Pru Cormorant." When Wally didn't respond, Anthony added, "The English teacher at the high school."

"Right." Wally grabbed a picture and studied it. "How does Baker know her?"

"He claims that she's always hanging around him and his wife when they go to the VFW or the American Legion." Anthony grinned. "Mr. Baker is convinced that Ms. Cormorant has a crush on him."

"Interesting." Wally tucked that info away and said, "Okay. Now that the women in the photo have been tentatively identified, let's get started on the contract offer."

As he explained the mayor's proposal, including the K-9 officer that Martinez verified she'd had training on how to handle, Wally mulled over what Anthony had found out. Could Pru Cormorant have done something to get rid of Edie Baker so that she could date the woman's husband?

CHAPTER 19
CAN'T FIND MY WAY HOME

Skye woke with a start and gazed groggily at the laptop in front of her. She was seated at the RV's tiny kitchen table with her head resting on her arms. After being up and down all night with the twins — she'd just get Eva to sleep and CJ would start crying — she must have dozed off when she sat down to review the psych reports that Piper had completed the past couple of weeks.

Before sitting down, Skye had phoned the twins' pediatrician, Dr. Fellows. She'd been concerned that the babies' restlessness was due to her recent attempt to wean them off breast milk and onto formula, which she was trying to accomplish prior to returning to work full-time.

Dr. Fellows had asked several questions, then assured Skye that the babies' sleep patterns were still developing. The pediatrician had said that the twins should sleep fifteen or sixteen hours a day, but those hours

293

might be sporadic. She'd also mentioned that one advantage of them transitioning completely to formula was that they would probably sleep longer stretches of time during the night.

Now, as Skye stifled a yawn, she really hoped the doctor was right. If the torture of one twin awake every hour between ten and six a.m. was a new pattern, even with Dorothy's help, she'd never make it. After all, they couldn't expect the housekeeper to be up all night with CJ and Eva and take care of them during the day too.

Getting up at the crack of dawn to be at school by 7:20 a.m. was bad enough. But doing it without sufficient rest would be a problem. Skye had always said she could be a morning person if morning was considered a minute before noon. And she hated to think of how she'd handle difficult staff and parents if she'd been awake with cranky babies.

Speaking of which, she rose from her chair, stretched out the kink in her back, and walked over to the bedroom to check on the twins. Both were peacefully napping in their bassinets and she fought the urge to rouse them.

Dr. Fellows had insisted that naps didn't cause them to sleep less at night. In fact, the pediatrician had assured Skye that it was exactly the opposite. The more they kept to their scheduled naps, the more likely they would sleep longer at night.

Skye blew kisses at her babies, then headed back to the table to resume reading Piper's reports. However, before she took more than a couple of steps, there was a knock on the door.

Afraid the noise would wake CJ and Eva, Skye hurried over and looked through the window. Judy Martin stood on the little metal porch with a wrapped gift in her hands.

Judy was the town librarian and engaged to Anthony Anserello, one of Wally's officers. She and Skye had become good friends during Skye's frequent visits to the Scumble River Library and Skye was looking forward to having her as a fellow police wife.

Easing open the door, Skye put her finger to her lips and whispered, "Come in. The twins are sleeping, so we need to keep it down."

Judy gave her a thumbs-up and removed her jacket. As Skye hung the garment in the foyer closet, she admired the vintage purple swagger coat with its oversized moonstone plastic buttons. Although the petite brunette's distinctive style wasn't one that Skye could wear, she admired it on her friend.

Once Skye closed the bedroom door, she offered Judy something to drink. The librarian's sandy brown ponytail swung back and forth as she declined.

She and Skye took a seat on the sofa, and after Judy gave Skye the package she'd been holding, she said, "I wanted to get this to you before all the Christmas hubbub started."

"What is it?" Skye fingered the crisp black-and-white paper.

"It's a going-back-to-work present." Judy grinned. "I know your maternity leave doesn't officially end for another month, but since you've started going into school a few days a week, I decided you needed to have it now."

"That is so sweet of you." Skye *tsked.* "But with your wedding coming up, you shouldn't be spending money on me."

Neither Judy nor Anthony made huge salaries and Skye knew they were paying for their own reception. She made a mental note to find a way to help them out.

"Just open it." Judy nudged the gift perched on Skye's knees.

"I can't imagine what you got me." Skye untied the shiny white ribbon, tore away the paper, and opened the flaps. Inside was a smaller box.

"Keep going." Judy giggled.

Lifting the lid of the smaller box, Skye gasped. It was a silver bracelet similar to one she'd recently given away. But instead of her sorority's letters engraved on the dangling disk, this one had an image of St. Monica, the patron saint of mothers.

"Thank you!" Skye immediately slipped the bracelet on her wrist.

"I had my aunt take it with her on her trip to Italy." Judy touched the medallion. "She held it up during the Papal Blessing so it's consecrated by the pope."

Skye blinked away a tear. "What an amazing gift."

"You are so worth it." Judy hugged her, then sat back and said, "Is that your phone vibrating?"

Skye dug the cell from her jeans' pocket and swiped. It was a text from Wally. She saw that she'd missed an earlier message from him warning her to avoid Homer, but evidently, things had changed, since this text asked if she could find a sitter and get to the station by two to help with Beilin's and Homer's interviews. He'd added there was someone else they needed to talk to afterward and he'd explain about that in person.

She frowned. Who could she get to take

care of the twins? Her mom had taken this week off work, but she'd be busy preparing for the extended family's huge Thanksgiving party tomorrow. Carson wasn't getting back into town until later. And Dorothy had said she was hosting the holiday at her house and would be cooking all day. Skye was out of options.

Sighing, she looked at her friend and said, "Sorry. I just need to let Wally know I can't help out the PD this afternoon."

"Why is that?" Judy wrinkled her freckled nose.

"All my babysitters are unavailable."

"I'll do it," Judy offered. "The library's closed and Anthony is pulling a double shift. He won't be home until after midnight."

"Wally can get along without me," Skye demurred. Although she really wanted to be there when Wally talked to both men, she wasn't about to impose on her friend. "I'm sure you're busy enough getting ready for tomorrow."

"Nope. Anthony and I are going to his folks' house, and all his mom wanted us to bring was a French Silk pie, which I baked this morning."

"Well . . ."

"We're pals, right?" Judy asked, and when Skye nodded, she said, "Friends are like boobs and I'm the real sort, not the fake kind."

"You definitely are, but that doesn't mean I should take advantage of you," Skye protested.

"If I agreed with you about that then we'd both be wrong." Judy smirked, then ordered, "Let Wally know you'll be there and go get ready." She jumped to her feet. "I remember where everything is from the time Anthony and I babysat last month."

"Okay." Skye sent a quick text, then headed toward the bedroom to change clothes and put on some makeup. She paused at the door and said, "I really appreciate it. It's one thirty and the first interview is at two, then there's a second one, and maybe a third so I could be as late as five thirty or six."

"No problem." Judy gestured to the fridge. "As long as there're enough bottles we're golden." She glanced down at the black cat inching its way from under the couch. As he twined around her ankles, she added, "Okay, Bingo. And enough mushy food for you."

The feline meowed his agreement, and chuckling, Skye hurried away. Fifteen minutes later, she was ready, but before she left, she explained that she was weaning the twins from breast milk and told Judy the proportion of each to use for their feedings. Then thanking her friend again — for both babysitting and the bracelet — Skye got in her SUV and drove away.

As she headed to the station, she wondered about the identity of their mysterious third interviewee. She still hadn't come up with a viable candidate by the time she got to the PD. Pulling the Mercedes into a spot near the building, Skye trotted into the garage. She made it a habit of entering the PD this way because if she used the front entrance chances were that she'd be delayed by whoever was dispatching. They would want to chat about how fast the twins were growing or the weather or some bit of gossip, and Skye would end up being late.

Once she was inside the station, she hurried down the hall, but when she neared the break room, she slowed as she caught a glimpse through the window of Anthony sitting with Beilin Quinn at the long rectangular table. The young officer was staring at the contractor as the man spoke on his cell phone. Every time Beilin thumped the table to make a point, Anthony flinched and fingered the gun on his belt.

Wondering why Wally wasn't with the suspect, Skye jogged toward the stairs to the second floor. However, before she got to them, Wally met her at the bottom of the steps. His hair was standing on end and his shirt collar was open.

Skye would bet the farm that she'd find his missing tie on the floor of her husband's office. When he got frustrated, he had a bad habit of taking it off and throwing it across the room.

"Hard day?" Skye closed the gap between them and gave him a hug.

"Yep." Wally laid his cheek on the top of her head and said, "I'm juggling contract negotiations, several suspects for Jerita's murder, and we finally might have a lead on Edie Baker's whereabouts."

Skye's heart skipped a beat. "Really?"

He hadn't said Edie's body. Maybe the poor woman was still alive.

"You remember I told you that Martinez was viewing security recordings from the grocery and dollar stores?" When Skye nodded, he continued, "There was a section that showed a woman, who Gerald Baker identified as his wife, in the dollar store the morning of Edie's disappearance. And it's possible she went off with an individual that she met there."

"Met as in a deliberate plan or someone she casually ran into at the store?"

Wally shrugged. "There's no way to tell. But Gerald Baker identified the other woman in the picture with Edie and said she'd been hanging around him and his wife at various VFW and American Legion events. Possibly coming on to him."

"Wow!" Skye had long since stopped believing that nothing could surprise her, but she hadn't seen that coming. "Who was it?"

"Pru Cormorant."

"You're kidding me!" Skye gasped. "Corny has a crush on Mr. Baker? Or maybe they're having an affair and he didn't want to admit it. I don't think I told you that she's improved her appearance and the rumor around the teachers' lounge is that there's a man in her life. A married one at that."

"I figured we'd head out to Pru's house as soon as we finish interviewing Beilin and Homer and find out what she has to say about it all." Wally rubbed the stubble on his jaw. "I thought maybe since you knew her from school, she might be more willing to talk to you."

"I'll give it a try, but we're not exactly friends, so . . ."

"Well, we'll see what happens." Wally put his hand on the small of Skye's back and guided her toward the break room. "Right now, let's deal with Beilin."

The minute Skye and Wally walked through the door, Anthony jumped to his feet.

Not quite saluting, the young officer said, "Chief, Mr. Quinn has been Mirandized, signed the acknowledgment form, and declined representation."

"Good job." Wally nodded toward the exit. "Go ahead and get back on patrol."

"Yes, sir."

He dismissed the young man, turned to Beilin, and said, "Thanks for coming in. I wanted to bring you up to speed on our investigation."

"Great." Beilin frowned. "But why all the rigmarole with my rights and all?"

"I also have a few questions for you, and our city attorney insists that we Mirandize and tape anyone we interview." From the cabinet next to the sink, Wally took out an old-fashioned tape recorder, pushed a button, and said, "Please state your full name and address."

Beilin complied, then asked, "Why don't you use your phone to record the interview?" Beilin asked.

"The lawyer vetoed that idea because my cell isn't city issued."

The contractor flicked a glance at Skye.

"Why are you here, Mrs. Boyd?"

Before Skye could speak, Wally explained her status as the psych consultant.

"Oh. Okay." Beilin nodded. "I guess I did hear something about that."

Skye took the chair next to the contractor and put her hand on his arm. "Nothing you say here will be shared with anyone else. The only reason the content of this interview will ever be made public is if you go to trial for your wife's murder."

"You can't imagine that I . . ." Color drained from Beilin's face. "What reason would I have to kill her?"

Skye opened her mouth but closed it, not sure how to answer.

Wally ignored Beilin's question, sat across from him, and said, "Here's what we know so far. Although your house had been broken into previously, just a few minor items were missing and there was only some petty vandalism. In addition, nothing was stolen the day of Jerita's murder. Correct?"

Beilin nodded, then said, "Well, maybe her iPhone. I thought it was in her handbag, but when I went to get it out this morning, only the case was there."

"And you didn't think that might be a good thing to mention to me earlier?" Wally's ears reddened and Skye could tell he was barely holding onto his temper. "I don't suppose you brought in the purse and case?"

"It's in my truck." Beilin scrubbed his eyes. "There's just so much to think about. I meant to bring it in when I got here, but I forgot." He half stood. "Shall I go get it now?"

Wally waved him back into his seat and said, "After we're done, I'll walk out with you and put it in an evidence bag."

"Sure." Beilin perched nervously on the edge of his chair, cleared his throat, and said, "So . . . uh . . . what have you found out so far?"

"Earl Doozier's story has been confirmed by his fingerprints, and quite frankly, he has no motive. Plus, I seriously doubt Earl would have stuck around and phoned for help if he'd killed your wife."

"I still don't trust him," Beilin muttered.

"Oh, I don't trust him, but I also don't think he's our murderer." Wally shot Skye a glance and said, "However, we do have a more viable suspect, one who does have a creditable motive." Before Beilin could ask, Wally added, "I can't share the name of that person, but another possibility has come to light and that has raised some questions."

"I want to know who you think killed my

wife." Beilin pounded the table.

Skye was impressed at how easily Wally ignored the contractor's outburst and turned the tables as he said, "Let's start with where you were when you told Jerita you were working from dawn to dusk on our house."

"Uh." Beilin licked his lips. "I . . . Well . . ." He squared his shoulders. "The thing is, a month ago, I started construction on a second home."

"Seriously?" Skye glared at the contractor. "You promised to finish our place before accepting another job."

"Your house is almost done and I would have lost out on this one if I couldn't get things underway before the weather got bad," Beilin protested.

Wally put his hand on Skye's arm and she knew he was urging her to keep her cool. She blew out a breath and nodded her agreement.

"We'll need to check with your other employer to verify your story." Wally made a note, then said, "Now that you've answered that question, why didn't you tell me the real reason that you left Chicago and moved to Scumble River?"

Beilin looked down at the table and mumbled something Skye didn't catch.

"What?" Wally asked, leaning forward. "You need to speak up."

"I don't know what you mean." Beilin continued to study the tabletop as if it held a map to a Scumble River gold mine.

"Jerita told her boss, who is my sister-in-law, that she left the city to make sure her daughter was protected," Skye said softly. "And Loretta was under the impression it wasn't just from the normal dangers of city life. She believed that there was a specific threat Jerita was trying to avoid."

"It's possible." Beilin shook her head sadly. "If she could, Jerita would have encased Jenna in Bubble Wrap."

Skye wrinkled her brow. Clearly, it wouldn't be easy to get Beilin to talk about specifics. Glancing at Wally, Skye silently requested permission to take over the questioning. He gave a slight nod and sat back in his chair.

"Can you give me an example?" Skye asked.

"Once, in preschool, another little girl took Jenna's snack and licked it. Then before the teacher could stop her, Jenna ate it." Beilin shrugged. "Jerita wanted to sue the school and the teacher for neglect."

"I see." Skye turned so that she was focused entirely on the contractor. "Then going after our school district and Principal Knapik wasn't the first time she brought a lawsuit against someone."

"Nah. Just the first time she had a good case." Beilin's eyes hardened. "I think she ended up becoming a paralegal so schools and teachers would be more afraid of her and give her what she wanted for Jenna."

"Any other instance of Jerita's overprotectiveness?" Skye asked.

"She was convinced that someone was going to snatch Jenna." Beilin sighed. "After a woman tried to talk to Jenna on the El, Jerita wouldn't take any form of public transportation. She watched Jenna go into the school and met her at the door when it was over."

"So Jenna was only out of her sight when she was in class," Skye murmured.

"Uh-huh." Beilin thrust out his chin. "And it was a lot more difficult to control that in the city."

"So nothing more specific?" Skye asked. "You're saying that Jerita was just paranoid."

Beilin blinked rapidly, ran a hand over his hair, then cleared his throat, and said, "Yes."

Skye was pretty darn sure he was lying. She nudged Wally's calf with her foot and gave an almost imperceptible shake of her head.

"Would you be willing to allow us to search your house?" Wally asked. "Maybe we could locate something among Jerita's things that would give us more of a clue about anything specific she feared in regard to Jenna."

Beilin screwed up his face. "Well . . ."

"It would be very helpful, and if we could eliminate that area of the investigation, we could concentrate on the other suspect."

Skye wasn't fooled by Wally's smooth tone. She could see the tension around his mouth.

There was a slight hesitation, then Beilin answered, "Fine. But I want to be present when you search and I don't want Jenna there."

Wally raised an eyebrow at Skye, who shrugged. Beilin's demands weren't outrageous.

"Sure," Wally agreed. "But we need to do it sooner rather than later."

"How about the day after Thanksgiving?" Beilin offered. "Jenna and I are going to my folks for the holiday and I plan to leave her with them over the weekend so I can finish up a few things with your house." He grinned at Skye. "If all goes as planned, you should be able to move in the first week of December."

"Awesome!" She smiled back at the contractor. He seemed like a nice guy and she really hoped he hadn't killed his wife.

"Friday morning works for me," Wally agreed, then looked at Skye and asked, "Can you get a sitter?"

"Dorothy is available." Skye shook her head. "I was hoping to do some Black Friday shopping. You do realize we have literally no furniture for our new house?"

"Well, if you can't make it . . . But if we start at eight, we'll probably be done by ten." Wally patted Skye's hand. "Plenty of time to shop, right?"

"Of course." Her eyes slitted. "How long can it take to furnish a thirty-five-hundred-square-foot home?"

"Don't forget the apartment over the garage," Beilin added helpfully.

"Of course not." Skye glared at both men. "What's another six hundred or so square feet?"

CHAPTER 20
ALREADY HOME

Skye studied Homer through the partially closed blinds covering the break room window. He'd arrived a few minutes ago. Skye had volunteered to keep an eye on the high school principal until Wally was done talking with Dante. She wasn't sure what the men were arguing about, but she hoped whatever it was wouldn't take too long to settle.

Turning her attention back to Homer, she narrowed her eyes. Unaware that he was being observed, the principal's usual bluster was absent. Still wearing his topcoat, he sat slumped in a chair with his head in his hands. His typical overbearing presence was hidden beneath a layer of defeat and several days' worth of facial stubble.

A teeny tiny part of Skye was sorry for the man, but not enough to try to make him feel at ease. And as the minutes ticked by, Homer grew more and more agitated, fuss-

311

ing with the crease of his brown dress pants, tugging at the cuffs of his dress shirt, and shuffling the soles of his Hush Puppies against the floor.

Skye was afraid that any second he would bolt from the police station, but luckily Wally arrived before the principal decided to make a break for freedom.

"Ready?" Wally asked, and when Skye nodded, he held open the break room door for her to enter first.

Homer glanced up as Skye walked into the room, then glanced behind her at Wally, and evidently frightened by their ominous expressions, he whined, "I didn't want to do it."

"Which part?" Skye crossed her arms. "Setting up Earl or killing Jerita?"

"What? No!" Homer yelped. "I didn't kill that woman or anyone else. I meant involving Earl Doozier. I heard you brought him in here, and I figured he told you about that little call I made to him."

"Little call!" Skye barely stopped herself from lunging across the table. "You lured that poor guy to a murder scene to save —"

"Let's stop here and make everything nice and official," Wally interrupted, gently tugging Skye down onto a chair and sitting next to her.

He'd left the recorder on the table after Beilin's interview and now he popped in a fresh tape and switched it on. Wally announced the date and time, told Homer he was being recorded, then asked him to state his name and address.

After the preliminaries were complete, Wally said, "Why don't you give us your side of what happened that day, Homer? I'm willing to keep an open mind."

Skye raised an eyebrow, but remained silent.

"I didn't kill her." Homer gazed at Wally as if the chief were the last bullet in a gun and Homer was surrounded by zombies. "I merely went over to her house to persuade her to reconsider her lawsuit. Shamus ordered me to offer her whatever she wanted to make it all go away, which was exactly what I intended to do."

"And when Jerita refused, you murdered her." Skye slapped the tabletop with her open hand. "Then you decided to kill two birds, or lawsuits, with one knife, and you phoned Earl to come be your patsy."

"Yes. I mean, no." Homer slowly shook his humongous head. "I mean, you're trying to mix me up. I admit that it crossed my mind that if I got Earl over to the Quinns and you all thought he was the

313

killer, he wouldn't have time to pursue a lawsuit against me or the school." Homer's cheeks hollowed as he sucked in a huge gulp of air. "But the woman was dead when I got there."

"That woman has a name," Skye snapped. "It's Jerita Quinn, not the ones you've been calling her since she got the best of you."

"Okay, sure." Homer looked confused at Skye's anger, then repeated his declaration of innocence. "Mrs. Quinn was dead when I got there."

"So you arrived at the Quinn house and . . ." Wally encouraged.

"I'd called the day before to ask her to talk to me. She refused to come to the school for a meeting, but she said she'd speak with me at her house at eight thirty." Homer dug a wrinkled white handkerchief from his pocket and used it to wipe the sweat from his forehead. "She told me I had twenty minutes to convince her because she had to be at work by nine."

"Were you on time?" Skye asked, knowing Homer's propensity for tardiness.

"On the dot." Homer grimaced. "That woman — I mean, Mrs. Quinn — scared me."

"Then what?" Wally waved his hand for the principal to continue.

"I rang the bell two or three times, but no one came to the door." Homer toyed with a scrap of paper lying on the table. "Then I tried the knocker a few times and I might have shouted."

"That must have made you angry." Skye raised a brow. "Her standing you up like that, especially with Dr. Wraige breathing down your neck."

"Yeah, of course it did. That woman was ruining my life!" Homer's usual belligerence made a brief return appearance, then his shoulders slumped. "I tried phoning her, but she didn't answer either her home number or her cell." He frowned. "I had given up and was walking back to my car when I heard a sound from the backyard."

"What kind of sound?" Wally asked.

Skye pursed her lips. Homer's story seemed an awful lot like Earl's account.

"Maybe the squeak of a gate or some leaves rustling." Homer shrugged. "Who knows? At that point, I wasn't really trying to identify the noise. I just headed back there to see if it was Mrs. Quinn."

"So you've marched around the corner of the house and you saw . . ." Wally prodded.

"Nothing at first." The hairs sticking out of Homer's ears waved like antennas when he shook his head. "Then I spotted the playhouse and I thought maybe Mrs. Quinn was cleaning it or something."

"Seriously?" Skye sneered. "That's the best your imagination could do?"

Wally chuckled, then said, "So, Homer, what was your next move?"

"I walked over to the fence, looked toward the playhouse, and saw Mrs. Quinn lying there with the knife sticking out of her temple." Homer's ruddy cheeks paled. "I knew I'd be the police's number one suspect since Skye would no doubt rat me out about the lawsuit."

"It's my civic duty." Skye smiled sweetly.

"Don't play dumb." Homer glared at her.

"I would never play dumb with you, Homer." Skye clicked her tongue. "You're too good at it for me to win."

Homer ignored her taunt and continued, "So, after thinking it over for a couple of minutes, I realized that if the police had another suspect, it would keep the heat off of me. That's when I called Earl. Once I heard him arrive at the front door, I made some noise to get him to come into the backyard, then I took off through the trees, circled around to my car, and left." Homer looked back and forth between Skye and Wally, then asked, "You believe me, right?"

Unfortunately, Skye did believe him. His

story sounded exactly like what a self-centered rat like Homer would do in that situation.

She was about to nod when Wally asked, "Then why did we find your pumpkin seed hulls inside the house?"

"How do you know they're mine?" Homer bluffed. "Do they have my name on them?"

"No." Wally leaned back in his chair. "But they do have your DNA."

"How . . ." Homer trailed off, then a light dawned in his eyes, and he pointed a finger at Skye. "You went through my trash. That's why that paper from the lawsuit was missing, but the rest of the garbage was still there."

Skye kept her expression deadpan and didn't respond to Homer's accusation.

"Speaking of that." Wally's smile was predatory. "What you wrote on that page makes a mighty good piece of evidence toward your motive."

"Look, the Quinns' back door was open, so I went inside to see if the killer was still there." Homer twitched his shoulders. "I must have spit out those hulls without realizing what I was doing. It's become a habit and I don't even notice anymore."

"There's no way on God's green earth you were looking for the murderer." Skye stared at Homer until he swallowed audibly. "You were looking for Jerita's phone to get the recording she made of you."

"And her cell phone just happens to be missing," Wally said, leaning toward the older man. "If you turn it in now, I might be able to talk Mr. Quinn out of pressing charges for burglary."

"I didn't . . ." Homer stammered, then glanced at Skye, who shook her head and gave him an I-don't-believe-you stare. "Okay. I looked for it, but it was gone. There was just the case in her purse. I figured Mrs. Quinn had it in her pocket, but by then Earl was pounding on the door and I had to get out of there."

"Will we find your fingerprints match those we took from the scene?" Wally asked.

"No. I wore gloves." Homer spoke into his chest. "My hands get cold really easy so I always have a pair in my coat pocket."

"Then what did you do?" Skye raised a brow.

"Like I said." Homer ran his fingers along the scarred tabletop. "I made sure Earl would go around to the backyard and I took off."

Wally and Skye continued to question Homer, but they couldn't shake his story. Finally, after he was fingerprinted and given a warning not to travel out of town, they allowed him to leave.

As soon as Homer was gone, Skye and Wally headed over to Pru Cormorant's house.

On the way, she asked, "How do you want to handle this?"

"Your guess is as good as mine." Wally blew out a breath. "It's not as if I've ever had to ask a suspect before if they kidnapped a woman in order to date that woman's husband."

He turned into a neighborhood within walking distance of the high school. The homes were older, mostly from the fifties and sixties, and had spacious lawns. The area hadn't been in any of the tornados' paths so the trees and landscaping remained intact.

Pru's house was a well-maintained, beige-brick ranch with an attached two-car garage. The driveway looked as if it had been recently resealed, the yard was leaf free, and the sidewalks sparkled as if they'd just been power washed.

All of which Skye could have predicted. What she hadn't expected was the extensive Thanksgiving decorations. There was an elaborate wreath on the front door, a colorful turkey in the picture window, and a birdbath on the lawn holding a pretty arrangement of pumpkins.

Wally parked the cruiser by the curb, and he and Skye walked up the sidewalk. Before they could ring the bell, the front door was flung open and Pru stood blocking their view of the house's interior.

"Hi!" Skye attempted to make this seem like a friendly visit. "Wow! Your decorations are gorgeous. Did you do them yourself?"

"Of course." Pru folded her arms. "That's the only way to be certain they're done correctly."

"I bet you could get almost all the materials from the dollar store in town," Skye said, hoping that avenue of discussion would lead the way to what they really wanted to ask the woman.

"Most of them." Pru's expression was smug. "I try to shop local."

"Me too," Skye said. "It's too bad we don't have any clothing stores."

"They probably wouldn't carry your size anyway." Pru stared at Skye's hips. "I remember when the Elegance Boutique was in Scumble River. They never had anything over a twelve."

"Maybe that's why it closed." Wally put his hand on Skye's back and shot Pru a look that said *I dare you.*

"Hmm." Pru's lips tightened and she demanded, "What are you two doing at my home anyway?"

"May we come in and discuss it?" Skye asked, trying to edge her way over the threshold.

"No." Pru didn't budge.

"Fine." Wally shrugged. "I suppose we can come back with a warrant."

Skye wondered if he was bluffing.

"I have no idea what you're talking about." Pru's voice cracked.

"We have you on the dollar store's security recordings with Edie Baker the day she disappeared." Wally raised an eyebrow. "It shows her getting into your car, and she hasn't been seen since."

Now Skye knew he was bluffing because the recordings hadn't caught the two women in the parking lot.

"Her golf cart ran out of charge so I gave her a ride home." Pru met Skye's skeptical gaze, but then looked away.

"Buzz." Wally's smile was smug. "A dollar store clerk drove it back to Bord du Lac with no problem."

"It must have had a short or a loose wire or . . ."

"Let them in, sweetheart," a feminine voice called out from inside the house, then

Edie Baker joined Pru in the doorway. She slipped an arm around the English teacher's waist and declared, "It's time to tell the truth and shame the devil."

"And by devil, I assume you mean Gerald," Skye guessed.

"Pru said you were a smart one." Edie smiled and gestured them inside.

There were very few wrinkles on Edie's beautiful face, and her baby-blue eyes sparkled as she looked between Skye and Wally.

The interior of the house was as artfully decorated as the exterior, and when the four of them took seats at the kitchen table, Skye admired the centerpiece. It was a ceramic pumpkin sitting on two thin slices of a tree trunk and filled with colorful fall flowers.

She pointed to the arrangement and said, "How lovely. You're really talented."

Edie took Pru's hand and said, "That's how we first met. We were both buying things from the craft aisle at the dollar store and started talking. Then we kept running into each other at various VFW and American Legion events."

Skye glanced at Pru and the English teacher explained, "Cooking for one is a waste of time and the fundraising dinners are homemade food at a reasonable price for a good cause." Pru's warm smile transformed her normally unattractive countenance until she was almost pretty. "My father was a Korean War veteran and used to take me with him to the VFW and American Legion before he died."

"We saw each other at least twice a week for the past year or so." Edie gazed fondly at Pru. "And we fell in love."

"But you were afraid to tell Gerald," Skye deduced. "I expect a man with his view of the world would not gracefully grant you a divorce if you wanted to leave him for a man, let alone another woman."

Edie nodded. "Our marriage had been over for years, but I had no good motive to get free from him before I met Pru."

"The irony of life is that by the time you're old enough to know your way around, it's difficult to go anywhere," Pru said softly.

"Mrs. Baker, you don't seem, uh . . ." Wally trailed off and sent Skye a pleading look.

"What my husband is trying to say is that you don't appear to have dementia." Skye shook her head at Wally, who was sometimes too much of a gentleman for his own good.

"Probably not." Edie giggled. "I've always been a bit scatterbrained, but when I decided that I couldn't handle Gerald's endless ranting about how everyone was wrong about everything, I might have faked it a little. Just enough to get him to stop talking to me." She clapped her hands. "What Gerald never realized was that women are part angel. But once our wings are broken, the other part comes out and we use a broomstick to fly instead." She winked. "We're flexible like that."

"Good to know." Wally glanced uneasily at Skye.

She nodded her agreement with Edie's statement, but remained silent.

"I believe she has undiagnosed attention deficit disorder," Pru stated. "I'd like to get her to my physician for an examination. Since Gerald thinks all doctors are charlatans, he's never taken Edie to one. But because we hoped everyone would think she was dead, it would have been hard to explain her presence at the medical building if someone spotted her."

"That's why you talked to me about Edie that day at school," Skye guessed, then not waiting for Pru to confirm her deduction, she looked at Edie and asked, "Wasn't it more difficult to pretend you had dementia once Gerald hired a caregiver for you?"

"Nope." Edie giggled again. "After Krissy

caught me leaving on my neighbor's golf cart, which, by the way, I had permission to use while she wintered in Florida, I told her the truth. And once Krissy knew the situation, she said that everyone deserved to be with the people they loved and not just who they were stuck with because they made one bad choice. In fact, she helped me plan my escape."

After kissing Skye goodbye in the parking lot and promising to be home by six, Wally walked toward the police station, swearing under his breath about filthy liars as he entered the building. He'd held it together in front of his wife, but this was one of those days when the supply of pseudo cusswords was insufficient to meet his needs and he just had to bring out the actual expletives.

With the possible exception of Earl Doozier — which was mind-boggling on its own account — every single person associated with Jerita's murder *and* the missing person case had either outright lied or hidden an important fact.

And it was no consolation that despite Krissy Ficher's blatant deception they'd been able to find Edie Baker, because now that he knew her whereabouts, he wasn't sure what to do about that knowledge. Both the no-longer-missing woman and Pru had begged him not to reveal Edie's location to her husband, but Wally hadn't been able to make any promises.

Edie was well over twenty-one and at least seemed to be in her right mind, but she had been reported missing by her legal husband. Did that give Baker the right to know what had really happened? Wally didn't think so, but would have to check with the city attorney to be sure.

Neither Mrs. nor Mr. Baker had done anything illegal. There was no theft; she'd had permission to borrow the golf cart from her neighbor. And there was no filing a false police report; Baker had genuinely thought his wife suffered from dementia and had wandered off on her own.

Thankful that at least he didn't have to worry about arresting either of them, Wally stomped down the hallway, climbed the stairs, and flung open his office door.

Mulling over the list of calls he needed to make to untangle all the lies he'd been told, Wally marched into his office. Then when he glanced toward his desk, he nearly had a heart attack.

Shouting "What the fu . . . dge!" he shot back into the corridor.

Then as Wally stared at it, the huge black dog occupying his chair raised its furry head from where it had been resting on the desktop. It had a long black beard and hairy eyebrows, making it look like Homer Knapik and Grizzly Adams had had a love child.

Wally slammed the door closed and jumped as a voice behind him said, "I see you met Arnold."

Wally turned, saw Martinez, and after his heart stopped racing, asked, "Arnold?"

"As in Schwarzenegger," she explained. "Mayor Leofanti dropped him off about an hour ago. He's our new K-9 officer." The young woman looked over her shoulder in the direction of Hizzoner's office and whispered, "But I don't think Arnold's had much training."

"Of course he hasn't." Wally rolled his eyes, then edged past Martinez. "Please remove the dog from my office while I speak to the mayor."

It wasn't that Wally disliked dogs, but he'd had a bad experience as a child. Afterward, he'd never been exposed to them again so he hadn't had a chance to warm up to animals of the canine persuasion. But even if he had, he wouldn't want a dog sitting behind his desk. What if the creature ate an important report or peed on his perfectly broken-in chair?

When Wally entered the mayor's lair,

Dante scowled and snarled, "What now?"

"We never agreed on the dog." Wally crossed his arms. "My staff said they'd take the bonuses versus raises in salary along with the increased uniform allowances and the removal of the part-timer's hour cap, but we were still discussing the K-9 officer."

"I had to strike while the dog shit was hot." Dante mirrored Wally and crossed his arms too. "My friend is going out of business, and if I didn't take Arnold, we'd have lost our chance."

Wally argued, "Officer Martinez tells me that the dog isn't trained."

"That isn't true. While his training isn't completed, we got him cheap to make up the difference." Dante beamed. "These animals go for up to twenty thousand dollars. Arnold was only a tenth of that."

"You spent two thousand bucks on a partially trained dog that we have nowhere to house?" Wally shot Hizzoner a death glare. "Send him back."

"No returns." Dante picked up the phone. "Close the door on the way out."

"I'm dropping the dog off at your place," Wally threatened. "I hope your wife is okay with a large, hairy guest for Thanksgiving."

Wally stomped over the threshold and slammed the door behind him. Rolling his

329

eyes, he nearly ran into Martinez. She had the dog on a leash and was squatting in front of it, cooing into its floppy ear.

Leaping up, she said, "I . . . uh . . . overheard what you said to the mayor and I'd be glad to take Arnold home." She took a breath, then in a rush continued, "I've been planning to get a dog, so I have all the stuff he'll need, even some food."

"That would be great." Wally gave her a stern look. "But this isn't permanent, so don't get attached. He only stays until we figure out how to send him back to the guy who scammed the mayor."

"The thing is" — Martinez bit her lip — "I'd love to have the opportunity to take whatever class is necessary to complete his and my training."

Wally considered her words. He had nothing against using a K-9 officer, and in reality they probably were stuck with the animal. If it could be trained, it would be a useful addition to their police force.

Martinez and the dog both turned dark pleading eyes up at Wally and he gave the animal a pat on the head before asking, "What breed is this guy anyway? I thought police dogs were German shepherds or Doberman pincers."

"He's a giant schnauzer." Martinez

scratched the dog behind his ears and he wagged his tail. "Schnauzers are intelligent, reliable, brave, loyal, bold, and easy to train. Plus they hardly shed at all."

Wally had never seen Martinez so excited or so confident. He liked her self-assurance and it was clear her enthusiasm would be an asset in learning to handle the dog.

Hoping he could squeeze some money out of the police budget, he said, "If we can find the finances for the training, I'll give it a chance. Any idea what it would cost?"

"Thank you, sir." Martinez hugged the dog. "I think the course is three weeks and the fee is about six thousand dollars. Maybe if we don't have the resources, I could do a fundraiser or something."

"We'll talk about it more after the holiday," Wally said. He wouldn't mind just paying for it out of his own pocket, but then Dante would expect him to pick up the slack anytime the department ran short.

"Yes, sir." Martinez kept a hand on the dog's collar.

Remembering Skye telling him he was rude, before he headed to his office Wally added, "Have a good Thanksgiving."

"You too, sir." Martinez's voice followed him down the hall.

Taking a seat behind his desk, Wally

scrubbed his face. It had been a doozy of a day, and before he could go home he needed to talk to the city attorney, which was never a quick call. Wally sighed and picked up the telephone.

After a lengthy discussion, Wally translated the legalese that the lawyer had spouted to mean that Gerald Baker had no right to know where his wife was located. If Wally wanted to be a nice guy, he could let the man know she was safe and had left him on her own accord, but was in no way to reveal where she was living.

Another long conversation with the attorney resulted in the man confirming that he'd be able to get a warrant to track Jerita's cell phone. But due to the holiday, it wouldn't be issued until Friday.

In an ideal world, Wally would drive out to Bord du Lac and give Baker the news about his wife in person. But in this reality, it was five thirty the day before Thanksgiving, and investigating a murder trumped Wally's more compassionate inclinations. He soothed his conscience by telling himself that Baker's reaction would more likely be anger rather than sorrow.

Dialing the man's number, Wally fought off a feeling that he was being selfish. Although he'd vowed to work more reasonable hours and put his family first, sometimes it was tough to find a balance between his responsibility to the job and his commitment to Skye and the twins. But in the end, his wife and kids had to come first.

"Mr. Baker," Wally said as soon as the man answered. "This is Chief Boyd and I'm happy to tell you that your wife is alive and well."

"Where is she?" Gerald demanded. "Are you bringing her home?"

"Unfortunately, Mrs. Baker doesn't wish to return." Wally steeled himself for the man's outrage, and he wasn't disappointed.

"You know as well as I do that she isn't mentally fit!" Gerald shouted. "She can't make those types of choices."

"Do you have a power of health attorney or guardianship?" Wally asked. Edie had said he didn't, but the city attorney had told Wally to make sure of that fact. "If so, I'll need to see the paperwork."

"She's my wife and I don't need some document to make you tell me her location," Gerald sputtered. "I have a right to know."

"I'm afraid you don't." Wally's voice was sympathetic. "But I can assure you that Mrs. Baker is in a safe place. It appears her dementia may have been exaggerated to

333

mislead you, but she is fine."

Gerald ranted for several minutes, threatening to sue the police, the city, and Wally, then in a flurry of cursing hung up.

Wally's next call was to the crime lab to ask if they had the ability to track Jerita Quinn's cell phone to find out its location. The techs had already left for the day, but the receptionist promised to have someone contact him first thing Friday morning.

During the holiday, the techs were on call only for emergencies. Wally assured the woman that was fine since he wouldn't have a warrant until then anyway.

The clock was rapidly ticking toward six and Wally searched his mind for anything else that needed to be done today. With Thanksgiving tomorrow, this was probably his last chance to reach anyone still working and even that was a long shot.

He pulled a legal pad toward him, picked up a pen, and considered what he'd learned from the interviews he and Skye had conducted throughout the afternoon. An important question was whether Homer was telling the truth. It was possible that he'd concocted that whole extravagant story to cover up murdering Jerita Quinn.

What did they know for sure? One, Jerita was murdered in the backyard with a knife from her own kitchen. Had the murderer forced his or her way in with a gun or had Jerita invited him or her inside? But if the killer had a weapon, why use a knife?

Two, how did Jerita end up outside? Again, had she been forced or had she been showing the killer the elaborate playhouse?

Homer wasn't the brightest bulb, but was he stupid enough to clean his prints from the knife and then leave evidence like his pumpkin seed hulls behind? And why wipe off the weapon if he was wearing gloves? Unless of course he killed her, then put his gloves on to search the house. Still, neither scenario sounded like a man who would forget the pumpkin seed hulls.

Okay. Homer wasn't in the clear, but how about Beilin? Was he lying about why they left the city? And had he really just noticed his wife's cell phone was missing or had he destroyed it because it held something that incriminated him?

Wally thumped his forehead with the heel of his hand. He should have confiscated the vic's phone the day she was murdered. He couldn't believe that he'd made such a rookie mistake.

In his defense, he'd thought the crime scene techs had taken it, but that wasn't a good excuse. It was his job to make sure of

335

the details.

Clearly, the lack of sleep was getting to him. It would be so much better once they moved into the house and the twins could be in their own rooms. As it was, they were inches from his and Skye's bed, and every time they whimpered or turned over, he and Skye both bolted awake, which wasn't good for either of them.

Yawning, Wally scrubbed his eyes and groaned when he remembered that they had to wait until Friday to search the vic's house. The delay gave Beilin ample time to destroy anything he didn't want the police to find. An image of the big bonfires that the contractor used to get rid of trash that accumulated as the new house was being built popped into Wally's mind and his shoulders slumped.

He supposed he could have insisted Beilin let him examine the place immediately, but that would have involved attempting to secure a warrant. And Wally wasn't at all sure the city attorney could get one since they really didn't have much to show probable cause. Unfortunately, Skye's conviction that Beilin was lying wasn't exactly hard evidence.

Wally growled in frustration. What he really needed was more information. Infor-

336

mation he couldn't get until after Thanksgiving. Although he normally loved living in a rural area, the fact that there was no judge or crime scene tech available until Friday was aggravating. But in such a small county, there just weren't enough personnel to staff either the courthouse or the lab 24/7.

Sure, there were people on call, but his situation didn't qualify as an emergency. And insisting that it was vital would only make enemies he didn't need. The Scumble River PD depended on the county resources too much to burn those kinds of bridges.

Wally glanced at his watch. It was quarter to six and he was out of ideas. Sighing, he closed up the Quinn file and got to his feet.

Coming to an abrupt halt on his way to the door, he went back and picked up the phone. There was one more call he wanted to make. Krissy Ficher had lied to him, which was obstruction of justice. And while he had no intention of having her prosecuted for the crime, he did intend to threaten her with arrest for actively impeding an investigation. A good scare might stop her from doing something like that again.

Smacking the desk when her cell went directly to voicemail, Wally blew out a frustrated breath and left a message for her to be at the PD Monday at ten thirty sharp. He wanted to convey the consequence of her actions to her directly rather than via a voicemail message.

Exasperated, Wally headed downstairs, stopping in the front office to alert the dispatcher that he was going home.

Lonny, the guy subbing for May while she was on vacation, looked up from the computer and said, "Through for the day, Chief?"

"Yep." Wally nodded. "I'll be off radio, so call my cell if there's an emergency."

"Will do." Lonny gave him a half salute, then answered the ringing phone.

As Wally started to leave, the dispatcher held up a finger, indicating he should wait.

Lonny listened for a few more seconds, then said, "It's the medical examiner."

The dispatcher handed over the receiver and Wally asked, "Dr. Norris, did you find something?"

His heart leaped with the hope that she had a lead for him to follow. Whatever she had to say must be important because her shift would have ended an hour ago.

"Unfortunately nothing more than I already told you." Dr. Norris chuckled. "Sorry to get you all excited, but I wanted to give you a heads-up that my complete report will be popping into your email anytime now."

"So a little light reading for the holiday," Wally joked to mask his disappointment. "Why are you still at the morgue this late the day before Thanksgiving?"

"Under the best of circumstances, I'm a bit of a workaholic, and since I don't have family in the area it's even worse." Dr. Norris's tone was light, but Wally could hear the underlying loneliness.

"Well, if you don't have any other plans, why don't you come to my in-laws for dinner?" he asked.

He knew that May wouldn't mind his impromptu invitation. She always invited anyone who would be alone for the holiday to join them and she'd be happy to set another plate at one of her many tables.

"I couldn't impose on your family like that," Dr. Norris protested.

"My mother-in-law would insist."

"Well . . ." Dr. Norris hesitated, then said, "I was dreading the thought of eating a frozen dinner in front of the television set."

"No need for that, Dr. Norris." Wally gave her May's address.

"Since I'm joining your family for dinner, you better call me Doris Ann."

"Terrific." Wally added, "See you at one

339

p.m. tomorrow and don't even think of bringing any food. My mother-in-law would not appreciate it."

"Is a bottle of wine safe?" Doris Ann chuckled. "One of my many talents is that I drink well with others."

"Wine is fine, but beer would be better," Wally teased.

"My kind of people. And I know the perfect brand. Pine Belt Pale Ale. I brought a supply back from my last trip home to Texas."

"Perfect." Wally hung up the phone grinning.

He'd looked up Dr. Norris after his first contact with her. She was widowed and in her late fifties. With her bringing his dad's favorite beer, maybe she'd lure Carson away from Bunny Reid. He *had* to be getting tired of the ditsy redhead by now.

Whistling, Wally headed out of the station. Maybe something was finally going right.

CHAPTER 22
HOME FOR THE HOLIDAYS

Skye was not a fan of snow. Unlike her Mother, who adored the stuff, she thought a white Christmas was vastly overrated. And a white Thanksgiving was just ridiculous. Especially in Illinois, where there was a good chance there would also be a white Easter.

She had always thought of snow not as a winter wonderland, but as a substance that made driving dangerous and ruined her expensive shoes. Although, she'd never really understood what a pain in the butt it was until she attempted to carry a baby down icy metal steps while being pelted from every direction.

Granted, before Skye attempted her descent, Wally had sprinkled the stairs with salt, but she was still afraid that she'd fall. And evidently Eva did not enjoy her first experience with the winter's unwanted gift either because she was screaming her head off.

Behind Skye, Wally had both CJ and their contribution to the Thanksgiving feast. CJ was happily cooing at the flakes and Skye wondered how she managed always to be carrying the twin who was crying.

After settling the babies into their car seats, Skye and Wally climbed into the SUV and headed toward her parents' place on the other side of town. The streets weren't bad yet, but if the snow continued to fall, they would be by their return trip. Especially the country roads.

Ten minutes later, Wally pulled the Mercedes behind Gillian's minivan and got out of the car. "Looks like your mom and dad have a full house." He opened the back door of the SUV, unbuckled CJ, and scooped him into his arms.

Skye did the same with Eva, then said, "Yep. Thanksgiving is the only holiday that both the Denisons and the Leofantis always celebrate together. Plus all the extra people Mom invites. It's always quite a crowd."

"Be careful." Wally did a quick shuffle to remain upright and CJ chortled, waving his little hands in the air. "I'll come back for the Crock-Pot."

"Good idea." Skye slowly stepped toward

the sidewalk. "Salt doesn't work on gravel so the driveway is going to get treacherous. I sure hope no one falls."

"Well, at least we'll have a doctor available if they do." Wally smiled.

Skye shook her head. "You do know that insanity doesn't so much run in my family as it strolls through, taking its time to get to know each of us personally? Is Dr. Norris prepared for that?"

Wally had told her about inviting the ME, which was fine — no one should have to be alone on a holiday. But his scheme to hook the woman up with his father had *Danger, Will Robinson* written all over it.

"I have a feeling not only will Doris Ann be okay with it, she'll love it." Wally grinned, then stopped and pointed at the yard, which was swathed in a mantle of pure white, with only the occasional paw print to mar its pristine surface. "Wow! That's really beautiful. It looks like a Christmas card."

"You know I don't like snow." Skye scowled. "It may be pretty, but not pretty enough to make up for the fact you have to hike through it, shovel it, and scrape it off your windshield."

Wally ignored her words and said, "Look at those evergreens."

"Dad planted them the week after my

parents moved into their new house." Skye stopped to calculate. "That would have been over forty-three years ago. I hadn't even been born yet." Skye glanced at the wind-break of firs that looked like flocked Christmas trees. They bordered the property on three sides and were a good twelve feet tall.

Continuing onto the back patio, Skye noticed her mother's concrete goose no longer wore the pilgrim getup it had on last week. The cement fowl now sported a button-down jacket over a dickey, a red necktie, a skirt, and a hat. A tiny umbrella with a brightly colored parrot handle rested along its wing. Skye wrinkled her brow. What in the world did this costume mean?

Wally nudged Skye's shoulder and asked, "Why is May's goose dressed like Mary Poppins?"

"Shoot!" Skye clutched Eva so tightly the baby squeaked. "Mom found out about Dorothy, and she's ticked her friend's going to be our nanny."

"You didn't tell her Dorothy was going to be our live-in housekeeper?"

"Not yet. I was waiting for the right time." Skye inhaled sharply. "But someone spilled the beans, and my money's on Vince."

Her brother had a big mouth and loved to stir up their mother. He'd probably offered that tidbit to May when he'd broken the news that he, his wife, and their kids were spending the holiday in Chicago at Loretta's family celebration instead of at his mother's.

With visions of future revenge dancing in her head, Skye entered the house, pausing in the utility room to add her coat to those already piled across the washer and dryer. Then with Wally following closely at her heels, the foursome advanced into the large kitchen where eager hands took the twins from their arms.

While Skye took the babies' jackets off, Wally returned outside. When he got back, he handed Skye the Crock-Pot, then removed his own coat.

Walking over to May he said, "I hope you don't mind that I invited Dr. Norris to dinner."

"Of course not." She patted his cheek. "I told you when you called last night that I'm always happy to have another guest. I put her right next to your father." May winked. "Like you said, we can't let that poor woman spend her Thanksgiving alone."

Skye rolled her eyes. Now her mom was in on Project Matchmaker.

"You're the best, May." Wally hugged Skye's mother, then walked out of the kitchen.

Watching him leave, Skye wondered what it would take to change the tradition that allowed the men to sit in the living room watching TV while the women did all the work preparing the meal. Probably an apocalypse.

Shaking her head at the blow to feminism, Skye greeted everyone, then nodded to the slow cooker and asked, "Where shall I put this?"

Her mother was standing at the sink draining potatoes in a colander, and after she looked around, she said, "Set it on the table under the picture window. There's a plug underneath the sill." May peered suspiciously at the Crock-Pot and wrinkled her nose. "You were supposed to bring the cranberry sauce. What in the world is that?"

"Cran-apple chutney." Skye went to put the slow cooker down. "I thought I'd try something new."

May *tsked.* "What happened to the nice slices of jelly like we always have?"

"No one really likes that stuff, so I made this. It has fresh cranberries, honey, orange juice, cinnamon, cider vinegar, and a dash of ground ginger. And it's warm so it won't make the turkey cold."

"I see." May sniffed, turned back to the sink, and muttered, "Good thing I bought a can of cranberry sauce."

Skye's aunt Kitty was stirring gravy at the stove, while her aunt Minnie had the oven door open and was basting the turkey. She kissed both of them on the cheeks and said, "What do you want me to do?"

"Grab an apron and start wrapping the rolls in foil," May ordered before either of Skye's aunts could speak.

Skye wondered why she had even bothered asking. The only task her mom ever trusted her with was warming up the dinner rolls.

As she started tearing off sheets of Reynolds Wrap, her grandma Cora spoke. "How's the house going? Will you be in before Christmas?"

"Fingers crossed," Skye answered quickly.

Her grandma was seated at the kitchen table, and Skye shot her an innocent look. She didn't want to discuss the murder, and she'd bet dollars to doughnuts that's where this line of questioning was headed.

Along the counter bisecting the kitchen from the dinette, her twin cousins, Gillian Tubb and Ginger Allen, sat on stools and rolled silverware into napkins. They weren't allowed to do any actual cooking either.

"Do you think your contractor killed his wife?" Gillian smirked at Skye.

Ginger snickered. "Trust our cousin to

347

hire a murderer."

Skye ignored the jab. "It's hard to say." She could tell they had already heard all about Jerita's death. "So far there's no evidence against Beilin."

May rolled her eyes. "It was probably Earl Doozier. If you weren't protecting him, he'd be under arrest. He left the scene of the crime."

A voice rose, echoing off the cocoa-colored walls and the freshly scrubbed tile floor. Kitty's daughter-in-law put her hands over Eva's ears and Cora did the same with CJ.

Ginger spoke above the roar. "But it's usually the spouse, isn't it? That's the way it is on all the TV shows, and the reporters say that too."

Skye tore off another piece of foil. "Ginger, I don't know how to break this to you, but the media is not a reflection of reality."

That seemed to give Ginger and Gillian something to think about, and they whispered back and forth between themselves for several minutes.

May finished at the sink and moved the bowl of boiled potatoes to the counter. As she added milk and butter she asked, "Ginger, Gillian, where are your husbands?"

Gillian sighed. "They're defending Scumble River from the invasion of vicious deer and venomous pheasant. In other words, hunting."

Before anyone could comment on Gillian's statement, the outer door slammed, and footsteps sounded from the utility room. Charlie and a woman Skye didn't recognize walked into the kitchen. The woman was in her fifties, wearing a pair of black slacks and a black turtleneck with a thigh-length pumpkin-colored cardigan. She had a coordinating scarf looped around her neck and her makeup was subdued. Ash-blond hair was styled in a smooth bob that stopped right below her chin.

"Hi." The woman moved forward and smiled at everyone. "I'm Doris Ann Norris."

"Nice to meet you, Dr. Norris." Skye held out her hand. "I'm Wally's wife, Skye."

"Call me Doris Ann." The medical examiner gave Skye two six-packs of beer.

Skye wedged the cartons in the already overstuffed fridge, then introduced the ME, who greeted each person with a warm hand-shake.

May smiled and said, "Dinner will be ready soon. Would you like Charlie to escort you to the living room?"

"Dr. Norris and I aren't together. We just arrived at the same time." Charlie shot May a sharp look.

"Of course not." May frowned at Charlie. "I just meant that Dr. Norris could join Wally and his dad. I understand that she's originally from Texas just like them."

Skye examined her mother's expression. May had been thrilled that Bunny had elected to have dinner with her son, Simon, and his girlfriend, Emmy. Skye, on the other hand, had been surprised that Carson had chosen to join their family's celebration rather than eat with his girlfriend. Either the twins were a huge draw or his relationship with the redhead was cooling down.

As Charlie and Doris Ann left, the women started talking. Skye listened to her female relatives speculate about the medical examiner, but they stopped abruptly when the ME reappeared in the doorway.

Doris Ann eyed them all coolly, then grinned. "I think the real fun is probably out here." She walked over and linked arms with May. "So who carves the turkey around here? Because I'm really good at cutting up bodies." She winked. "You know, just sayin'."

Once the food was ready, the men put up two long folding tables in the living room. Then three card tables were crowded into what had been Vince's room before May took it over as her den, and all the leaves were installed in the dinette table. Once the seating arrangements were finished, everyone grabbed a napkin roll of silverware and filled their plates from the food set out buffet style on the counter and on the table under the picture window in the kitchen.

It was the younger generation's job to fetch drinks and disburse the hot rolls and butter. Skye was happy that her cousin's children were now old enough to take their turn as servers, and even happier that the boys were pressed into duty with the girls. That was a huge change from her generation's experience.

In the past, the guys had always claimed the living room tables, the women had camped out in the kitchen, and the kids had taken the card tables in the den. This too was slowly changing, and finally more and more couples were eating together.

When the feeding frenzy started, Skye slipped away to give the twins a bottle of the breast milk she'd pumped that morning and combined with baby formula. Once they were fed, she put them in the portable cribs May kept in Skye's old bedroom. With the babies napping, she returned to the kitchen and Wally handed her an empty plate and a silverware roll.

After they got their food, they found two chairs together between May and Cora and sat down. Skye immediately cut into her turkey and savored the flavor. She had been lucky enough to nab a piece with crispy brown skin and she planned to enjoy every bite.

Okay, she had hidden the piece under a pile of less desirable dark meat before anyone else went through the buffet line, but she counted this as the one advantage of being chained to the kitchen.

Just as Skye put a big forkful of sausage dressing into her mouth, May leaned toward her and said, "I thought you were trying to lose the baby weight. I'm sure stuffing isn't on your diet."

Skye swallowed, but before she could tell her mother to mind her own business, Wally scowled at May and said, "Skye is perfect the way she is and her doctor was very pleased at her last checkup."

From the other end of the table Doris Ann added, "You know, May, your diet isn't only what you eat."

"What do you mean?" May asked, a look of confusion on her face.

"Your diet consists of what you hear, what you read, and the energy that the people around you release." Doris Ann raised her eyebrow. "We should be far more concerned about the emotional and spiritual meals we put into our bodies than the physical food."

May grunted, pursed her lips in disapproval, and turned to talk to her sister, Minnie Overby.

"That's very interesting, Doris Ann. Thank you." Skye shot the ME a grateful smile, then said to Wally, "And thank you, honey." Skye touched her husband's hand. "You are so sweet."

As she continued to eat, Skye looked around. Gillian and Ginger were chatting with her cousin Kevin's wife, so Skye turned to her grandmother and whispered, "What do you think of Dr. Norris?"

"She looks like a smart cookie." Cora took a sip from her coffee cup, then winked. "She'd probably make a mighty good mother-in-law."

"Seriously?" Skye shook her head. She hadn't realized that Wally had enlisted so many members of her family to help him with his plan to switch his father's affections from Bunny to the ME.

"Bunny's not a bad gal." Cora's wrinkled face took on a faraway expression. "But she'd have trouble fitting into Carson's life when he goes back to work full-time. She'd be miserable as a CEO's wife."

Skye pondered her grandmother's words. What she said was true, and Carson had as much as admitted that himself before he left for his board meeting. It probably was best if her father-in-law and Bunny drifted apart, but Skye just hoped that neither would be hurt.

Talking to one of the Leofanti relatives, Doris Ann's voice rose above the others. "The best thing about the good old days is that I wasn't old or good."

Skye grinned. The ME's view of the world was certainly unique.

After dinner, the women cleaned up and did the dishes while the men watched football on TV, played cards, and napped. That still hadn't changed, and Skye doubted that it ever would. At least not without a major rebellion from her female relatives.

The afternoon drifted by. Little groups would form, chat, then drift into other clusters. Skye noticed her cran-apple chutney had not only been eaten, the Crock-Pot was completely empty. She made a mental note to inform May of its success.

The snow had continued to fall, and by six, Skye was antsy to get home. She liberated Wally from her Uncle Dante, who was extolling the virtues of the city's new K-9 officer, and they said their goodbyes.

As they drove over the now treacherous roads, Skye was thankful for the Mercedes. The heavy SUV made the short trip between her parents' place and the RV a lot safer.

Still, Skye was clinging to the armrest and jumped when Wally suddenly broke the silence. "Doris Ann and my dad seemed to really hit it off. He offered her a ride to Texas on the corporate plane next time he goes down for a meeting."

"That's great." Skye bit her lip. "Do you think his and Bunny's relationship is fading out?"

Wally didn't answer for a while, but as he turned into their driveway he said, "It might be. I don't have anything against Bunny," he chuckled, "except her son. But I don't think she'd enjoy the straitlaced part of Dad's life."

"Well" — Skye glanced in the back at their sleeping babies — "I don't think anyone would have thought we fit together too well either, but we seem to be doing just fine."

Early Friday morning, as Skye cautiously descended the RV's steps, the roar of an engine turning into her driveway startled her, causing her foot to slip. She clutched the railing, wondering why no matter how much salt Wally applied, the metal stairs still remained icy.

Peering down the driveway, Skye watched as her father's old blue truck bumped over the snow-covered gravel. It rattled to a stop behind her SUV and she carefully made her way over to the pickup.

Without turning off the engine, Jed rolled down the window and said, "Hey."

"Hi, Dad. What are you doing here so early? It isn't even seven thirty yet."

"Ma and I have been up since five," Jed said, then took a quick peek behind Skye and asked, "Where are the twins?"

"Dorothy's taking care of them today." Skye explained, "I'm meeting Wally to search Beilin Quinn's house. We're hoping to find some clue about his wife's murder. And after that, I'm going shopping for furniture."

Wagging his tail, Chocolate, her father's Labrador retriever, hopped onto Jed's lap, stuck his head out the open window, and licked Skye's face. She scratched him behind his ears and told him he was a good boy, but wrinkled her nose at the aroma of wet dog wafting from the cab.

"About Dorothy." Jed frowned. "Your ma's not too happy about you hiring her."

"Really?" Skye said noncommittally. She'd managed to avoid that particular conversation at Thanksgiving, but knew she'd have to have it eventually.

"Your ma's worried." Her father pinned Skye with a sharp look.

"About Dorothy taking care of the kids?" Skye knew that May could put the cloud in any silver lining, but Dorothy was one of her best friends. Her mother might be upset with Skye for hiring Dorothy rather than allowing May to be their granny nanny, but she shouldn't be worried about her BFF taking care of the babies.

"Nah." He gave a quick shake of his head and then mumbled, "Your Crock-Pot."

Jed's steel-gray crew cut was hidden by a

plaid cap with the earflaps folded up. His brown Carhartt jacket was open, revealing a blue flannel shirt, and his hands were bare. No farmer ever buttoned a coat or put on a pair of gloves until the mercury stayed below the zero mark on the barn thermometer for at least a week.

"Mom was worried about my slow cooker?" Skye asked. Even for May that was a bit much. "What? Did she think we wouldn't eat without it?"

"You ran off so lickety-split yesterday, Ma thought something might be wrong."

Jed's faded brown eyes squinted as he gazed out the windshield. Only citified wimps wore sunglasses. His face was tanned and leathery. It looked as if he should be out in the summer heat, not driving around in the snow.

Skye chuckled. "Tell Mom we're all fine. You know the older I get, the earlier it gets late." She tightened the red wool scarf she had wound around her throat and adjusted her earmuffs. "And I wanted to get home before the roads got any worse."

"I figured that was it, but you know your ma. That woman's a champion worrier." Jed pushed Chocolate aside and handed Skye her Crock-Pot, then before cranking up his window, he said, "Stay warm."

As she watched her dad leave, Skye muttered, "I'll try, but twenty-eight degrees is too dang cold for November." Instead of climbing back up the RV's slick steps, she put the slow cooker on the floor in front of the Mercedes's rear seat, slid behind the wheel, and said to herself, "If this keeps up, we'll be frozen by Christmas and living in igloos by the time spring rolls around."

Instead of turning on the radio, Skye drove in silence past the ice-encased trees and snow-covered fields. It was nice to have some time to herself with nothing but the sound of the SUV's tires rolling over the blacktop.

A few hardy souls were out sprinkling their driveways and sidewalks with salt, but most of the houses were surrounded by pristine white yards untouched by man or beast.

As she turned toward the police station, Skye glanced at the downtown area. There wasn't a single car parked along Basin Street. Evidently there was no Black Friday open-at-dawn nonsense for the Scumble River stores.

To Skye's right, the spire of St. Francis Catholic Church seemed to float above the commercial buildings, sparkling as if dusted with powdered sugar. Listening closely, she could hear the bells calling the faithful to the daily morning mass.

Skye turned into the PD's parking lot, and when she drove near the front of the station, she saw Wally jogging out of the building. He gestured for her to pull up to the curb, and when she complied, he opened the rear door and threw a backpack with evidence collection kit stenciled across it into the back, then hopped into the passenger seat.

As he buckled up, he said, "Beilin called a few minutes ago and asked that we not arrive in a squad car. It seems Jenna refused to stay with his folks. Her cousins have her scared to death that the cops will arrest her for killing her mother."

"But she was at school during the TOD." Skye wrinkled her brow, trying to come up with a likely scenario where a five-year-old committed matricide. "What the heck did they say to her?"

"No idea." Wally shrugged. "But Beilin mentioned that the cousins in question are teenagers, so the possibilities are endless."

Skye was about to question Wally further when a snowplow rumbled past them in the opposite lane and Wally said something under his breath.

"What?" Skye shot him a questioning

360

glance before turning her gaze back to the road.

"Plowing is a waste of city money," Wally grumbled. "We only got a couple of inches and all the plow does is make the road slipperier."

"Isn't it laying down salt?" Skye squinted into the rearview mirror.

Wally shook his head. "Nope. The only reason that snowplow is even out is that Hizzoner wants everyone to see their tax dollars working. You know, he barely won the election a couple of weeks ago. And that was with only a write-in candidate opposing him."

"Really?" Skye knew Dante had won, but not that it had been so close.

As Skye guided the SUV onto the Quinns' street and slowed in front of their house, Wally said, "Park in the cul-de-sac at the end."

"Why not at Beilin's?" she asked, but complied with his directive.

"Another one of Beilin's requests," Wally said as he slid out of the SUV and grabbed the evidence collection kit from the back of the car before jogging around the Mercedes to open Skye's door. "Even though we aren't in a marked car, he doesn't want us to park in his driveway."

Wally held Skye's elbow as they hiked the two blocks to the Quinn residence. Once they had safely navigated the icy front steps, he rang the bell and waited. There was no answer and he rang it again, then once more.

When there was still no response, Wally snarled, "Golldang it! If Beilin's made a run for it —"

"Wait." Skye pointed to a note taped to the window. She retrieved the paper, scanned it, and said, "According to this, the door's unlocked. Beilin and Jenna are waiting in the playhouse and he wants us to text him if we have any questions. He'd also like us to let him know when we leave so they can return to the house."

"Seriously?" Wally shook his head. "Beilin's demands are starting to tick me off."

Skye didn't respond to Wally's comment. She could understand his frustration, but also could see Beilin's point of view. He was trying to protect his child from a truly awful situation.

As she and Wally entered the home, Skye asked, "Won't Beilin and Jenna be cold out in the playhouse?"

"Nah," Wally answered absently as he scanned the foyer. "It has gas, electric, and running water. They spared no expense for that child."

"Oh." Skye sincerely hoped that Carson wouldn't try to spoil the twins with a similar model. Then when Wally didn't move, she asked, "What exactly are we looking for?"

"Any kind of notes or letters that might explain why Jerita thought moving here would protect Jenna from whatever she feared in Chicago."

"Okay." Skye glanced around the open-concept house. From the foyer area, it was one huge room. A kitchen occupied a third of the space and the rest was furnished with couches, chairs, and occasional tables. One end held a huge stone fireplace with book-cases on either side. "I'll start by going through the books. Lots of people stick things between the pages."

"I'll search the bedrooms." Wally handed Skye several evidence bags. "Put anything you find in these."

"Gotcha." Skye headed toward the shelves. Over her shoulder she asked, "How many bedrooms are there? Oh. And should I search the kitchen?"

"Three, plus two offices." Wally stepped into a hallway, but his voice floated behind him. "And yes, when you finish with the great room, see if there's anything in the kitchen or the powder room."

Skye put on a pair of plastic gloves, then

spent the next hour picking up books, holding them open, and shaking them. She thanked her lucky stars that neither of the Quinns appeared to be big readers and the shelves were far from crowded.

When she finally reached the last volume on the bottom shelf, she saw that there was a cabinet underneath and opened the door. Inside was a stack of albums.

Sitting cross-legged on the floor, Skye pulled the top album onto her lap. As she flipped through its vinyl sleeves, she noticed that there were random pockets throughout the scrapbook that were empty. Examining them closer, Skye saw that several of the plastic pages had been ripped from the binding, then repaired with clear tape and replaced.

Of the seven albums, two were devoted to Jerita and Beilin's wedding and their honeymoon. However, the five remaining books represented each year of Jenna's life. And those were the ones with missing pictures.

Getting to her feet, Skye went in search of Wally. She found him in what she guessed was Jerita's office. Although there was nothing on the screen, he was staring at the desktop computer's monitor as if in a daze.

"Wally," Skye called to him from the doorway, unwilling to startle a man with a gun. "Beilin said they'd been vandalized, right?"

Turning toward her, he blinked, then said, "Yes. I believe he told me it happened a few weeks ago."

"Did he say what had been damaged?"

"No." Wally stepped closer to her. "Why?"

Skye held up one of the albums that was labeled *Jenna Age One.* "There are missing pictures in five scrapbooks and some of the pages look as if they were torn from the album. I just wondered if these were the items that were damaged when their house was broken into."

"I'll text him and ask." Wally unhooked his cell phone from his belt.

While Wally tapped in Skye's question, she gazed around the small office. Jerita's paralegal certificate hung on the wall alongside several other credentials. It seemed that she was also a licensed esthetician and travel agent.

As they waited for Beilin's answer, Skye walked around the room. A pile of empty frames with smashed glass were stacked on top of a filing cabinet. Frowning, she took a quick tour of the rest of the house.

Several exposed hooks were scattered among the master bedroom and the great room walls. Skye bit her lip. What was with all the absent pictures?

Wally's phone chirped and he read the text to Skye, "Albums were torn up and framed photos were smashed. Snapshots were missing."

"I wonder what that means," Skye murmured softly, then looked at Wally. "It has to have something to do with why they moved here."

Wally was busy tapping the screen of his cell and explained, "I'm asking for details about the missing pictures."

Skye joined Wally at the computer and peered at the monitor. Although she could hear a whirring sound, nothing seemed to be happening.

"Why isn't it turning on?" Skye asked. Her grasp of how computers worked was weak at best, but she knew something should be on the screen. "Shouldn't there be a twirling hourglass thingy to tell you it's loading or booting or . . ."

"I have no idea." Wally frowned, then said, "I'll have to get it over to the crime lab and have the techs take a look at it."

Wally's cell cheeped again and he read out loud, "The pictures were all of Jenna. Just her alone. The ones with Jerita and Beilin weren't touched."

"Hmm. That's got to mean something."

Skye tapped her fingertips on the computer tower, then jerked them away and warned, "Maybe you better turn this thing off. It's getting really hot."

Wally leaned forward, sniffed, and quickly pressed the Off button. The evidence collecting kit was on the desk chair and he dug through it. After a second, he plucked a small flashlight from its depths, switched it on, and shined it into the tower's vents.

"Do you see anything?" Skye asked.

"I think so." Wally quickly unplugged the computer from the electrical outlet, then disconnected all the cables running from the tower and the monitor.

After taking a multipurpose tool from his utility belt, Wally used its tiny screwdriver to remove the tower's hard plastic casing. A few minutes later he slid it up and Skye's mouth dropped open when she looked over his shoulder and saw what was there.

A folded sheaf of papers had been stuffed on top of the fan. The pages had a blue backing just like every legal document Skye had ever seen.

Wally put on the pair of gloves he'd discarded while he'd worked on removing the casing, then carefully lifted up the pages and placed them on the desktop. Once they were flattened, he began to flip through them.

Skye crowded next to him and gasped. It was a surrogacy contract.

Wally huffed out a surprised breath. "Well, that explains the autopsy results."

"What do you mean?" Skye asked without looking up from the document.

"This morning, just before you got to the station, I was rereading Doris Ann's final report and saw something that I hadn't noticed before. It stated that Jerita had never given birth. I thought it was an error and intended to phone the doc after we finished here and ask her to reexamine the vic."

"Hmm. Let me see something." The contract's fine print was difficult to make out and Skye had to squint. "Look at the name of the surrogate."

Wally leaned closer and read, "Kristina Ficher Hovery. So what?"

"Isn't Edie Baker's caretaker named Krissy Ficher?" Skye asked. Then when Wally didn't react, she said, "As in Kristina."

"Sh . . . shoot!" He continued to read, then said, "According to the contract, the surrogate must be married and have already had a successful pregnancy. Romano Hovery signed in the spot designated for the surrogate's husband."

Skye had continued to flip the pages of the contract and froze when she saw a section highlighted in bright yellow. Pointing to it she read out loud, "Upon the birth of the child, the surrogate and her husband shall immediately relinquish full custody of the child to the intended parents. In addition, it is the specific intent of each and every party to this agreement that the surrogate and her husband shall not have any legal rights toward the child and that neither party is the legal parent of any child conceived and born pursuant to the conduct contemplated by this agreement. Any child born pursuant to the conduct contemplated by this agreement shall be morally, ethically, legally, contractually, and otherwise the child of the intended parents for all purposes."

"If the surrogate tried to get the child back, that would explain why Jerita was anxious to get Jenna out of Chicago. She might have thought that the woman wouldn't find them here."

Wally tapped his cell phone screen, then said, "There's an obituary for a Romano Hovery that states he died nine months ago and his wife is listed as Kristina Ficher Hovery. But there's no mention of a son or

369

daughter. Of course, Krissy could have lied about having had a successful prior pregnancy."

"Oh my gosh! I'll bet when her husband died, Krissy went looking for her child." Skye covered her mouth. "Remember what Edie told us Krissy said to her?" When Wally shook his head, Skye reminded him. "Edie said that Krissy told her that everyone deserved to be with the people they loved, and not just who they were stuck with because they made one bad choice."

"So if Jerita refused to allow Krissy to take Jenna, Krissy might feel justified in killing the woman keeping her from her daughter."

CHAPTER 24
WON'T GO HOME WITHOUT YOU

Skye and Wally just stared at each other for a couple of seconds before Skye finally asked, "Do you think Beilin knew about Krissy?"

Wally raised an eyebrow and gave her an *Are you seriously asking that?* look.

Skye blew him a raspberry and said, "I didn't mean about the surrogacy. Of course he knew about that. I meant did he know that Krissy was in Scumble River? And if what we think happened really happened, did Beilin know Krissy was trying to get Jenna back?"

"It's possible he didn't." Wally pursed his lips. "I'm thinking that Jerita could have taken the surrogacy contract from their safety deposit box to show Krissy that she had no legal rights, then hidden it in the computer until she could return it. But why keep it a secret from her husband?"

"Because he might have allowed Krissy to

371

be a part of their lives?" Skye guessed. "It wasn't the same for him as it was for Jerita. There wasn't another man saying he was Jenna's father, but Krissy would certainly be trying to claim the role of Jenna's mother."

"I just texted Beilin to come in here." Wally crossed his arms. "It's time he answered all our questions honestly and in person."

They waited several minutes, but Beilin didn't respond. With each passing second, Skye could see Wally getting angrier and angrier.

Finally she said, "I'll just go outside and get him. Jenna has seen me at school with Piper, so I shouldn't scare her."

"Fine." Wally followed Skye to the French doors leading from the kitchen out to the deck. "But if he's not in here in five minutes, I'm coming out there and arresting him for obstruction."

Skye nodded her understanding, stripped off the plastic gloves she'd been wearing, shoved them in her pocket, and headed out toward the playhouse. Making her way through the gate, she walked up to the cute little door with the heart-shaped window and knocked. When there was no answer, she stepped inside.

She hadn't realized the playhouse was so large. Not only could she stand upright, it appeared to have two or maybe three rooms. The one she was in at the moment was furnished like a parlor. There was a child-sized sofa with a coffee table set for a tea party. On the table were two cups: a small one that still held a bit of chocolate milk and a larger one with a moist film on the bottom.

Calling Beilin's name, Skye followed a narrow hallway toward the rear of the structure. Suddenly a shiver ran up her spine. Something didn't feel right. It was too quiet. Even if Beilin wanted to protect Jenna, he should have responded to Skye's shouts.

Before she could turn to leave, a woman stepped in front of Skye. The woman held a softly snoring Jenna draped over her shoulder and a gun in her free hand.

She scowled at Skye and demanded, "What the hell are you doing here?"

"I'm . . . I'm . . ." Skye tried to come up with an answer that wouldn't get her killed, but her mind refused to cooperate. Although she had never seen the woman before, Skye was certain the woman was Krissy Ficher.

"You're what?" Krissy walked around Skye, blocking her exit.

"Is Jenna okay?" Skye didn't like how the girl seemed more deeply asleep than normal.

"My daughter's fine." Krissy's gaze flicked toward the girl hanging over her shoulder. "Jenna's just taking a Benadryl nap. When Beilin went inside to get her for the tea party, I slipped a few of the crushed pills into her milk."

Before she could stop herself, Skye warned, "Diphenhydramine can impair motor skills, judgment, and memory in children for up to three days. She may be woozy and uncoordinated when she wakes up. Make sure she drinks lots of water."

"Shut up!" Krissy screamed. "You sound like that bitch from social services who took Jenna's brother from me after my husband died. I'm a good mother."

"Sorry," Skye said quickly. As unlikely as it seemed, in her job as a school psychologist, she'd actually had conversations like this before. Although they hadn't occurred at gunpoint, at least she was prepared to handle the woman's hostility. "I certainly never meant to question your parenting skills."

Krissy ignored Skye's words and whined, "Then that social services cow talked me into signing the adoption papers by telling me that when I wasn't in my right mind I might hurt him. I haven't been able to find him yet, but I will now that I have Jenna. She told me that once I had one baby, I'd find the other one."

"Who told you that?" Skye asked, confused. "The social worker?"

"Don't be stupid. It was Princess Diana." Krissy's voice was awestruck, then she blinked and snarled, "Now I'm going to ask you one more time. What are you doing here?"

"I'm a neighbor," Skye said quickly, her heart racing. More than likely, Krissy was schizophrenic and having hallucinations. How in the world had she passed the mental exam to become a surrogate? Then again, women were often asymptomatic and undiagnosed until their midtwenties, so Krissy's first episode could have only recently occurred. Probably after her husband died. "I brought food over for Beilin. By the way, where is he?"

"My fiancé is sleeping. I put a little zolpidem in his brandy. The advantage of being a caregiver for the elderly is that I can help myself to some of their meds without anyone even noticing." Krissy eyed the door behind Skye. "I have a wheelchair in the van for him, but I needed to get Jenna situated first."

"But —"

In a blink, Krissy's mood changed and she shrieked, "You must really think I'm stupid." Her mouth flattened and her face turned red. "You're the police chief's wife. I saw your picture online."

"True, Wally is my husband." Skye's voice cracked. "But we live across the street and I'm just —"

"Liar. Beilin is building you a new house by the river. You're living in an RV next to it until it's finished." Krissy blocked Skye's attempt to edge around her by pointing her gun at Skye's head. "I should just shoot you now. You and your husband have ruined everything."

"I don't know what you mean." Skye retreated until she was pressed against a door leading to what she assumed was another of the playhouse's rooms.

"Edie called me to let me know you'd found her." Krissy waved the gun in the air. "Then when the chief left a message demanding that I come to the police station today, I knew he'd figured it all out."

Skye forced herself to remain composed. She couldn't rush the woman. Jenna could get hurt in the struggle. Stalling for time, she asked, "What did he figure out?"

Krissy snapped, "That Beilin and I were meant to be together with our daughter, but Fake Mother wouldn't divorce him and leave."

"By Fake Mother, you mean Jerita?" She needed to keep the other woman talking. Wally would be out here soon. He'd only given Beilin five minutes to get into the house and it had to be longer than that since this nightmare with Krissy had begun.

"Yes. Once Romano died, Princess Diana said that I was supposed to be with my real soul mate, Beilin."

"Did she tell you that in words?" Skye glanced over the woman's shoulder. Had she seen someone at the front door's window?

"Of course not." Krissy rolled her eyes. "She only talked to me once, and then when they medicated me, she never spoke again. Finally, I stopped taking the pills and Princess Di started sending me signs."

"Like what?" Skye forced herself to look at the woman.

"The day I buried Romano, I saw Beilin and Jenna at the restaurant where we had the funeral luncheon. Fake Mother wasn't with them so I knew that empty chair at their table was meant for me."

"Oh." Skye flicked a glance at the door and saw it inching open. "Anything else?"

"Yes. In Chicago, I worked as a nanny, and one afternoon when I went to pick up my charges after school, Jenna was waiting in the same line as those kids. She smiled at me and asked me to tie the ribbon in her hair." Krissy's tone had become dreamy. "That's when I started to follow her."

Holy crap! It was difficult to keep up with Krissy's constantly shifting reality.

Skye was speechless for a moment, then said, "And Jerita saw you and panicked."

"Yes." Krissy petted the sleeping child's back. "Fake Mother tried to hide Jenna from me, but Princess Diana sent me another sign."

"She did?" Skye asked.

"Yes. I kept looking online, and finally a story popped up about Beilin's new construction company. It was all about how your old house had been destroyed in a tornado and your new place was his first project." Wonder dripped from Krissy's words. "So I moved to Scumble River and Princess Diana guided me into getting a job with the Bakers. It was only Saturdays and Sundays so I could watch Jenna during the week. I was even able to break in and get some pictures of her. But most of them included her fake mother so I didn't want them. I figured the good ones were all on Fake Mother's phone so I took it after I got rid of her."

"That makes sense." Skye kept her voice agreeable. "She'd be the one taking the photos."

"Right." Krissy smiled happily. "Then it turned out Edie really didn't have dementia, and I knew I was supposed to help her find happiness. And once I did that, Princess Diana would guide me to mine."

"But why did you kill Jerita?" Skye asked.

"When I was sure that I was really supposed to be Jenna's mom, I contacted Fake Mother and explained. But she kept yapping about the contract that I'd signed." Krissy's voice held a burning rage.

"That's just how paralegals think," Skye soothed, trying to both calm and stall the woman. "Everything has to be in black and white for them."

"I gave her several chances." Krissy shook her head. "I told her to make an excuse to leave Beilin and then everything would be fine because I knew that he loved me."

Wally had eased into the playhouse and was advancing toward Krissy.

"I take it Jerita said no?" Skye was intent on keeping Krissy talking so Wally could get the jump on her.

"When she invited me over here, I thought she was finally coming to her senses." Krissy scowled. "But then Fake Mother showed me a copy of a page of the contract that said I had relinquished all rights to Jenna. It was then I knew that she'd never do what she was supposed to do. She was going against Princess Diana. She was as bad as Camilla."

Camilla? The woman Prince Charles ended up marrying after he and Diana got divorced? Skye had never been a royal watcher, and after this conversation she never would be.

Afraid to make a mistake talking about the royal family, Skye ignored that part of Krissy's delusion and asked, "So what did you do?"

Skye figured since Krissy was so talkative, she might as well try for a confession.

"I pretended to agree and asked if I could see where Jenna played so I could have it as a memory." Krissy patted the sleeping girl again. "When Fake Mother walked outside, I grabbed the knife from the butcher block on the counter and followed her. She turned her back to point out the playhouse's size and I hit her with the butt of my gun, then I stabbed her in the temple." Krissy shuddered. "I didn't want her to come back as the undead Fake Mother."

"Why didn't you just shoot her?" Skye asked. Wally was right behind Krissy. Another step and he'd have her.

"I was afraid the noise would bring out the neighbors." Krissy sighed. "I know that woman across the street watches Beilin." Krissy lowered her voice as if to tell Skye a secret. "I think she has a crush on him, but he's mine."

Skye searched for a way to keep Krissy engaged. "Well, he is a nice-looking man and very charming."

"You like him too?" Krissy's mouth fell open, then she snarled, "Well, you can't have him." She waved the gun in Skye's face.

"No. No. I don't want him." Skye's blood was roaring in her ears. "He's not my type."

"Shut up!" Krissy suddenly flew into a rage and backhanded Skye across the mouth. "I see now that Princess Diana is testing me with you."

Skye felt her rapidly swelling lip and tasted the blood. She could see Krissy's thoughts were zipping from idea to idea like a fly in a bug zapper. The woman was starting to lose whatever part of reality she'd been able to hold onto before this. Her moods were changing from second to second and her physical movements were getting jerkier and less controlled.

Krissy nodded to herself. "Princess Diana wants me to execute you to prove that I'm her loyal subject."

"Why would she want me dead?" Skye blurted out, then bit her tongue. That had been stupid.

Krissy ignored Skye and continued to babble to herself. "I was so happy when I found Jenna. And it was perfect because since I'd been watching them, I knew that Beilin and Fake Mother weren't getting along. So it was obvious that he didn't love her and was ready to see that I was his soul mate, not her. Then I arranged to run into him in the supermarket and he paid for my groceries when I didn't have enough money so I knew he loved me."

Krissy refocused on Skye and pointed the gun at her. Wally raised his own weapon and nodded to Skye. She tensed, ready to duck.

Krissy slid Jenna to the floor and propped her up against the wall, then grasped her gun with two hands.

As she stepped closer to Skye, Wally pressed his weapon to the back of Krissy's head and yelled, "Freeze!"

"Nooooo!" Krissy screamed and Skye

heard the sound of a gun being cocked. "If you don't leave before I count to three, I'll shoot her."

Wally stood perfectly still as if he'd been tagged in a game of statues and Krissy turned toward him to gloat. "That's better."

"Okay. You win. I'll leave."

While Wally was distracting Krissy, Skye felt behind her until she located the doorknob. She sent a prayer of thanks when it turned and she could ease it open without a sound. Once it was a few inches from the frame, she allowed herself to fall backward.

As Skye hit the floor, it sounded as if the world had exploded, and Krissy crumpled onto Skye. She shoved her off and scrambled away.

As soon as Krissy hit the ground, Wally ran into the room. Beads of sweat stood out on his top lip and the expression on his face was a combination of rage and absolute terror.

His gaze frantically sought Skye as he demanded, "Are you all right?"

"Except for a bruised tailbone and a split lip, I'm fine."

While Skye checked on Jenna, Wally handcuffed Krissy to the door. Turning to where Skye was squatting in front of the unconscious little girl, he said, "Darlin', you scared the living crap out of me."

"Me too." Skye glanced at Jenna and the man passed out on the child-sized princess bed. "You'd better call an ambulance for these two."

"On the way." Wally blew out a long breath. "I radioed for backup and EMTs as soon as I looked through the window and saw what was happening."

"Did you hear Krissy's confession?" Skye asked.

"Every word." Wally's smile was frightening. "She'll probably end up somewhere for the criminally insane, but even Loretta wouldn't be able to get her off scot-free from this."

EPILOGUE:
TAKE ME HOME TONIGHT

Skye stood in the foyer of the new home directing traffic. There were delivery people going in and out, as well as friends and family who had come over to help them move from the RV to their dream house. May had resigned herself to Dorothy as the twins' nanny, and along with her friend, she had all four of her grandchildren, as well as Bingo in the garage apartment.

Jed, Vince, Loretta, Uncle Charlie, Trixie, Owen, Judy, and Anthony were all busy hauling boxes or assembling furniture, but each of them occasionally snuck upstairs — some to play with the babies and others to play with the cat.

A man wheeling a dolly with a large dresser strapped to it paused next to Skye and grunted, "Where's this go?"

"The master bedroom." She gestured to her right. "At the end of that little hallway."

It had been ten days since Krissy Ficher

385

had tried to kidnap Jenna and Beilin. Luckily neither of her victims was any the worse for the sedation she'd slipped in their tea party drinks. And Beilin had come through with his promise to finish construction and have Skye and Wally moved into their new place the first week of December.

Skye had assured the contractor that they could wait if he wasn't feeling up to working, but he'd insisted he was fine. Fortunately, Jenna had no memory of Krissy, and in order to make sure she didn't hear anything at school, she was staying with Beilin's parents until after Christmas.

Beilin had confided in Skye that he thought by that time, the holiday excitement would make Krissy's actions old news. Skye disagreed and explained that no matter how long Jenna was away, it was highly likely that someone would mention the incident to her when she returned to school.

Skye had given Beilin the name of a therapist near his folks who could help him explain the situation in a way his daughter could understand and accept. She could only hope he would take her advice and contact the woman.

Now, as Skye watched her new home coming together, she said a silent prayer for Jerita's soul, and for Beilin and his daughter.

Pushing away the sadness she felt for the Quinn family, Skye directed the placement of the dresser, then returned to her post in the foyer. This was a big day for her own family and she was determined to enjoy every second of it.

Wally was wrangling all the toys and baby equipment they'd managed to amass since living in the motor home. The amount of paraphernalia was mind-boggling, and this was before all the gifts the twins would get for Christmas. Skye made a mental note to donate at least half of the current stuff to the Stanley County Women's and Children's Center.

As Wally hauled a bassinet over the threshold, he asked, "Didn't you order cribs for CJ and Eva?"

"Yes." Skye checked her clipboard. "They've already arrived and are in their rooms."

"Then why do we need the bassinets?" Wally wiped a drop of sweat from his brow.

"I thought we could put them in our room for a while in case the twins have trouble sleeping in their new surroundings."

"No." Wally reversed directions. "We are not starting that. The bassinets are going into the attic."

Skye chewed her lip. "You're right." It was

exactly what she'd advise someone else to do. "But I'm warning you that when they cry, it'll break your heart."

Several hours later, everything had either been delivered or moved, and Skye was taking a vote on what kind of pizzas to order when the doorbell played Jim Croce's "Time in a Bottle." She quickly glanced at Wally and blinked away a tear. As promised, he'd found the perfect song for them.

Before Skye could get to the door, it opened and Homer Knapik sauntered into the room holding a huge basket with a shiny red bow.

He made his way to Skye, thrust the gift into her arms, and muttered, "Thanks."

"For what?" Skye asked as she examined the basket's contents.

There were two bottles of cabernet sauvignon, several types of sausages, various cheeses, a sleeve of wheat crackers, a box of chocolates, and a package of cookies. The gift had to have cost Homer a couple hundred bucks.

"For getting Beilin and Earl to drop their lawsuits." Homer pulled at the collar of his dress shirt. "And for getting me off the hook by finding Mrs. Quinn's killer."

"So you no longer mind that I'm a dead body magnet or that I help the police with murder investigations?" Skye couldn't resist taunting him a little after all the grief he had given her about working for the cops.

"Nah." Then as he marched back to the foyer, Homer added, "But don't let it go to your head." He paused to give her his signature glare. "And don't for one minute think that anything between us at school has changed." With that parting shot he stomped out of the house, letting the door bang shut behind him.

Skye crossed her arms and gazed heavenward. Homer was still the same jerk he'd always been, and she'd bet money that by the time she returned to work, he'd have forgotten all about how she'd saved his sorry butt.

Everyone had stopped talking when the principal had barged in, but once he was gone conversations restarted. At least until a second guest arrived.

This time when "Time in a Bottle" played, the visitor waited for them to answer the door. Skye was shocked to see Beilin Quinn on their porch holding a gift bag, but she and Wally moved aside and the contractor crossed the threshold.

Glancing at the crowd, he asked, "Could we talk somewhere a little more private?"

"Absolutely." Skye handed Trixie the pizza

menu and said, "Can you call in the order while we talk to Beilin?"

"Absolutely." Trixie took her cell phone from the pocket of her jeans and gave Skye a thumbs-up.

Beilin followed Skye and Wally into the currently empty fourth bedroom, and as soon as the door was shut, he asked, "What's going to happen to Krissy Ficher?"

"It's hard to say." Wally leaned against the bare wall. "Her attorney, who thankfully is not my sister-in-law, will probably plead her as not responsible by reason of insanity. A court-ordered psychiatrist will evaluate her and my guess is that the doctor will find her incompetent to stand trial."

"What happens after that?" Beilin frowned.

"My best guess is that she'll be remanded to a hospital and medicated. If the meds work she'll be sent back to jail to go on trial." Wally shrugged. "After that, it's anyone's guess. But she did confess, so it's likely she'd be convicted at that point."

"Did she say anything after she was arrested?" Beilin's shoulders drooped.

"Just that she had punctured the squad car's tire so you'd have a chance to escape from Sergeant Quirk, and she couldn't understand why you didn't try to get away."

"You know, when we found out that it was too dangerous for Jerita to get pregnant because of her heart problem, I wanted to adopt." Beilin gazed at the ceiling. "But because Jerita was afraid the biological mother would try to get the baby back, we decided to use a surrogate. We had already had a few surrogacies fall through and we weren't getting any younger so although I knew we should have gone through a reputable agency, Jerita didn't want to take the time. And now I'm a single forty-eight-year-old father raising a five-year-old daughter on my own."

"I understand." Wally nodded. "I was concerned with being an older father too." He put an arm around Skye. "But my smart wife told me that being a more mature parent was a plus. We don't sweat the small stuff because we know it all usually ends up just fine."

"I hope you're right." Beilin sighed. "I did contact that therapist and we have an appointment for the week after Christmas for her to help me explain why Krissy killed Jerita."

"Good." Skye let out a breath. "It'll be tough, but keeping secrets from kids rarely works out well." She paused, then added, "And I think your decision to keep Jenna in our regular education classes versus putting her into the gifted programs is the right one."

"Yeah. From what Ms. Townsend explained about the results of the evaluation she conducted, Jenna will be happier where she is."

"I'm glad you had a chance to meet with Piper and go over the testing." Skye gave him an encouraging look.

"Me too." Beilin nodded, then said, "I'll let you two get back to your friends and family in a second, but I wanted to thank you both for saving my daughter from that lunatic." He handed Skye and Wally the gift bag he'd been holding. "And for trusting me to build your house. I hope you have many happy years here."

Skye lifted a beautiful brass plaque from the tissue. The lettering read: "Bless this house and all who enter."

Skye gave the sign to Wally, then stepped away from him and hugged Beilin. "Thank you so much."

They walked the contractor to the front door, and after he left, Wally said, "Even though Krissy is clearly mentally ill, I still don't understand why she did what she did. She barely knew Beilin, so it couldn't be that she was madly in love with him. And

Jenna was never her daughter."

Skye was silent for a moment then said slowly, "I think that Krissy was convinced that she wouldn't ever be content without Beilin and Jenna."

Wally put his arm around Skye's waist. "Which just goes to show you, it's a mistake to put the key to your happiness in someone else's pocket."

"Exactly." Skye kissed Wally. "We are all responsible for our own emotions. No one can make you feel one way or the other." She ruffled his recently barbered hair. He'd finally gotten time to have Vince cut it and she was still trying to get used to its shorter length.

"Well." Wally winked. "Once we get rid of all our guests and get the twins asleep, I bet I can make you feel really good."

"I bet you can too."

She couldn't believe her good fortune. She had the love of her life, precious twin babies, and had just moved into her dream house. It didn't get any better than that.

ABOUT THE AUTHOR

Denise Swanson is the *New York Times* bestselling author of the Scumble River mysteries, the Deveraux's Dime Store mysteries, and the Chef-to-Go mysteries, as well as the Change of Heart and Delicious Love contemporary romances. She has been nominated for *RT Magazine's* Career Achievement Award, the Agatha Award, and the Mary Higgins Clark Award.